TO LOVE SOMEONE

BAYTOWN BOYS

MARYANN JORDAN

Cover design by: Graphics by Stacy

ISBN ebook: 978-1-947214-74-3

ISBN: print: 978-1-947214-75-0

❀ Created with Vellum

ABOUT THE AUTHOR

I am an avid reader of romance novels, often joking that I cut my teeth on the historical romances. I have been reading and reviewing for years. In 2013, I finally gave into the characters in my head, screaming for their story to be told. From these musings, my first novel, Emma's Home, The Fairfield Series was born.

I was a high school counselor having worked in education for thirty years. I live in Virginia, having also lived in four states and two foreign countries. I have been married to a wonderfully patient man for thirty-five years. When writing, my dog or one of my four cats can generally be found in the same room if not on my lap.

Please take the time to leave a review of this book. Feel free to contact me, especially if you enjoyed my book. I love to hear from readers!

Facebook
Email
Website

f

Author's Note

Please remember that this is a work of fiction. I have lived in numerous states as well as overseas, but for the last twenty years have called Virginia my home. I often choose to use fictional city names with some geographical accuracies.

These fictionally named cities allow me to use my creativity and not feel constricted by attempting to accurately portray the areas.

It is my hope that my readers will allow me this creative license and understand my fictional world.

I also do quite a bit of research on my books and try to write on subjects with accuracy. There will always be points where creative license will be used in order to create scenes or plots.

He pushed open the glass doors that led from the worn-tiled lobby of the Veterans Administration Hospital in Norfolk and stepped into the sunshine. He rubbed his hand over his beard as he tilted his head back, letting the sun beat against his closed eyes, the warmth knocking off the air-conditioned chill and sterile scent that had settled over him.

Dropping his chin, he pulled his reflective sunglasses from their perch, one stem tucked into the front of his T-shirt. With a flick of his wrist, he snapped them open before sliding them onto his face. A lock of hair fell over his face, and out of habit, he tucked it behind his ear. He jogged down the steps at the front of the building, his boots sounding out a heavy tap on the concrete.

A few people scooted out of his way, but most were used to the eclectic patients and visitors that spent time inside the hospital. Still, the expressions on their faces as they quickly moved to the other side of the sidewalk didn't surprise him. Tall, bulky, tattoos. Jeans that were clean but faded and leather boots that were scuffed, broken in, and comfortable. The black leather jacket with patches sewn on the front and sleeves sat easily on his shoulders. His motorcycle helmet was held in one hand. His hair and beard were clean but long and shaggy.

And honestly? He didn't give a fuck what anyone thought.

The news from the hospital had been good, and he felt like celebrating. By himself... he didn't have anyone to celebrate with. That particular fact, he did give a fuck about. He might be a loner but didn't always like being alone.

Continuing to stalk to the parking lot, he stopped by his bike, strapped on his helmet, unlocked the saddle-bags to double-check his belongings, and swung a long, muscular leg over the bike, settling his ass onto the seat. He started the motor, revving the engine before pulling out of the parking lot. He had no particular destination in mind, not unusual for him. He often got onto the road and veered in whatever direction seemed to make sense at the time.

Now, the idea of heading to the beach, finding a bar with decent burgers and beer, and watching the sunset over the water appealed to him. Entering into traffic as he merged onto the interstate, it didn't take him long to get to Virginia Beach. He shunned the main board-walk area and continued along Shore Drive until he got to the less-commercial area that faced the Chesa-peake Bay. He knew he was close to the Naval Amphibious Base Little Creek, but his time in the

Navy had not been spent as a prestigious SEAL who trained there, instead having served as a firefighter on a ship.

Passing the family restaurants and ones catering to tourists, he found a no-frills bar on the beach. Stepping inside, he scanned the interior, satisfied with the evidence it was exactly what he desired. The patrons looked up, but after their first curious glance, no one paid attention to him. The back of the bar overlooked the water, and after ordering his burger, fries, and beer at the counter, he headed outside. There were high-top tables and chairs near the railing. Choosing one at the end of the deck, he was glad there were few people around, preferring to enjoy the sunset without the conversations of others interrupting.

It didn't take long for the food to come, and he devoured it, realizing he hadn't eaten since the previous evening. Bloodwork at the hospital required him to fast, so he'd had no breakfast. The testing lasted through lunch, and now he was sure the burger and fries tasted as good as any he'd ever consumed. But then, with a thick, medium-rare burger, crispy fries, and cold beer, how could you go wrong?

With his meal complete, he leaned against the back of the chair and propped his feet onto the rails of the fence around the patio. Staring out over the water, he spent several minutes letting his mind drift with the ebb and flow of the surf. The sun was setting, brilliant colors beginning to streak across the sky. He'd always paid attention to his surroundings. He liked the soothing motion and sounds of the ocean and wasn't embarrassed to admit it. *Well, if I had anyone to admit it to...*

As he continued to drink his beer and stare out over the water, a long bridge that stretched into the horizon captured his interest. The Chesapeake Bay Bridge Tunnel.

Picking up his phone, he scrolled through saved emails. Not that he got many, and most he deleted, saving only the very few that meant something to him. It didn't take long for him to find the one he was looking for. The one from Zac Hamilton. His finger hovered over the button for only a few seconds before he clicked on the email.

Joseph, I figured you'd get this email no matter where you were or what you were up to. I came back to Baytown on the Eastern Shore of Virginia. Coming home wasn't bad considering a bunch of my friends came back after their service as well. I took the job of Fire Chief, then became a paramedic, and now I'm the EMS Captain. Not bad for a Squid. Wanted to let you know that we've started an American Legion here. It's a laid-back, easy way of life on the shore and sure as fuck a great place to call home. So, besides checking in with you, I'm extending an invitation. If going home wasn't what you wanted it to be or the wandering I know you're probably doing isn't keeping you busy, give Baytown a chance. I sent a note to Jason as well, hoping he'll make it here. Got a lot of new blood moving in, many out of the service who need a good place to call home. Anyway, hope

you're well and if you're ever on the Eastern Shore, look me up. Zac

He took another long drag from his beer before setting it down on the table. Scrolling through his emails again, he came to one that came in about a year later from another Navy bud.

Joseph, believe it or not, I took Zac up on his invitation and came to Baytown. Didn't figure I'd stay, but fuck, the people are nice. Starting a business, got a place to live. I know you're a drifter, but if you're ever out our way, come on by. I can always use an extra pair of hands. Jason

His eyes lifted from his phone screen, and he scanned the distance over the water. He knew what was on the far side of the bridge. The Eastern Shore. Baytown. Friends. Maybe some work. *Hell, it's not like I've got anything else I'm doing.* The sun was still setting, and he considered waiting until the next day before trying to cross the long bridge. But the more he stared into the distance on the other side of the bay, a longing built deep inside, pulling at him.

Tossing plenty of money for his meal and a tip onto the table, he planted his booted feet on the floor, grabbed his helmet, and headed out to the parking lot. Once more throwing his leg over his bike, he revved the engine and roared down the road, stopping only to pay the toll at the beginning of the bridge.

The sun was disappearing into the horizon to the west behind him, but the streaks of color to the east offered enough illumination that he noticed the beauty surrounding him. The seventeen miles of bridge that connected the mainland of Virginia with the Eastern Shore offered a unique opportunity to feel completely connected to the Chesapeake Bay. The mostly-still water reflected the color and sparkles with a few whitecaps crashing against the pylons or the rocks near the tunnel entrances. Two underwater tunnels offered the multitude of sea vessels entering the Bay on their way to Norfolk or Baltimore the opportunity for unimpeded progress.

Traffic was light and he wondered if it was always this way. When he'd looked on a map, the Eastern Shore was little more than a narrow peninsula dotted with small towns and rural farmland.

While the beauty of the water and the skies surrounded him, he still wondered why he was making this trip. *To see a couple of old Navy buddies? To discover a new place?* Or maybe it was just one more stop in his long quest of trying to find a place to call home. *Home. Do I even know what I'm looking for?* "The ache for home lives in all of us. The safe place where we can go as we are and not be questioned." The quote from Maya Angelou ran through his mind and he grit his teeth, knowing the ache for a home burned in him but had no idea if he was destined to always search, never find.

Pushing those thoughts down, he focused on the cool breeze and salt air, allowing them to fill his senses. *I sure as hell have tried a lot of other places, so this is just one more to discover.*

Evening had descended by the time he crossed the last mile of the bridge to Fisherman's Island. Now, the long straight road ahead brought out the urge to let loose his desire for speed, but the sight of a patrol car sitting in the median kept him in check. The last thing he wanted was to be stopped. It was his experience that law enforcement looked on the outside of him and made certain assumptions. Having to call Zac and Jason to get him out of jail was not a great way to start his visit.

Passing a grocery store, the only major store he'd seen, he turned at the first traffic light he'd come to, seeing the sign pointing toward Baytown. He was careful to slow down to follow the speed that decreased as he neared. Giving in to the desire to take a look around before contacting Zac or Jason, even at night, he drove around the perimeter of the town, surprised that it only took him a few minutes to complete the task. *Christ, did Zac really grow up in this tiny-ass town? And Jason decided this was the place to land?*

He'd passed a pub on the main street, and a little liquid courage seemed like a good idea. Parking just down the street, he locked his bike, grabbed his helmet, and stepped inside Finn's Pub. His shoulders immediately relaxed as his gaze scanned the interior. The pub looked as though it retained the original look and appeal of days gone by. A dartboard hung on the wall to the right and an old fireplace and sofa sat on the left. Old brickwork walls and wooden floors looked to be from the previous century. A polished wooden bar ran the length of the right side with tall, mismatched chairs. The left side of the bar held tables and booths.

It was a slow night, which worked for him as he walked to the end of the bar and took a seat. The music was loud, but voices could still be heard. Laughter, the sound of camaraderie, and the antics of the two men behind the bar, whose looks were so similar they must be related.

"Looks like you're new around here," one of the men said, his smile wide. "Well, you've come to the best fuckin' bar on the Eastern Shore."

Just then, the other man walked up and shoved the first one in the shoulder. "Aiden, shut the hell up. You know this is a family establishment."

"Chill, Brogan! Look around, man. You see any kids in here?"

"Will the two of you stop arguing and get the man what he wants to drink? By the way, brothers dear, the books are finished, and I'm getting ready to head home to Gareth and little Finn."

The quick verbal exchange had only taken a few seconds, but the man sitting at the bar felt his lips twitched upward, something that used to happen more often but now was rare. It didn't take a genius to figure out that Aiden and Brogan were brothers and the beautiful woman who'd taken command must be their sister. He could appreciate her beauty, but with the wedding band sparkling on her finger and the mention of a child, he simply nodded his appreciation and ordered a beer. Leaning against the back of the stool, he enjoyed his drink and continued to observe the easy camaraderie between the two barmen and the pub patrons.

He must've given off the vibe that he wasn't there for conversation because other than checking to see if he wanted another drink, he was left to himself. Finally, he glanced at the old clock on the wall and knew he could not put off the real reason for him coming any longer.

Tossing money onto the bar, he offered a chin lift to the largest brother still slinging drinks and headed outside to his bike. By now, darkness had settled over the sleepy town, the street lamps casting gentle light on the quiet street. Pulling out his phone, he checked the GPS and knew he didn't have far to go but didn't want to leave his bike unattended. Even in a small town, trust was hard to come by.

It only took a moment to drive the three blocks back through town, turning at the corner where he saw Jason's auto shop. And right next door was the lighted window of a small tattoo shop. Unsure if the door was unlocked, he was surprised when it opened easily. Walking inside, he spotted a familiar face even if Jason's outward appearance was more like looking into a mirror than a Go Navy advertisement.

The man in front of him was wearing a tight T-shirt, faded jeans, and heavy boots. His long hair was pulled back in a ponytail and his face was covered in a shaggy beard. Jason Boswell. One of the few friends he'd made in the Navy and stayed in contact with. He waited as the uncertainty that crossed Jason's face morphed into recognition.

Suddenly, Jason jerked and he gasped. "Joseph? Joseph Hernandez?"

2

Hearing his name coming from his friend's lips, Joseph grinned and barely had time to lock his legs into place as Jason rushed forward to envelop him in a bear hug. They slapped each other's backs before separating, Jason still shaking his head.

"Fuck, man," Joseph laughed, his gaze locked on Jason's long hair. "Look at you."

"Me? Hell, you're no fuckin' Navy regulation, either."

For a few seconds they simply stared, Jason's expression still holding disbelief, and Joseph figured his own was much the same.

"The last time Zac tried to get you to move out here, you were hitchhiking somewhere in Texas," Jason finally said.

Joseph nodded and hefted his shoulders. "I could say I was just in the neighborhood, but hell, while Virginia isn't remote, the Eastern Shore sure as fuck is."

"So, are you just passing over or really thinking about staying?"

"Got no plans at all. I was traveling my way east, working a few jobs, when I needed to stop over at the Veterans Hospital in Norfolk." Joseph shrugged and ran his hand through the scruff of his beard.

"Are you okay?"

Jason's voice was instantly full of concern, something rare in Joseph's experience. And, he silently admitted, was nice. "Yeah, yeah. I got sick a few months ago and just never got over it. I figured if I went to a veterans' hospital, then I could get treated. I looked at a map and realized how close I was to the Eastern Shore, so I figured it was time to check out what you and Zac have been talking about."

Jason leaned around and flipped the lock on the door, turning off the 'Open' sign, and motioned toward several chairs in the corner near the front desk. Taking him up on his silent invitation, he sat while Jason grabbed two bottles of water from a small refrigerator.

Jason settled into a seat nearby and handed one of the bottles to him. "I gotta tell you, man, if you need anything, you only have to ask."

Taking a sip of cold water, he nodded. "Thanks." He leaned back and allowed his gaze to drift around the small shop. "I see your garage is next door. How's business?"

Jason laughed. "When I first came out here, I had the idea that I'd open the garage, get enough people to work in it and run it, and then I'd do nothing but oversee the garage while mostly working in the tattoo shop. But damn, this town was so desperate for a garage that also had a tow truck, and I was constantly working just to keep up with the demand. I've got two other mechanics who work for me, and we're busy all the time. It didn't take long to discover that there was a lot more mechanic business than tattoo business. I'm only doing tattoos on the weekends. I'm busier during the summer when vacationers are around but definitely not enough for tattooing to be my full-time job."

He peered closely at Jason considering his words didn't match up with the smile on his friend's face. "You okay with that?"

Jason shrugged, and his smile widened. "I love the artistic outlet that this business allows, but I don't want to run it all by myself anymore. Plus, I've met someone and am no longer willing to work all the time. I've now got something else to live for."

His brows lifted in surprise, but from the expression on Jason's face, it wasn't hard to see that the man was truly happy. He took another swig of water and thought about the changes that had occurred over the past couple of years. He already knew that Zac was married, and from what Jason was saying, he might not be long in following.

Jason leaned forward, leaning his forearms on his knees. "If you're thinking about hanging around Baytown for a while, are you looking for work?"

He jerked his chin back. "Hell, man, I just got here." Jason's question caught him by surprise. He'd only planned on checking in with two old friends. But suddenly, the vision of the long bridge-tunnel over the Chesapeake Bay came to mind. The sunset. The long stretch of road. The tiny town. The friendly pub. He opened his mouth to say that he had no plans on staying but instead blurted, "I know Zac was the Fire Chief and is now the Rescue Captain. I figure I could volunteer when needed since I have some experience from the Navy."

He blinked, wondering where that idea came from. Before he had a chance to take the words back, Jason nodded.

"He'd be glad to have you, I'm sure."

The idea of just sitting around waiting to answer a fire call would not be enough. Casting his gaze around the shop again, he said, "I'm going to need to work to keep my sanity. Are you serious about wanting somebody to work here?"

Jason's grin widened even further. "Hell, yeah! It's only part-time, but as far as I'm concerned, you can take over most of the tattoos. It won't take up all your time, so anything you want to do to work part-time in the garage is perfect also."

Relief moved through him at the idea of not hitting the road immediately again. The thought of staying in Baytown, at least for a little while, held appeal. *Damn... I haven't even seen it in the daylight.* But if the Bay at sunset was anything to go by, it'd be a nice place to stop until he figured out his next move.

Jason stood and tossed the empty water bottles into the recycle bin. "Have you got a place to stay?"

"I just fuckin' decided to stay," he laughed. Jerking his head toward the street, he said, "I saw a campground a couple miles down the road. I can ask if they have a camper to rent."

"Well, why don't you crash at my place? I've got an apartment over the shop that needs to be rented."

Stunned that Jason seemed to have an answer for everything, he asked, "Are you sure?"

"Absolutely. I'll show it to you, and then I'll head across the street to see Rose."

He looked across the road and saw an ice cream shop with a sign declaring 'Sweet Rose'. Grinning, he said, "Rose… pretty name."

Jason nodded and his face lighted as he nodded with enthusiasm. "Pretty lady." He flipped off the lights and started walking toward the back of the shop, calling over his shoulder, "Come on up, and I'll show you around. There are stairs from the back area of the shop. There's also an entrance from the alley behind, but I rarely use it."

Following upstairs, he was shocked when he walked into the apartment. The wooden floors had been refinished and the walls were freshly painted. A sofa and two comfortable chairs faced a wide-screened TV mounted on the brick wall. Glancing to the right, he could see a small kitchen with new appliances. "Fuck, man, this is nice."

Jason grinned and slapped him on the back. "Well, if you decide to call Baytown home and need a place to stay, I'll rent it to you."

"I never stay anywhere very long, you know that."

"Yeah, but eventually, we all have to settle down. And I'm telling you, Baytown is a nice place to settle."

He grunted his response. Considering he'd never found a place to settle, he doubted Baytown would be any different. But passing some time here while catching up and helping out a couple of old buddies, this apartment made for a nice temporary home. *Sure as hell beats a camper.*

"I'll pay rent for the time I'm here, so just let me know what it will be."

Jason nodded, then pointed out the two bedrooms, both outfitted with queen-size beds and a dresser. The bathroom, like the kitchen, had been completely redone and modernized.

Jason reached into his pocket and pulled out his keys, fiddling until he'd worked two off the key ring. Handing them to Joseph, he said, "One is for the shop and one for the apartment. Make yourself at home. I know there's no food in the refrigerator, but you passed a grocery store as you came into town. Plus, for break-fast, you can't do better than Jillian's Coffeehouse or Stuart's Pharmacy. Tomorrow, come on down to the garage, I can put you to work, and we'll find Zac."

The events of the day had happened so fast, Joseph barely had time for his brain to catch up with every-thing Jason was offering. He'd come on a lark, arrived unannounced, and already had a place to stay and an offer of work. He reached out his hand, hoping his appreciation came through in the handshake and back slap given and received.

Walking back downstairs after Jason, he waved goodbye and watched his friend jog across the street and go through a door next to the ice cream parlor. Looking up, he could see the lights on in the apartment above and smiled. Heading to his bike, he emptied the saddlebags, checked the locks, and made his way back upstairs.

It only took a few minutes to stow his toiletries into the bathroom and put his few clothes away. Sitting on the side of the bed, he pulled off his heavy boots, the clomp echoing off the wood as they dropped to the floor. He walked back to the living room, sat on the sofa, and flipped through channels. But he felt restless. Not finding any show or sports on TV worth watching, he turned it off, sitting in the quiet, letting his mind wander.

A rolling stone, he'd traveled to many places in the few years since he'd been out of the Navy. He'd find a place, find a job, and work until the urge to move on took over. Texas oil field. Louisiana shrimp boat. Georgia peach orchard. Tennessee whiskey distillery. He'd traveled to many other places, but the ones where he'd stopped and worked were the ones that stayed most in his mind. *And now, Baytown. Wonder how long this will last?*

The fatigue of the day settled over him and he felt older than his years. Glancing around, he was stunned that he was so quickly ensconced in a large, furnished apartment. Driving into town, he'd considered sleeping under the stars if needed.

He hefted his body from the sofa and flipped off the lights before walking straight into the bathroom. A shower washed off the travel and the scent from the hospital. Stepping out, he wiggled his toes on the thick, plush bathmat and grinned, wondering if Rose had contributed to Jason's apartment. He found the towel to be equally as plush and dried off quickly. He pulled on clean boxers and crawled into bed, surprised at the soft sheets, comfortable mattress, and fluffy pillow.

Having pulled a book from his pack, he reclined and read until his eyes grew tired. Turning off the lamp on the nightstand, he slid down, still stunned at the turn of events. When he'd driven into town, he figured a small, used camper would be where he laid his head, never imagining that he'd end up being offered a nice place to stay. Already Baytown was offering a respite.

Closing his eyes, he allowed the fatigue to pull him under.

Bolting upright in bed, Joseph looked around. The early light of dawn shone through the slats of the blinds, and for a moment, he had trouble remembering where he was. Even with as many places as he'd traveled, he usually woke instantly, knowing his surroundings. But having slept so soundly all through the night, he blinked in confusion while feeling completely refreshed.

He scraped his hand over his face, a smile hinting at the edges of his lips. He tossed the covers back and headed into the bathroom. Taking care of business, he dressed in his standard uniform of jeans, T-shirt, and boots. Walking through the living room, he grabbed his leather jacket, keys, and wallet, then headed down the stairs and through the shop. First order of business... breakfast.

Eschewing his bike, he decided to walk but determined to move his bike to the alley later so that he'd be able to use the back stairs. The light of day gave evidence to a street full of little shops, a bank, lots of businesses, and a library. He spied the green awning with the sign of Jillian's Coffeehouse & Galleria, but as he neared, his steps slowed. Peering through the window, he could see people bustling around, greeting each other, laughing, talking, and sitting at small tables crowded together. *Not my scene.*

He turned and headed in the other direction toward Stuart's Pharmacy. Entering, he discovered it was exactly what he'd hoped for. A small-town drugstore with the pharmacy in the back, aisles filled with items to purchase on the right, and a small diner on the left with booths and tables.

Sliding into the last red vinyl-covered booth, he barely had a chance to look at the menu before a matronly server in a pink uniform popped by. She was already pouring coffee before he had a chance to speak. Her gray hair was teased and sprayed into a bouffant, barely moving as her head bobbed when she greeted him warmly.

"Hey, sugar, I'm Doneeta, and I'll be serving you today. Well, today and any other day you come in for breakfast. I don't even ask anyone if they want coffee anymore. Been doing this job for over twenty years and never met somebody who didn't want coffee in the morning! Course, some people prefer tea, but I figure a big boy like you would want his strong coffee."

Startled at her greeting, he nodded his thanks. "I'll take your breakfast special. Extra-large."

"I'm not surprised. A boy your size has gotta fill up in the morning. My Harvey, God rest his soul, was a big man. He liked a breakfast that would get him going in the morning." She leaned down and winked. "Marlene ended up ordering too much bacon along with the sausage this week. Since you're getting a breakfast special, we'll throw them both onto the plate!"

He nodded his thanks again, and she bustled off to pour more coffee. He'd barely taken a sip of the hot, strong brew when his seat was jostled. Jerking his head around, his gaze landed on Jason, followed closely by Zac. He jumped to his feet, greeting Zac the same way he was greeted by Jason the previous evening. After hugs and back slaps, the two men slid into the booth across from him.

Jason yelled out, "Doneeta, make that two more of whatever this guy is having!"

"You got it, sugar! Lordy, Lordy, Marlene! We're going to get rid of all that extra bacon!"

Grinning, Joseph shook his head and focused his attention on his friends. Zac's dark hair was still trimmed short, swept to the side. The familiar, easy-going smile was on his face, and Joseph wondered if it was due to being out of the Navy, having a job he enjoyed, or being married. *Hell, probably all three.*

"I can't believe you're actually here, man," Zac enthused, his smile wide and eyes roaming over Joseph's face. "What have you been up to?"

"Traveling. Working. I'd stay awhile somewhere and then get the urge to move on."

"And home?" Zac prodded.

Snorting, he shook his head. "What home?" The last thing he wanted to do was talk about the place where he grew up. If the look on his face wasn't enough to let someone know that was a conversation he wasn't going to have, he felt sure the tone of his voice certainly gave evidence. But he didn't have to worry about these two.

That was probably why they'd become friends in the first place. He and Zac met when they worked on the same ship as Navy firefighters. Jason came around soon after as a mechanic. Somehow, the three of them bonded one night in a port after getting rip-roaring drunk. Zac talked about his mother's death and his father's alcoholism. Jason's parents had been killed while he was in the middle of the ocean on a Navy vessel. Joseph spilled his guts about his relationship with his parents. It might have seemed fucked up, but the three of them had been friends ever since.

"Well, you won't find a better place to call home than Baytown," Zac said, leaning back in his seat, drumming his fingers on the tabletop.

"Not looking for a place to call home, guys. Just looking for a chance to reconnect with old friends and a place to put my head at night for a while until I feel the urge to move on."

Jason held his gaze. "I'm telling you, Joseph, this place will get into your blood. You think it's just one of your many stopping points on your travels? It'll be hard to say goodbye."

He looked up in gratitude as Doneeta interrupted by placing their plates onto the table. He was starving, but he also wanted to halt the conversation that he knew wouldn't come true for him. Fuckin' happy endings were for others.

For several minutes, the three shoveled in the super-sized breakfast special. Eggs, bacon, sausage, biscuits and gravy, grits, hash brown potatoes, and Doneeta kept the coffee coming. When their plates were finally clean, the three men leaned back and groaned in satisfaction.

"Jason tells me that you'd like to volunteer with the fire department," Zac began.

"It's something I can do, and I'm more than happy to help."

Jason leaned forward, his forearms now resting on the table. "I talked to Rose last night after I got home, and she had an idea. Actually, I can't believe I didn't think of it at the beginning. Since I only need some tattoo work on the weekends, and right now I have two mechanics working for me in the garage bays, where I need help is an extra person to run the tow truck. When a call comes in now, one of them has to stop working on a vehicle. And I'm telling you, calls for the tow truck come in all the time."

Joseph nodded slowly, liking that idea of staying busy. "I got no problem driving a tow truck. I've also got some mechanical knowledge from some of the jobs I've done. I worked on oil field machinery and the engine of the shrimp boat I was on for a while." Chuckling, he added, "Hell, when I worked at the whiskey distillery in Tennessee, I helped them with their ancillary equipment."

A bark of laughter erupted from Zac. "Damn, you always could pick up something easily. If somebody showed you how it worked one time, that was it… you nailed it."

"You were the smartest person I'd ever met," Jason said, his eyes twinkling with mirth. "I always thought it was funny that you're such a fuckin' genius and loved hiding it."

He scowled and mumbled, "Not hiding it. Just not fuckin' flaunting it."

The other two laughed and his scowl deepened, only interrupted when Doneeta popped by again. He handed her a wad of bills to cover all three breakfasts plus a generous tip.

"Sugar, you're giving me too much," she protested, her brows raised to her bouffant hairline.

"No, ma'am. It's for you. Good breakfast. Good service."

Her eyes widened as she sucked in her breath. She reached out and rested her hand on his shoulder. "Well, Lordy be. My Harvey was a generous man, too. I'll share this with Marlene. I might have served, but she did the cooking."

With that, she bustled off again, and he turned back to the other two, seeing their wide grins. "Shut it," he rumbled, sliding out of the booth. The others followed, and the three men walked into the sunshine.

"I've got to get to the station. Come by sometime, and I'll show you the ropes." Zac tossed a wave and headed to his SUV.

Jason clapped him on the back. "If you're ready, we can head to the shop. We're just getting into vacation season, and I've got no doubt the tow truck will be called for soon."

With a nod, he slid his sunglasses onto his face and climbed into Jason's SUV. *Looks like my quick visit with friends is turning into a bit of a stay.* Strange, but that thought didn't scare him.

3

"What are you doing? This makes no sense!" With her hands planted on her hips and her fingers curling into fists, she wondered how everything could go so wrong. An errant strand of dark hair fell from her neat ponytail, most likely from swiping her hand over her face several times in frustration.

Samantha Collins stood in the middle of the lobby of Robertson's Veterinary Clinic, her gaze following Tom Robertson as he hustled back and forth between his office to the right of the reception area and out to his truck before returning and making the trip again with boxes in his hands. Tall and bespectacled, his short, dark brown hair was sprinkled with gray, and his usually warm eyes now avoided looking at her.

She'd arrived early like she had every day since he'd hired her. Today, instead of finding him prepping for the animals that would be seen, she found him emptying his office. After shock and disbelief shifted to the side and a tide of anger rode in full force, she jumped in front of the door, spread her arms out, and speared him with her glare. "Stop!" For a second, she wasn't sure if he was going to plow straight through her, but his feet halted even as he returned her glare. "What the hell is going on? Jesus, Tom, talk to me!"

His shoulders slumped as the air escaped his lungs in a rush. He dropped the box to the floor, his hands lifted to the side, and he shook his head. "Sam, I'm sorry."

"Tom, I don't know what you're sorry for. I don't know how to help or what to do unless you tell me what you're doing and why the hell you're doing it."

His eyes shifted to the side, staring out one of the large windows in the front of the clinic. He swallowed audibly, his Adam's apple bobbing, catching her attention for some inexplicable reason.

"I got a call last week that my father wasn't doing well. I didn't mention it because I thought there was time to figure out what I was going to do. I got another call yesterday that let me know that I was needed back in Boston. After I got packed up today, I was going to sit down and tell you all of this, but you showed up in the middle of me trying to get everything taken care of."

Her anger fled but frustration simply filled the empty space. "Okay. I'm sorry. I can see that you're upset about your father, and I understand." Sucking in a deep breath, she let it out slowly. "What I don't understand is what you're doing right now."

"I've got to go back to Boston and deal with my family. I have no idea how long it's going to be, so I made the decision late yesterday to simply move back."

"Temporarily?"

"No, Sam. I'm leaving the Eastern Shore."

She blinked, her gaze jerking around the room. "But... but... the clinic? The business is growing. We talked about hiring another vet so there'd be three of us! You're in the process of getting a vet intern!"

"I know, and I'm sorry." He sighed heavily again. "I just don't have any choice. But you're going to be taken care of. I called my attorney yesterday evening, and he's already drawn up all the paperwork. I'm leaving the business to you—"

"You can't do that!"

"I can, and I did. It's solvent, I promise. The books are good, the staff will stay the same, and the new intern will be here soon. I know it's going to be hard on you, and you'll be spread thin, but you can hire a new vet almost immediately if he wants to stay. And if not, it's spring, and new veterinarians will be graduating soon."

"This wasn't what I wanted," she said, her heart pounding and her stomach churning. She had been lured to the rural area in need of a vet, excited for the chance to practice medicine for an established clinic. Going to small farms, getting to know the residents and their pets, helping out at the shelter. After the years in the military, the ease of being a shore-life veterinarian was easy on her soul. The notion of running the clinic held no appeal. "I don't know that I can handle the pressure of trying to run this place by myself for a while."

"Sam, truly, I'm sorry. But I have no choice. I have to leave."

She stood unmoving for a moment, but no reply was forthcoming. Feet like lead, she stepped to the side, watching as he gathered the box from the floor and walked out the door. Her mind was whirling with the changes that had struck like lightning in the last fifteen minutes.

Tom walked inside again, and for once didn't head back into his office. Instead, he stopped right in front of her. She looked up and saw what appeared to be regret slashing across his face. Her emotions were churning, frustration warring with anger, and a large dose of fear mixed with disbelief. She had no idea what he observed staring at her. *Probably the mess that I'm feeling inside.*

There were no words to stop Tom from leaving considering it was a family crisis that was taking him away. Still unable to think of anything to say, she simply held his gaze.

"Sam, you're going to be fine. You're smart, competent, and caring. I know it's going to be rough until you can get help, but I left instructions for the staff. The new vet intern starts next week and can cover a lot of the smaller jobs."

She nodded, the motion more automatic than an indication of agreement.

He reached his hand out, and she hesitated only a second before grasping it in return. The professional handshake seemed incongruent with the loss of a colleague, but he surprised her when he bent and kissed the top of her head, mumbling, "Sam, I'm sorry. For… everything."

With that, he hustled around her and moved out the door. She followed on wooden legs and watched as he backed out of the parking lot and pulled onto the street, quickly disappearing into the distance.

What just happened? What the hell just happened?

Standing outside the clinic, she continued to stare as though that would bring him back. Robertson's Veterinary Clinic was not located on the main road that ran north and south through the Eastern Shore but was on a side road. The location was still easy to find while offering the animals that had to be boarded overnight due to surgeries a quiet place for their runs in the back. Tom had taken over the clinic from an elderly veterinarian in the area who'd retired years before. He'd built the practice and spent money improving the clinic. While the surgical area might not be considered state-of-the-art, it was more than adequate for what they needed. The office manager and receptionist, Annette, ordered supplies, handled the schedules, and kept things running. There was one vet assistant and one vet tech. Tom had wanted to hire another veterinarian but found it difficult to find someone willing to move to the Eastern Shore, so he'd been working on securing a vet intern.

She tilted her head back, letting the early morning sun land on her, trying to warm the cold, heavy weight of responsibility that had settled inside. With Tom gone, she knew her days off were gone as well. The clinic was closed on Saturday afternoons and Sundays, but as the only veterinarian in the area, she could get called in at any time. When that had happened in the past on weekends, Tom had given her a day off during the week.

Now, it looks like I'll be working seven days a week. Great. Just fuckin' great.

Another car pulled into the parking lot, and she watched silently as Annette alighted from her vehicle. One look at Annette's face and she could tell the intrepid office manager was already aware of what was happening. Not giving Annette a chance to greet her, she glared, her fists firmly planted on her hips again. "You knew. You knew and said nothing to me!"

Annette rushed over, her hands up in a placating gesture. "Sam, I'm so sorry. I didn't know anything for sure until yesterday evening. Tom had been talking all week about not knowing what to do, but he swore me to secrecy."

"Secrecy!" She reared back, deciding to give way to the anger. "He's gone. Gone, Annette. I had no warning, no chance to prepare. Now, this whole business has settled onto *my* shoulders."

"We'll all help, Sam. No one else knows but me. We'll tell Susan and Tonya today when they get in. "

"When are we going to figure out how to make this work with just one veterinarian?"

"I took our schedule home last night, and I've been working on it—"

A growl erupted from deep within Samantha as she thought of Tom confiding his troubles to Annette and not her. She couldn't decide if she was more hurt or pissed. She had wondered if Tom and Annette had more than a professional relationship, but that was only from a few glances she'd witnessed between them. In her late-thirties, Annette had been with the clinic for years.

Tall and thin, she was attractive, and it had crossed Samantha's mind that the two of them would make a good couple. That thought now made her wonder how Annette was handling Tom's departure.

Annette threw her hands up and plowed on. "I know you're upset, but I didn't know what else to do. I worked on the schedule, and the new vet intern will start on Monday. I looked over the résumé that Tom gave me, and Brentley should be a good fit. Native Virginian. From Virginia Beach originally. He's one semester away from graduating. He can do some of the minor surgeries like spays and neuters without your supervision. That'll keep things going until you can hire him or a new veterinarian."

Sam dropped her chin and stared at her sneakers, her head shaking back and forth slowly. With her eyes squeezed tightly shut, she wished she could turn back the clock to the previous hour when she was just waking, happy, satisfied, and at peace.

"Sam."

Annette's voice brought her back to the present, and she lifted her head, resignation settling heavy across her shoulders.

"Sam, honey, I promise, it'll be okay. Susan and Tonya are coming in this morning, and I shifted our morning appointments so that we'll have time to deal."

A snort erupted, and she shook her head again. "I guess I should be embarrassed. This is now my clinic, and you're handling things a lot better than I am."

Annette stepped closer and reached out to grab her hand, giving a squeeze. "I've had the week to start thinking about things and this was just dumped on you this morning, so don't feel bad. We'll get through this and come out still being the best veterinary clinic in North Heron."

"We're the *only* vet clinic in North Heron."

Annette waved her hand in front of her and rolled her eyes. "Details, details, let's not worry about details!"

She barked out a laugh, and it felt good to release the tension. Two more cars were pulling into the parking lot, and Sam sucked in a deep breath. "Okay, it looks like we're all here. I guess it's time to figure out what we're going to do."

By the end of the day, Samantha's brain was more scrambled than it had been that morning. She was grateful that Annette was so organized. And the memory of Tonya's angry diatribe at Tom's leaving so quickly without preparing them made her smile.

She'd spent time looking over the lawyer's papers. All she had to do was sign. Tom, true to his word, had left the entire clinic, debt-free, to her. She would need to change the name of the clinic, open new bank accounts and lines of credit, and re-set up payrolls and employee contracts. All of those items made her head spin, but between the attorney and Annette, she was assured it would be taken care of.

She had to admit Annette's schedule was good, but that was assuming the new vet intern was going to fit in well and be willing to jump in and work hard immediately. The last thing she wanted to do in the midst of everything else was to train someone new.

That evening, all four women left at the same time, which was unusual, but by the end of the day, they were drained. She locked the door and waved as Tonya's husband picked her up, their kids in the back seat waving as well. Annette and Susan pulled out right after, and Samantha was grateful her truck started on the first try.

On the drive home, it sputtered several times, but she stepped on the gas a little harder, and as usual, the engine caught, lurching forward. She leaned and rubbed her hand on the dashboard. "Come on, ol' Bessie. I can't afford to put you out to pasture and buy a new truck now even if I wanted to."

She soon made it to her home, small and temporary as it was. After she'd been hired by Tom, she'd jumped into working long days and sometimes long nights. She bought a mid-sized camper, parking it on the plot of land she'd bought. One of the older farmers had a section of his farmland that backed to the Chesapeake Bay. He'd thought about selling it for years and told her he knew he could make a mint off of it by selling it to a developer who'd want to put up a million-dollar home. Instead, he preferred it going to someone who needed it, and considering she came out every time his pigs needed a vet, he sold it to her for very little.

The camper was much smaller than a mobile home and yet large enough for her. A small sofa on one side faced a small TV. A dinette table with two booth seats next to a small kitchen. A double bed was at the end with a small bathroom and closet next to it.

Most importantly, she could look out the window over her bed and see the water. It wasn't much, but it was hers.

Pulling up next to her home, she climbed out and heard the familiar baying that always brought a smile to her face. With the farmer's help, they'd fenced in a large area that included a big doghouse, and when his bloodhound had puppies, he'd given one to her. Considering they were purebred, she'd been stunned by his gift. He'd sold the others but gave her the runt, saying it needed special care. Now, at a year old, the beautiful dog was already a big boy and loyal to the bone.

Walking to the gate, she unlatched it and let him out, laughing as he bounded around. "Come on, Frodo. Let's get some food."

She'd barely set the food dish onto the floor when he immediately dove in, his long ears dangling all about. Just watching him eat made her feel lighter than she had all day. Her phone rang, and she glanced at the caller ID. Smiling again, she hit connect.

"Hey, Dad."

"Hi, sweetheart. Your mom was just saying to me that she'd had you on her mind all day long so we decided to call."

She had no idea how her parents were able to do that. Somehow, across the miles, even when she'd been on the other side of the world, they always seemed to know when she was upset or worried. "As usual, Mom is right."

"Oh, dear, that sounds like a story. Hang on, let me put you on speaker since your mom's right here."

Her father had been a veterinarian in the rural mountains of Virginia for many years. Knowing her parents would understand, she started at the beginning of her day and talked all the way through the events. Neither offered empty platitudes nor did they trash Tom even though they were both irritated that he hadn't given her more warning. By the end of the conversation, she felt better. Somehow, simply unburdening herself made her feel more in control. Her parents' knowledge of the business was invaluable.

"Have you thought about a name for your clinic?" her mother asked.

"My staff and I bounced around a couple of ideas this afternoon when we were tired of thinking of everything else. I suppose Collins' Veterinary Clinic would work."

"That's kind of boring, don't you think?"

Laughing, she leaned over and rubbed Frodo's ears. "I guess it is. I really haven't had time to think about it."

"Well, it might seem silly in light of everything else you have to deal with, but I'd give it some thought. After all, it's going to be on your sign, your shirts, your logo, your business. Go with something fun!"

"I'll sleep on it, and we'll see what I come up with," she promised. "Thanks for calling, Mom and Dad. I really needed this."

She fixed a sandwich and grabbed chips and a beer, taking her dinner down to the beach with Frodo bounding along beside her. Smiling, she watched him move along, his nose to the ground, inspecting the area. "Any new smells since last night, boy?"

He looked up, his soulful eyes on her sandwich, and she laughed. "Hey, you had your dinner."

She sat on the sand and watched the sunset as she munched her dinner and finished her beer. A breeze blew over, lifting her spirits, and she sucked in a deep breath of salt air. Laying back, she watched the clouds catch the orange streaks of setting sunlight. After several minutes, Frodo came over, and she noticed a slight limp. Sitting up, she grabbed his paw, rubbing her fingers around his pads, finding a little sand burr. She pulled it out and rubbed his head. "That's the story of my life. Taking care of paws." Thinking of her larger animal clients, she laughed. "Well, hoofs and paws."

4

TWO MONTHS LATER

Samantha's phone rang, jolting her awake. She rolled over, her gaze landing on the time just as she connected the call. Six thirty. It wouldn't seem that early except she'd been up into the wee hours of the night with an emergency surgery when someone's beloved pet was hit by the family car. Now, with only three hours of sleep, she answered her phone with more of a yawn than a greeting.

"'Lo, Sam Collins."

"Sam, I'm so sorry to call this early in the morning. It's Lizzie. Lizzie Weston."

Samantha held the phone with one hand and rubbed her bleary eyes with the other. "Lizzie, what's wrong?"

"I had a couple of goats get out of their pen and into the pasture. I don't know what's happened, but... but... oh, Sam... they're dead!"

Lizzie's words had the effect of cold water dousing her, and she tossed off the covers, trying not to step on

Frodo as she headed into her bathroom. "Don't touch anything, and I'll be right out. Give me about twenty minutes to get there."

Disconnecting, she blinked a few more times as she stared into the mirror. Her dark brown hair stuck out in a sleep-messy nest around her head. She sighed, dragging a brush through the tresses, taming it into a ponytail. She had neither thick, curly hair nor straight, sleek hair. It wasn't luxurious or filled with red or blonde highlights. It was just brown. Plain brown. Wavy enough to stick out around her face when she perspired but otherwise totally unremarkable.

Leaning forward, she caught sight of the row of freckles across her cheeks. The similarity to the cover image of a childhood book she used to read, *Rebecca of Sunnybrook Farm*, struck her. The freckles were cute when she was a child but irritating as an adult. Especially an adult that looked much younger than she was. *God, I need more sleep!*

Shaking her head to dislodge the ridiculous early-morning musings, she splashed water on her face and grabbed her tub of moisturizer. She never worried with makeup but as much as she was outside knew that moisturizer and sunscreen were essential. Quickly finishing in the bathroom, she dressed in a pair of jeans, a worn T-shirt with her clinic logo, and a light jacket. Pulling on thick cotton socks, she looked down at Frodo sleeping.

"Damn, boy, I hate making you go out into your pen, but I have no idea how long I'm going to be gone." He groaned as he stood, and she grabbed some food before jamming her feet into her thick rubber boots and heading outside to secure him inside his pen. "If I can get away early today, I will." The past two months without Tom hadn't been easy, but she was getting used to long days and little sleep.

It took a few tries for her old truck to start, but it finally rumbled to life. There was sparse traffic on the Eastern Shore, and she made it quickly to the Weston Farm as the sun was beginning to peek over the horizon.

Lizzie's grandparents had owned the farm, and when Samantha had first come to the Eastern Shore, she met Beau Weston. His granddaughter, Lizzie, had convinced him that goats and alpacas would be money makers for them, and he indulged her whim. A whim that turned out to be right. Lizzie received the necessary permits for the alpacas, and even though Beau was now gone, she was running Weston farms with great ideas for her goat's milk soap and lotions, hair sales from alpaca shearings, and animal petting days.

Pulling off the road, she drove under the Weston Farms sign and followed the gravel drive past the large, beautiful, white farmhouse around toward the barn and pastures. Scott Redding, Lizzie's boyfriend, was standing outside waiting for her as were the County Sheriff, Colt Hudson, and three deputies. *What the hell is the sheriff doing here?* Glancing to the side, she also saw several of their friends offering support to a distraught Lizzie.

She turned off the truck engine but it continued to sputter and chug until it finally quit. She could see Colt shaking his head, staring at her, and had no doubt he was thinking she needed to get a new vehicle. In fact, as she looked at all of the faces standing there, she could see the same expression. "They can bite me," she grumbled to herself as she got out of her truck, trying to shake off the fatigue that was her constant companion. It seemed like all her money was going right back into the vet business, and considering she worked all the time, she had no idea when she'd be able to buy a new vehicle... even if she was willing to give the old one up.

Rounding the front of the truck, her gaze shot out to the pasture where she could see the animals lying on the ground. She jerked around and observed Lizzie's tearful face, her heart going out to her. "Oh, fuck, Lizzie. I'm so sorry."

"Please, Sam, tell me they didn't suffer."

Whenever an animal died, owners always begged to be assured that their pet had not suffered. Half the time, Samantha knew she was lying to them but figured the little bit of peace was a gift she could offer. In this case, having not examined the animals, she had no idea what to say, and shooting a glance toward the show of law enforcement nearby, she sighed heavily. "Lizzie, honey, why don't you let Scott take you back to the house? I'll take a look and... um... talk to the Sheriff. As soon as I know what we're dealing with, honey, I promise I'll come talk to you."

She waited until Scott nodded his appreciation and one of their friends, Katelyn, took Lizzie's arm, leading her back into the house. She walked into the pasture and knelt by the goats, the knees of her jeans instantly soaking up the heavy dew. Ignoring the wetness, she quickly ascertained that the goats were indeed dead. As she began her examination, Scott looked toward the others. "Colt, we gotta do something. This shit can't keep going. First, the property. Next, the animals. When the fuck is somebody going to come after her?"

What the hell? She shot to her feet, staring at the tight faces of the men standing around. "Obviously, there are things going on here that I had no idea about. Colt? I'm gonna let you tell me what you need from me."

Colt's jaw was tight as he looked down at her. "Sam, I need to know the cause of death. Accidental or intentional."

Nodding, she snapped on a pair of gloves and knelt next to the goats again. She began by examining their faces, pulling her phone out of her pocket to snap pictures. She withdrew blood samples, labeling them before placing them into her satchel. Vomit was on the ground nearby, and she scooped small samples, placing them into plastic bags. Moving to the other goat, she also took samples of fecal matter. Looking at the remains of cut plant limbs nearby, she pinched her mouth tight, anger filling her.

Standing, she turned toward the others. "Azaleas are the standard flowering bush of the south but well known to be poisonous to many animals, including goats. I remember Lizzie taking out all of the azalea bushes around the house when she decided to raise goats. Her grandfather hated to lose the pretty bushes that her grandmother had planted and loved, but he understood Lizzie's need to make the entire area safe. Obviously, the goats are penned and don't get to the house, but she didn't want to take a chance." She jerked her head downward to the clump of cut, half-eaten plants. "That's the source of the poison right there."

One of the deputies opened his mouth and said something stupid, but instead of replying, Samantha shook her head, letting Colt deal with him. Scott looked over and asked, "Why did the asshole put the plants out here when the goats were in the pen near the barn?"

"I'm afraid that's for you all to figure out. I can't begin to imagine what kind of person would poison defenseless animals." Air left her lungs in a rush, and her heart ached. It never got easier dealing with a sick or injured animal, and yet she never thought of leaving the profession. Looking back at Colt, she stared at the large, handsome sheriff. She had always thought him to be a bit cold, uncertain if it was the burden of his responsibilities or simply his personality. But now that he was engaged, having fallen in love with a wonderful single mother and planned on adopting her son, Sam noticed a softness about him that had been missing.

"You okay, Sam?" he asked.

She blinked, shaking her head, wondering if lack of sleep was making her mind wander. "Yeah, yeah. I'm going to head to the barn and check out the rest of the animals to make sure there's nothing else going on. Once you're finished out here, let me know. I'll take care of disposing of the goats after I talk to Lizzie."

She collected her sample bags and placed them into

her satchel before standing. Walking into the barn, it didn't take long for her to ascertain that all of the other animals were fine and healthy. Her heart was heavy, but she could not help but smile at the antics of the goats as they bleated and butted each other out of the way to get to her.

She eventually made her way to the kitchen door and knocked. Gaining Lizzie's permission, she stepped inside and accepted the cup of coffee that Scott handed to her with gratitude. Once settled around the table, Sam lifted her tired eyes toward Lizzie as the young farmer gushed her appreciation that Sam had dropped everything to come straight to the farm.

Shaking her head, Samantha smiled weakly and waved her hand. "Oh, Lizzie, I'm glad I could be here for you. I'm just sorry for the reason." She took another sip of the strong brew and cleared her throat. "Okay, let's get this done, and I'll take care of the goats for you."

She sucked in a fortifying breath, then explained the azalea clippings that she found and her assumption that someone had placed them there. "I've taken blood samples from both goats as well as samples from the vomit and feces nearby. This will let me know for sure if the azaleas were the culprit."

Scott stood and offered his hand. "Dr. Collins, we appreciate what you've done more than you can know."

"I can't say it was my pleasure but it was my job. I'm glad I could be here for you." She had met Scott a couple of times and wanted to remove the formality. "Oh, and by the way, call me Sam… everyone does."

He nodded and turned toward Lizzie, his face filled

with concern. Sam watched as he enveloped Lizzie in his embrace, and her heart squeezed with the exhibition of raw emotion between Scott and Lizzie. She turned away, placing her cup into the sink, a sense of loneliness threatening to overtake her. Clearing her throat, she offered a small smile before nodding goodbye.

Heading to her truck, her feet felt heavier as she forced her mind to the next part of her day. Planning to back up as close to the deceased animals as possible so that someone could help her move them into the bed of her truck, she climbed behind the steering wheel. The engine grinded and clunked over and over but didn't start. Dropping her chin to her chest, she sighed. *Damn, can this day get any worse?*

She started to pull out her phone, but Colt waved her off, already on his. It was a simple gesture, but she was grateful for any help. Thirty minutes later, she was leaning against her truck with her eyes closed when the rumble of a diesel engine and the crunch of gravel had her look up to see a tow truck pulling into Lizzie's drive. The door to the large truck opened, and a booted foot emerged. As the man climbed down, Sam's gaze strayed from the foot up to a muscular, jean-clad thigh, up to a fabulous ass, and continued to wide, thick shoulders. By the time he turned around to face them, she kept staring, realizing that the front was every bit as glorious as the back.

He was a big man, and that was saying something considering that many of the men she knew were big. His dark hair was wavy and long, pulled back into a ponytail at the base of his neck. What captured her attention was the blonde streak near the front. On any other man, that could look ridiculous, but on him? Pure hot.

His jeans were worn, his black T-shirt was tight across his chest, and his arms were a sleeve of tattoos. Not one to give in to flights of fancy, something about this man instantly sent vibrations straight through her body, waking up the reminder she'd had a long dry spell when it came to a roll in the hay for something more than trying to give an inoculation to a goat who'd head-butted her.

Scott tossed up his hand in greeting. "I see Jason has got you working in the garage today as well as the tattoo shop."

"Yep."

"We had a problem here this morning. I don't know if Jason filled you in, but Dr. Collins, the veterinarian, needs to deal with two of Lizzie's goats that were poisoned and killed."

Her gaze was still pinned on the man's face, noting his jaw tightened at Scott's words. The large man simply nodded.

"I wasn't sure if one of Jason's mechanics could see if he could get Sam's truck started now or if it was going to have to be towed. Since you're here, I'm assuming all the mechanics are busy."

The man simply nodded again, still holding Samantha's attention as though he was a magnet and she was pure metal. She licked her dry lips and waited for him to look her way.

"Well, since it's going to have to be towed into the

shop, I'll follow so that I can take Sam back to the vet's practice to get another vehicle. We'll still have to dispose of the goats."

"Don't worry about following," the man said, his gaze shooting toward the pasture. "I can get the vet to the office and can also deal with the goats." He walked straight past Samantha without looking down at her, instead turning around to Scott, and reached out his hand. "Keys?"

Surprised that he was asking Scott for her keys, Samantha stepped forward and pulled them out of her pocket, giving them a jingle as she held them out.

He jerked slightly as he looked down at her, seeming to notice her for the first time. His gaze raked up and down her before he asked, "Where's the vet?"

Being short, she was used to people sometimes overlooking her. Being female, she was used to occasionally being dismissed. But the blast of his dismissal hit her exhausted emotions and all of his sexiness fled. If she could have incinerated him with her glare, she would have. He may have been a foot taller than her, but she pulled herself to her full height, arched an eyebrow, and held his gaze. "I am."

The man didn't even try to cover up his incredulity. "You're Sam? The veterinarian?"

Planting her hands on her hips, Samantha cocked her head to the side. "Which stuns you more? That my name is Sam? Or that a female can be a veterinarian?"

The man held her gaze for a moment, then scowled and turned without answering, walking back to the tow truck. He deftly maneuvered it so he would be able to hook up her truck.

Glancing toward Scott, Samantha snorted. "The man doesn't say much, does he? And what little he does say, he manages to put his foot into his mouth."

Scott's lips twitched. "You can trust him, that's all you need to know. I need to go check on Lizzie."

She watched Scott return to the farmhouse and felt guilty. He had enough on his plate dealing with Lizzie and everything happening to Weston Farms and didn't need to take on Samantha's irritation.

She turned to let the truck driver know that he needed to back her truck up closer so they could get to the animals, but the sight in front of her caused her feet to stutter to a halt as her mouth dropped open.

The man had walked into the field and kneeled to pick up one of the heavy goats into his arms, cradling its lifeless body carefully, giving evidence that he understood the precious burden. He walked back and laid it gently into the back of Sam's pickup truck before going back into the field, and with just as much care, bringing the second goat's body.

Her breath was shallow, her focus entirely on watching his actions, strength mixed with gentleness.

Within a few minutes, he had hooked up her truck and walked past her, still not saying anything. He opened the passenger door of the tow truck, turned around, and looked at her. She blinked out of her reverie. Assuming his action was his way of saying it was time to go, she grabbed her satchel, walked to the door, and looked up. The truck was huge, and she was glad there was a running board. He stuck out his hand, and she placed her much smaller one in his, allowing him to give her a boost. With her ass planted onto the seat, she glanced at him. "Just so you know, my name is Samantha. But everyone calls me Sam."

"Joseph." Then he slammed the door shut before walking around to the driver's side.

Her cheeks puffed out. *Great. I get Mr. Fucking Personality to spend part of my morning with.* Tired and wishing she'd had another cup of coffee, she turned and faced forward. The memory of watching him carry the goats so carefully stuck with her, and she sighed. *At least he's nice to animals.* "So, was it my nickname or that I'm a woman that made you think I wasn't the veterinarian?"

"You look like you're barely eighteen."

Swinging her head around, she glared. "You're about eleven years off," she muttered, trying to ignore the way his presence filled the cab of the truck. Giving up, she looked out the windshield and counted the miles until they could be out of each other's company. Unfortunately, that took a while.

Joseph pulled into the driveway of another farm, and without telling Samantha what he was doing, climbed out and walked over to the fence and leaned a muscular arm on top of the post. He talked to the older man working in the field, obviously having more words in him than had been evident with her. The farmer nodded his head, handed Joseph a shovel, and the two men shook hands.

Walking back over to the truck, he climbed inside

and stuck the shovel behind the seat. "We can bury the animals on the back of his property."

Having no response to that and not being in control of her own vehicle at the moment, she remained quiet. They soon pulled to the side of the fence, and Joseph climbed out, grabbing the shovel. He walked to a far corner and began digging a hole in the soft dirt.

Feeling ridiculous sitting in the cab of the truck, she opened the door and climbed down. Walking over, she watched for a moment, trying not to be distracted by the flexing muscles and light sheen of sweat that covered his arms. Feeling heat inside that had nothing to do with the sun shining, she asked, "Do you have another shovel?"

"No."

"Well, then let's take turns digging."

"No."

"What is wrong with you? I'm just trying to help!"

He stopped and stood, his arm resting on the handle of the shovel, and even though his eyes were hidden behind his sunglasses, she felt the burn of his gaze move over her. "Nothing's wrong with me. You're the doctor. I'm just doing some of the grunt work."

She opened her mouth then snapped it shut, unable to think of her retort. It was obvious he was going to keep doing what he was going to do, so she turned and made her way back to her pickup truck. Unlatching the tailgate, she let it down. He had wrapped the two goats in an old tarp, and she gave a tug but knew it was futile. They were much too heavy.

A few minutes later, he followed but hesitated as

they stared down at the deceased animals. "You should wait in the truck."

A multitude of emotions as well as responses slammed into her all at once. *I'm a veterinarian, not a delicate flower. This is not the first death of an animal I've ever seen. Don't treat me as though I'm weak. I've been in the Army, I've seen death.* But before she had a chance to open her mouth and let the floodgate of comments flow, he pushed his sunglasses up onto his head, and she saw his eyes. Green with flecks of amber. Eyes that held emotion. Eyes that held concern.

Deflated, she sighed and shook her head. "Thank you, no. With only one shovel there's little I can do other than watch. But I can report to Lizzie that I saw this to the very end."

Something passed through his eyes, an emotion she couldn't define. But before she had a chance to think further on it, he flipped the sunglasses back down, shuttering his thoughts and any chance she had of divining more of the mysterious Joseph.

She grabbed one end of the tarp, and if he had planned on arguing that he could do it himself, she was ready for him. But he remained quiet, lifting the other end, and they made it to the hole, albeit somewhat staggering on her side. A trickle of sweat ran between her shoulder blades, and she wiped her forehead to keep the sweat from her eyes. Repeating their actions, they lowered the second goat into the shallow grave.

She knelt, her hand resting lightly on the tarp for just a few seconds, emotion moving through her. Poisoned. *Who the hell would have poisoned these innocent animals?* A heavy sigh left her lips as she stood. She stepped back, lifted her gaze to Joseph, grateful that he had waited patiently to give her a moment of grief. With a nod, she watched him shovel the loose dirt, covering the two carcasses.

Their task complete, they climbed back into the tow truck, silent as ever. Catching a glimpse of her head in the side-view mirror, she spied hair sticking out at odd angles around her face from the sweat. A smudge of dirt was on her cheek. Her hands and knees were dirty as well. She had no energy to attempt conversation, and while he was gorgeous, noticing that sweat and dirt only made him more sexy while she felt like a wet, dirty mop, she remained quiet.

He pulled past the sign for the veterinary clinic after she gave him directions and parked in front. She climbed out after retrieving her satchel and turned to look up at him behind the wheel. She hesitated, wondering if a tip was proper... or insulting. "Thank you, Joseph. I really appreciate the extra help."

"No problem," he rumbled. "Jason will call you about your truck."

The dismissal felt final, so she shut the door and watched as her beloved truck was towed away by the elusive Joseph. *Get a grip, girl. A great ass doesn't make up for an aloof, brooding personality.* She snorted as she walked into the clinic. *Okay, it almost does.*

Fatigue pulled at her, making every muscle ache, but she couldn't go home. Walking inside, she gave a quick rundown to her staff about the morning, then went back to the room where they had a large washing machine and dryer and small shower. Stripping, she jumped into the shower and in only a minute had washed off the dirt, sweat, and smell of goats. Changing into spare scrubs, she tossed her clothes into the wash. Heading directly to their small lab next to the surgical room, she prepared the blood samples to be sent out. She completed an initial toxicity screen before she had other client appointments scheduled.

When she got a break in the afternoon, she called Lizzie to give her an update. "It'll be several weeks before we get a definitive answer, but my examination was definitely plant toxicity."

After more reassurances from her that the goats would have died quickly, she was surprised when Lizzie asked, "Did you get your truck fixed?"

Samantha snorted. "The grumpy bear took my truck to Jason's, and he's working on it. I should be able to get it back tomorrow."

"Grumpy bear?"

"I know I shouldn't call Joseph that because he really was very kind this morning. But throughout the entire ordeal, he barely said a word to me. I think if he could talk only in single words or grunts, he would."

They said their goodbyes, and Samantha leaned back in her chair, scrubbing her hand over her face. Annette poked her head through the doorway, a sympathetic expression on her face. "You need to go home. Susan and Brentley can handle everything else this afternoon. Tonya is ready to leave, and she'll take you home. I can pick you up in the morning."

Nodding, she agreed. "You're right." Brentley was the

veterinarian intern, and he'd jumped in, easily joining their team. Standing, she placed her hands on her lower back and stretched.

It didn't take long to get home, and she turned toward Tonya, who waved away her thanks. "Sam, you're there for everyone... the least we can do is take care of each other."

Frodo began baying, and she hopped out of the car, waving goodbye. She laughed as she let him out of the pen. He ran around, sniffing all around her pants and boots. Even with a shower, she knew the large dog would be able to ferret out new smells. "I was at a farm today, boy. You're going to pick up lots of scents."

Hours later, exhausted, she'd had dinner and finished a book she'd been reading. Turning off the lights, she let her hand drift to the side of the bed, rubbing Frodo's ears.

The events of the day moved through her mind like competing movie scenes... Lizzie's distress and the anger when examining the goats mixed in with the image of Joseph gently carrying the deceased animals. Baytown and the Eastern Shore had no shortage of handsome men who were also kind, and it seemed as though most of them were happily married or engaged. *What about Joseph? Is there someone special waiting for him?* Remembering his earlier dismissal of her, she sighed. *Probably... a tall, long-legged, beauty... the opposite of me.* It wasn't false modesty. She knew she was passable in the looks department, but as a petite woman, she'd often wondered what it would be like for a man not to have to bend to kiss her. *Not that I have any men lined up to kiss me, anyway.*

As tired as she was, she chuckled at the image and wondered if she'd be able to sleep but soon drifted off, images of a muscular, green-eyed, handsome man filling her dreams.

5

Joseph woke the next morning, his cock hard and aching and his mind full of the dark-haired, dark-eyed, natural beauty that he'd spent time with yesterday. *A veterinarian. How the hell was I supposed to know who 'Sam' was?* Considering the fact that she looked more like a young college student, he'd assumed she was there helping on the farm or with the vet. While he lay in bed trying to forget his disastrous meeting with the beautiful Samantha, his cock wasn't about to let him.

He had noticed her as soon as he'd approached Scott. *Hell, who wouldn't notice her?* The top of her head would easily tuck under his chin. She was petite but had curves. Curves that were evident in the fit of her jeans across her ass, and the T-shirt that stretched slightly across her breasts, the words 'Hoofs and Paws' drawing his eye.

Tossing back the covers, he stalked across the floor and into the bathroom, hoping a shower would do the trick. Normally, his morning wood was something he could ignore. Just pure biology and anatomy. But today, the image of Samantha Collins stayed with him, and his cock wasn't going to listen to anything his mind said.

He scrubbed his body and washed his hair, but his dick still ached. Closing his eyes, he could imagine her kneeling in front of him, her luscious mouth taking him deep. He palmed his erection, sliding his hand up and down its length, wishing it was her and not his hand. It only took a moment before his release blasted out, washing down the drain. He came so hard he saw stars bursting behind his tightly closed eyelids and couldn't imagine what it would be like if he was deep inside of her. Snorting, he opened his eyes. *Like that would ever happen.*

Never a great conversationalist, there was something about her that short-circuited his brain. *She's got a doctorate degree, probably rich, and probably stuck up her own ass.* As soon as that thought hit him, he knew he was wrong. He hated people judging him without getting to know him, and he couldn't believe he was about to do the same thing with her. *Even if she was rich, it wouldn't matter. Hell, I know that better than anybody.*

Drying off, he stalked naked into the bedroom and jerked on clean boxers and jeans. Pissed at himself for trying to come up with a reason for not liking her, he pulled the T-shirt on over his head and ran his fingers through his hair.

As though he had no control over his thoughts, he remembered everything about Samantha. Her arms were toned, and observing her strain to lift the heavy tarp-covered animals, he could tell she was no stranger to physically demanding labor, even if it was more than she could handle on her own. For a second, his own mother flashed through his mind... he'd never seen her lift more than a martini glass.

Pushing that thought down, he settled his mind back to Samantha. The jeans she wore were worn at the knees. The rubber boots on her feet looked like they'd seen better days. She was hardly tricked out in expensive clothing, even for a veterinarian at work. And her truck. Her piece of shit truck. *Why wouldn't she dump it and buy a new one?*

Unable to come up with an answer, he shoved his feet into his boots and walked into the kitchen. He'd been in Baytown for two months and didn't have a definite plan on when to move on. Strange... but he didn't have the urge to roam yet, satisfied to earn his keep and help out his friends. He was still renting the apartment over the tattoo shop from Jason. Baytown was now in full vacation season, and he usually worked Friday evenings and Saturdays at the tattoo shop. Nothing very complicated. Nor very interesting.

Mostly for vacationing families, Baytown wasn't a haven for college students looking for a wild time. Usually, his tattoos were for someone on vacation who decided on a lark to get their child's name tattooed on their wrist or a Celtic cross on their shoulder. Sometimes it was more challenging. Two weeks ago, a group of bikers traveling down the eastern coast had stopped at the pub and several made their way to the shop, adding ink to their already-tattooed bodies.

Last weekend, it was a bridesmaid party. He made sure the women were not drunk and they knew what they were doing when they signed the forms. Three of them got butterflies, two of them got hearts and flowers, and the bride had her soon-to-be husband's name tattooed on her shoulder. *Hope like hell the marriage lasts or she'll be regretting that tattoo.*

Shoveling down the eggs and toast while standing at the counter, Samantha crept back into his mind, and he wondered if she had any tattoos. He'd seen her arms, clear as a baby's. The idea of inking something into her perfect skin had his cock twitch again. *Jesus, down boy.*

Besides his weekends offering tattoos, he still worked as the tow truck operator. Jason hadn't been wrong, there were plenty of calls. Throwing in the volunteer firefighting, he stayed busy. *Busy, but with no particular purpose.* He snorted, shaking his head. Since when did no purpose bother him since he got out of the Navy? He'd never found a vocation or even a job that held his interest for very long. Drifting had become a way of life.

Rinsing off his dishes, he headed downstairs and into the garage. He glanced to the side where he saw Samantha's truck. Finding Jason, he jerked his head toward the vehicle. "Is the truck running?"

"Yeah, Troy got it going."

"Is it *just* running or is it reliable?"

Jason's brows lifted. "What's your interest in Sam's truck? Has she decided to sell it to you?"

Chuckling, he shook his head. "Fuck, I wouldn't have that piece of junk. Why doesn't she get rid of it?"

"I don't know. She said one time she kept it for sentimental reasons."

"Let me know when it's ready. I'll tow it out to the clinic so she won't have to try to make arrangements to come get it."

Jason's brows lifted again, but he just shook his head and smiled. If Jason thought his request was strange, he didn't react. That was another reason they were good friends. Jason took him as he came, not questioning his every move. Not wanting to open himself up for the rare question that might come, he turned and hustled back into the shop.

That afternoon, he hooked up her truck and rolled out of Baytown, heading to the vet clinic. He turned off the main highway and rumbled down the lane. Looking ahead, he saw the large wooden sign. **Hoofs and Paws Veterinary Clinic**. He hadn't paid attention to it the previous day when every fiber of his being was pinpointed on the woman sitting in the truck cab next to him. One side of the sign was a carved relief of a goat, dog, cat, and what looked strangely like a llama. He shook his head and his lips twitched upward.

The one-story brick clinic filled his view, and a glance gave evidence to the number of cars in the parking lot. Uncertain where to leave her truck, he pulled to the side of the building. Climbing down from the tow truck, he walked around to the back and began offloading her vehicle.

"You brought my truck back?"

The voice behind him was barely heard over the roar of the tow truck, and he looked over his shoulder... and down. Samantha was right behind him, her gaze darting between him and her vehicle, a crease settling between her brows. Today, she wore a white lab coat and blue scrubs, her name embroidered over the right breast pocket. Her hair was pulled back in a high ponytail but several wispy strands had escaped and now blew in the breeze. Her fresh-faced beauty and curves offered a siren's call to him, but he was glad his sunglasses hid his perusal. Her dark, sharp eyes held a hint of fatigue, and he wondered how much rest she had gotten.

He simply nodded since the answer to her question was obvious and turned back to the task at hand.

"Why did you bring my truck back? I was going to get a ride into Baytown this afternoon to pick it up."

"Now you don't have to."

"I can see that. But I haven't even paid Jason for the work. Do I pay you?"

"Nah. You can pay Jason the next time you're in town." Her truck settled to the ground and he moved forward, then knelt underneath the front to unhook the chains. Once accomplished, he stood and placed the chains back onto the tow truck, assuming she had gone back into the clinic.

"Joseph!"

His name burst sharply from her lips, and he turned, tilting his head to the side as he observed her. A scowl crossed her face, and it surprised him that no matter what expression she wore, he was entranced. That thought caused a scowl to cross his own face as he jerked off his gloves, slapping the dust against his thighs. Not saying anything, he waited.

She opened her mouth then snapped it shut, her expression now morphing into confusion. She shifted her gaze from him back to her truck again, and her stance relaxed as it appeared resignation settled over her. "Thank you for bringing my truck back. I'm sorry I snapped. I wasn't expecting this, but it was nice of you to bring it all the way out here."

He didn't want her to apologize but wanted her to keep talking. Uncertain how to accomplish that feat, he inclined his head toward the sign by the clinic. "Llamas?"

She blinked, jerking slightly, her gaze darting between him and the sign and back again. "Excuse me?"

"You treat llamas around here?"

Sucking in her lips, she appeared to fight a grin. The wariness had fled and her beauty hit him in the gut with full force. A hiss escaped as his breath halted. It was the first lightness of spirit she had exhibited around him, and he wanted to see her face when a true smile actually filled her expression. *Christ, I could drown in her eyes.*

"It's actually an alpaca. And no, there's not a lot around here. You didn't see them at Lizzie's farm because they were inside the barn, but she actually has alpacas."

She shrugged, and he could have sworn a blush crossed her cheeks. "The man who made the sign for my clinic said that I needed a tall animal on that side to make it balance... I figured the alpaca was a good choice since I don't provide services for cows or horses."

She was babbling, but nonetheless, it only made her more attractive. *Fuck, the last thing I need is for her to seem more attractive.* For the first time that he could remember, he wished he had the gift of words. Flirting. Casual conversation. Anything to keep her talking.

Offering another nod while mumbling, "Samantha," which he hoped conveyed 'have a nice day' and 'good-bye', he turned and walked back to the tow truck, climbing into the driver seat. Glad to have room for a U-turn, he headed out of the parking lot, unable to resist looking into the rearview mirror. The beautiful veterinarian was still standing next to her truck, staring at him. Too far away to see the expression on her face, he decided it didn't matter. He liked remembering her large, dark eyes and blush-kissed cheeks staring up at him. He managed to keep his cock from twitching but had no hope of keeping the left side of his chest giving a little squeeze.

***

Samantha finished the spay on the seventh dog surgery of the day, and that didn't include the six cats she'd performed surgery on. Nodding toward Brentley, she stepped back, allowing him to finish the stitching while Tonya monitored the anesthetics. She jerked off her gloves and paper apron and tossed them into the biohazard disposal container before pulling off her surgical mask. Once a month, she offered a spay and neuter clinic at a reduced fee to encourage as many responsible pet owners as she could to make sure they didn't end up with unwanted puppies or kittens.

Stepping into her office, she glanced at the desk and saw Annette had laid the toxicology report on top. Without even sitting down, she grabbed it and read the report confirming that Lizzie's goats had ingested the cuttings from the azalea bushes resulting in plant toxicity. Even though it confirmed her suspicions, she didn't feel any better about it.

Flopping into her chair, she called the Sheriff's department, connecting directly to Colt's line. After giving him the information, he thanked her, and she'd almost hung up before he added, "Sam, you haven't been to an American Legion meeting in a while."

"I know," she sighed, leaning back in her chair, rubbing her forehead. "It seems like the last several meetings I've ended up with late calls or late surgeries."

"About the time that Tom left?"

"Yeah. Although, things are a lot better now that I've got a vet intern, and he's working out great. I know the next meeting is tomorrow night. I'll make it, especially since I've got a project to announce."

"Sounds good. See you there."

Disconnecting, she leaned back in her chair and glanced out the window, seeing her truck parked in its regular spot. The sight of it always brought back memories of her grandfather, the original owner, but now, all she could think of was the taciturn Joseph.

When she'd heard the rumbling of the tow truck earlier, she'd rushed out to see what was happening, stunned to see him bringing her vehicle back. Just like the previous day, she watched his door open, then first, his booted foot, followed by his thick, jean-clad thigh and perfect ass, before the rest of his body made it to the ground, ending with a fabulous back, wide shoulders, and a face that held eyes that seemed to peer deep inside of her. *He's the only man who's held my attention and that was just by climbing out of a truck.*

She scrunched her nose and shook her head at the memory of babbling about llamas and alpacas. *What is it about him? I've only been around him a couple of times, and he either makes me angry or I lose my senses.*

Brentley popped his head around the door frame, drawing her attention. He walked in and sat on the chair directly in front of her desk. Light brown hair, trimmed neatly. Fresh face. Five years younger than her. He lacked the weariness that came from years in the military resulting in the little lines emanating from her eyes that she spied every morning when she looked in the mirror. He was nice looking, and it struck her that at one time she might have found him attractive. But now, it was the rough appearance of a tow truck driver that had captured her interests.

"We got them all done. Damn, that was a lot."

She blinked, her attention dragged back to the subject he was referring to. "I know, and at the reduced fee, we don't make anything by the time we pay for the anesthesia, pain meds, antibiotics, and other supplies. But I feel like we're doing a community service."

He nodded his agreement, then cast his gaze out the window. Brows lifted, he exclaimed, "Hey, your truck is out there."

"The garage had someone bring it back to me."

He brought his gaze back to her and cocked his head to the side. "It's not my business, and I know it costs a lot to run a clinic like this, but you could afford a new truck, right? I mean, it would be a business expense for you."

She laughed and shook her head. "Are you afraid I won't be able to pay you once your internship is over? Well, that is if you decide to stick around."

A sheepish grin crossed his face. "No, no, that wasn't it. I was just curious, that's all."

"That was my grandfather's truck. He was a large animal veterinarian near Blacksburg. That was the last truck he owned before he died. My dad was just going to get rid of it, but I asked if I could have it. Dad kept it running for me when I was in the Army, and as soon as I got out, I couldn't wait to drive it. I figure I'll keep it running as long as I can, and then, when it finally dies, I'll park it out front, fill the bed with dirt, and put plants in it!"

Brentley barked out a laugh. "Park it right under the Hoofs and Paws sign... that'd be perfect."

It felt good to take a moment and laugh, and she felt some of the tension leave her shoulders. She stared at the young intern. *Young? He's only about five years younger than me but looks so innocent. Or maybe I just look as old as I feel.* Sighing, she pushed that thought away. "I was only kidding about paying you full salary when you graduate. You're doing a great job here, but I wonder if you're anxious to get to much bigger city practice."

He shook his head. "No, not really. I thought about

trying for a residency somewhere, but honestly, I need to start pulling in a veterinarian salary to pay off my student loans. I'm sure you know how that is."

Now, it was her turn to shake her head. "To be honest, that's why I joined the Army. I put in four years with Uncle Sam to alleviate my student loans. I'm not gonna lie and say that I joined out of a great sense of duty, even though both my dad and grandfather served. I really wanted to wipe out my student loans and being an Army vet was a great way to do it."

"Makes sense," he said, nodding. "I've got two more months of my internship here with you, and then I graduate. Right now, I like this area, and I like your clinic. Quite frankly, I really like working with you, too, Sam. Figure we'll have the conversation as the time gets closer, but I definitely want to let you know that, as of now, I'll apply for the full-time veterinary position."

Smiling her appreciation, they stood at the same time. She clapped him on the back. "You've been here as long as I have today. I'll let you finish the reports on the last neuter you did, and then go ahead and leave. I'll check with the others, then I'm heading out soon, too."

She soon sent the others home, locking up after Annette, who was the last to leave. She double-checked the animals that were spending the night after surgery, making sure they were all resting comfortably. She ascertained the back doors were secure and alarmed, flipping off the lights as she moved through the clinic. Walking back through the surgical area, her sharp gaze scanned the room, but, as usual, Susan and Tonya had the space spotless.

She walked into the pharmaceutical closet, again scanning the area, mostly to see that their supplies were well-stocked. Not OCD, she still liked the supplies to be orderly, and Annette kept the shelves neat. Moving to the medical refrigerator, she checked the vaccines, surprised to find that they seemed to be low on canine vaccines, including rabies, distemper, bordetella, and parvo, but remembered Annette saying that they should receive an order soon. Not giving it another thought, she walked out and secured the closet's metal door.

Setting the final alarm and locking the front door behind her, she headed toward her truck and grinned. Sliding into the driver seat, her hands smoothed over the steering wheel, and her smile widened. She turned the key and the engine rumbled to life. Letting out a breath she'd been holding, she grinned. "Okay, Bessie, let's get home before you become cantankerous again."

While she wouldn't call the drive back to her home pleasurable, her truck made it down the road, no hesitations, no sputtering. Once she'd let Frodo run around and sniff, she brought him inside and fed him dinner. Staring inside her refrigerator, it struck her that a trip to the grocery store needed to be added to her list of things to do. Opening the freezer, she breathed a sigh of relief. One of her clients who'd had trouble paying her bill was so grateful that Samantha had only charged her half-fee and had brought several casseroles to the clinic. She pulled one out and placed it into the microwave. Soon, her home was filled with the scent of spicy chicken enchiladas. Grabbing a beer, she sat at her little table and ate while Frodo kept an eye on her.

It wasn't late, so she took a chance to see if Jason was still in the shop. He answered on the second ring. "Hey, Jason, it's Sam. Thanks a lot for getting my truck going again."

"That old truck still has some life in her."

"I'm glad… it means a lot to me. I was going to come get it this afternoon so that I could settle my bill. Since Joseph brought it out, I'll come in tomorrow." Jason quoted a price, and she breathed a sigh of relief. "Thanks. I really appreciate it."

Disconnecting, she added stopping to pay the mechanic's bill onto her to-do list for tomorrow, along with finding the time to double-check the clinic's pharmaceuticals. Moving over to her small sofa, she sat down and Frodo jumped into her lap. She absentmindedly rubbed his head while flipping through channels, but nothing held her interest. At least, not on TV. Her mind was filled with the image of Joseph climbing down from the tow truck, all denim, heavy boots, and gorgeous body. And his smile. And the way her name sounded on his lips. She'd never known how wonderful it was to hear 'Samantha' rumbled from deep inside a man's chest.

Blowing out her breath, she shook her head. *I seriously need to pull out my battery-operated boyfriend tonight.* But even as the thought went through her mind, she knew it would never be as good as the real thing. Leaning her head back, she sighed. Her life was busy, but the pervasive blanket of loneliness was beginning to settle heavily. *Is it so bad to want someone to love?*

6

Joseph was in the tow truck almost all day. A car accident on the main highway outside of town. Three stalled cars, one in a parking lot and two still in their owner's driveways. An overheated engine on the beach road.

By the end of the day, he was hot, tired, and looking forward to a run on the beach, a shower, and maybe dinner at the pub. Walking through the garage office, Jason looked up and waved him over. "Yeah?"

"Don't forget about the AL meeting tonight."

He pinched his lips together and nodded, letting his breath out slowly. "Damn, I did forget."

"Come on... it's not like you've got a hot date waiting on you instead." A wide grin crossed Jason's face as he wiggled his eyebrows. "Or do you?"

"Quit being an ass. You know I don't."

"Good. Then you can come to the meeting, and we'll get something to eat at the pub afterward."

Not having an excuse to skip the meeting, he nodded

and headed up to the apartment to shower. Changing into clean jeans and a T-shirt, he glanced into the mirror and swiped his hand through his still-wet hair. Thinking about the meeting, he had to admit he was looking forward to it even if he had forgotten. The American Legion chapter in Baytown served the two-county area and former servicemen and women came religiously. In the couple of meetings that he'd been to, he'd met veterans having served mostly in Vietnam, Korea, and the Middle East, representing a diverse group that ranged from their early twenties to their nineties. The oldest member was in a wheelchair and was ninety-eight years old. He had served in WWII as an eighteen-year-old.

He had thought the AL meetings would be stiff, boring, mostly administrative. But he found that they had a chance to talk, plan new community service projects, and build camaraderie. Hell, he'd never been around so many people since getting out of the Navy.

Walking into the AL meeting room that evening, his gaze scanned the area, recognizing many of the faces. He wandered around to the side, not surprised to find Zac standing next to the table loaded with donuts and coffee.

"How the hell do you stay so fit when you eat like you do?" he asked.

Zac grinned around a large bite before swallowing. "Metabolism. Well, that and running." He leaned forward and whispered, "But keep this a secret. Madeleine's on a health kick, and we haven't had donuts in the house for a while. I figured I'd get my fill of them here."

At the mention of Zac's wife, he couldn't help but grin in return. Zac had grown up in Baytown, and now that Joseph was here, he'd met Zac's original group of childhood friends and many of the others who'd moved here to settle. Good men and women, all of them, some with roots spreading deep as evidenced by their spouses and parents being part of the AL or auxiliary.

As he and Zac shifted to the side so that others could grab a donut, Jason joined them. "I'm lucky. Rose owns an ice cream shop, and on top of that, she's pregnant. No strict dieting in our house!"

Joseph glanced to the side, narrowed his gaze, then with a chin lift to his friends, grabbed a water bottle from the table. Walking over to one of the older members sitting by himself, he loosened the top before handing it to the man. "I thought you might like something to drink, sir."

The older man nodded, his eyes lighting, offering his thanks before taking the bottle in his shaking hands. The water threatened to spill out of the top, so Joseph reached out to steady the bottle on its way to the man's lips. After a long sip, Joseph replaced the lid and quietly handed the man a napkin so that he could discreetly wipe the few drops from his chin.

Nodding his appreciation, the older man said, "I try to never miss an AL meeting. Best people in the world are the vets right in this room."

Joseph opened his mouth to agree when the man

looked past him and grinned widely, saying, "And the prettiest."

Surprised at that comment, Joseph twisted his head around, seeing Samantha standing just inside the door, her wide-eyed gaze pinned on him. Her hair was down, the dark waves falling over her shoulders. *Beautiful... damn, she's beautiful.* He had no idea how long she'd been standing there watching him, but then, he also had no idea why she was there. "Excuse me," he mumbled, turning and walking directly toward her. Her gaze never left him as her head tilted back when he neared. He'd meant to just greet her, but curiosity took over. "What are you doing here?"

Her body jerked slightly, and she blinked. "What do you mean?"

"This is an American Legion meeting."

She blinked again. "I know."

"It's for members. Ve—"

"Geez, Joseph. I know. It's for vets."

"Yeah, Samantha. Vets... veterans... not veterinarians."

Her hands landed on her hips, and by now, he should've recognized the fighting stance. "First, you don't think I can be a veterinarian, and now, you don't think I can be a veteran. For your information, I'm both!"

Skirting around him, she stomped away, heading toward the front of the meeting room. He dropped his head back to look toward the heavens, but with his eyes closed all he could see was the image burned into his brain of her beautiful, dark, and very angry eyes shooting darts at him. *Am I destined to put my foot in my mouth around her?* Before he had a chance to seek her out and apologize, the Chapter President called the meeting to order. As he made his way to a seat, he grimaced. *Probably just as well... I'd only fuck things up again.*

Ginny McFarlane opened the meeting, rapping the gavel on the podium. Jason, the Sergeant at Arms, marched forward with Colt bearing the colors. Everyone stood, and then the Lutheran minister offered the prayer. The Empty Chair held everyone's attention for a moment as the POW/MIA flag was placed in the chair. The Pledge of Allegiance and Preamble to the AL Constitution were spoken in unison, then the President rapped the gavel once more.

He admired the way Ginny, one of the Baytown police officers, efficiently ran the meeting and inwardly winced again. He hadn't seen Samantha at the few previous meetings he'd attended, and it never dawned on him that she'd been in the military. *Veteran... Veterinarian... vet... and now, she thinks I'm an idiot as well as sexist.*

Various reports were given, duties were assigned, and new projects outlined. Just when he thought the meeting was almost over, Ginny surprised him by asking Samantha to come forward. His gaze followed her every move from the time she stood, slipped out of the aisle she had been sitting in, and made her way to the podium. His lips curved slightly as he watched her bend the microphone down to her level even though Ginny was not very tall.

"As many of you already know..." she began, her gaze finding his, "I served with the Army Veterinary Corps, including a year's tour in Afghanistan. The dogs I took care of were IED-trained."

His breath caught in his throat at the idea that she'd spent a year in a war zone. Her voice was steady, her face calm, and yet he noticed her white-knuckled grip on the edge of the podium.

"The first thing I want to mention is that I now volunteer some of my time with the Save-A-Vet Organization. This organization is run through Lackland Air Force Base and is a wonderful program to help our military war dogs be adopted out to loving families. I'm not here to plea for money or for any support other than to let you know about this organization. If there's anyone here who is interested or knows of someone who would like to apply to adopt a former military dog, I have the information. Plus, you can always ask me questions here or stop by my Hoof and Paws Veterinary Clinic.

"I have also been asked to approach the Service Committee about a fundraiser for our local animal shelter. I provide services to their worthwhile organization and they're always in need of assistance. I'll be working with the committee to brainstorm ways the AL can help. If you have any ideas, please contact me or one of the members."

She released her grip on the podium and made her way back to her seat. Joseph's breath left his lungs, and he realized he'd been tense the entire time she was speaking. He wasn't sure if she hated speaking in public or it was the subject. *Afghanistan. Worked with IED-trained dogs. What did she see and do over there?* There was a lot more to the beautiful veterinarian than what he'd assumed. He winced again and wondered if that was going to be a typical reaction when it came to fucking things up when talking to Samantha.

The last item of the meeting that Ginny reviewed was the upcoming elections. "We have a lot of new blood that has come into our area and would love to see you take a leadership role. It doesn't have to be as one of the main officers, but there are plenty of ways to serve with our AL chapter. If interested, let me or one of the other officers know."

Once they were dismissed, he looked for Samantha, determined to make amends. But as he moved closer, he could see she was surrounded with others asking questions about the dog program. A clap on his shoulder had him swing around, his gaze landing on Luke, the new medic at the county jail.

"Joseph, I'd like to get some new ink. I know the shop isn't open all the time, and my work schedule is pretty screwy."

"Don't worry about it, man. You let me know when you're available, and I'll make the time for you." The two men shook hands and walked out together as Jason made his way closer.

"You two heading to the pub?"

Going to the pub after an AL meeting was a habit that Joseph learned many of the members followed. Often, their wives and friends would meet them there. Part of him wanted to go home, hide away in his apartment, and wish that he could roll back the hands of time before he opened his mouth and insulted Samantha. Instead, he nodded. After all, maybe a beer and some laid-back time with his friends would help erase his embarrassment. "Sure, that sounds great."

Thirty minutes later, he was finally relaxing while ensconced in the bar. Aiden placed a beer next to his, and a small, feminine hand with short, blunt fingernails reached past him, fingers curling around the mug. Twisting his head, he was surprised to see Samantha. He immediately slid out of his seat, offering it to her. She hesitated, her gaze going from the tall barstool up to his face, then nodded her thanks as she placed a sneaker-clad foot onto the rung and hauled herself up into the chair. It didn't escape his notice that he was still taller than she was, even in the chair.

"I want to—"

"I'm sorry I—"

They both began speaking at the same time, and while he wanted to get his apology out, he said, "Please, go ahead."

She sucked in her lips and pressed them tightly together for a moment, then sighed. "I wanted to apologize for snapping at you earlier. Your assumption isn't unusual. Most people I meet are surprised that I was in the military. I definitely shouldn't have responded so rudely." Her face contorted with a grimace. "I'm usually a decent person, Joseph. I have no idea why I've been so prickly lately."

Already shaking his head, he said, "Samantha, I'm

the one that needs to apologize. I stuck my foot in my mouth… big time. It seems to be a habit around you."

Her head tilted to the side and she held his gaze. "A habit just around me?"

"Yeah, it seems to occur mostly around you."

Her brow furrowed as her top teeth landed on her bottom lip, thoughts working behind her dark eyes. "Why me?"

He shrugged and looked down at his beer, the room growing hotter as the conversation made him nervous.

She sucked in her lips again, then placed her hand on his arm. "You were really good with that older veteran… the one in the wheelchair. Some people aren't so comfortable with the elderly."

He tried to ignore the feel of her touch on his arm burning like a hot brand. "It's nothing." He didn't want praise for being a decent human being. He held her gaze longer, hoping she would keep talking to him and that he'd manage to have a conversation that didn't involve pissing her off.

Just as he opened his mouth again, she jumped and pulled her vibrating phone out of her pocket. Answering, she said, "Dr. Collins." She dropped her chin to her chest, her eyes closed slowly, and a sigh escaped her lips as she listened. "Okay, I'll be out." She disconnected, and he could swear there was regret in her eyes when she turned her gaze back to him and said, "I've got to go. Call out to the clinic. A client's dog tried to jump over their barbed wire fence. Unsuccessfully, I might add."

She slid from the barstool but halted as his hand

jerked out toward her, landing lightly on her arm. "You shouldn't go out by yourself so late at night."

A soft smile slipped over her face as she shook her head. "I'm the only vet... *veterinarian.* I'm pretty sure there are no such things as set hours. Anyway, I'll be fine."

She smiled at him, and he felt a deep longing to see her lips curve upward more often. Especially if it was directed toward him. Her face appeared even younger. And more beautiful. Little crinkles emanated from her eyes and a few tiny freckles were more noticeable as her cheeks lifted slightly with her smile. *Christ, I want to see that smile more often.*

She turned and started toward the door when his attention was snagged by two young women stepping into his line of vision. One was wearing a plastic tiara with a sash that proclaimed Almost Hitched while the other's sash proclaimed Best Maid of Honor.

Giggling stupidly, the one who seemed the most trashed tossed her hair over her shoulder. "The guy over at the bar said you do tattoos. I want to get my fiancé's name tattooed right over my heart."

The girl next to her leaned in and offered a drunken wink which resembled more of a rapid blink to get something out of her eyes. "She means she wants it right on her boob. I told her while she's at it she should get a nipple piercing, too."

Another girl stumbled over, blurting, "I told her to get a clit piercing, but now that I see you... damn, I'll strip and you can pierce any part of me you want to!"

One of them shifted to the side, and he saw

Samantha standing behind them, her eyes not giving away any of her thoughts. She simply lifted one eyebrow slightly, turned, and headed out of the pub.

Growling, he opened his mouth to shut them down when Brogan stomped over to their end of the bar and glared at the three women. "You're cut off. Go back to your hotel and sleep it off, ladies."

All three dropped their sloppy smiles and walked out grumbling. Ginny followed, murmuring, "I'll make sure they get there without getting into a vehicle."

Jason walked over, and Joseph looked at him, shaking his head. "I probably just cost your shop some money, but I was going to turn their asses down."

"Don't worry about it, man. We don't work on people who are inebriated, and I seriously doubt they'd want to go under the needle when sober." Jason looked to the side and smiled, lifting his arm as Rose walked directly to him, wrapping her arm around his waist.

After smiling at her husband, she turned and smiled at Joseph. "I saw you talking to Sam."

"Uh-huh."

"She's sweet."

He turned back to his beer. "Uh-huh." She laughed, and he couldn't help but glance to the side, seeing both her wide smile and Jason's grin.

She patted his shoulder and said, "Okay, okay, I get it. You don't want to talk about Sam."

"Uh-huh."

Rose giggled and leaned up on her tiptoes to kiss the underside of Jason's jaw. "I'm going to go say goodbye to the girls and then we can head home, sweetie."

Rose waddled away after Jason kissed her lightly as his hand rubbed her pregnant belly. Then, he turned back to Joseph. "Seriously, man, what's up with you and Sam?"

"If I wasn't gonna talk to Rose about it, why do you think I'd talk to you?"

Jason didn't reply but just held his gaze. Sighing, Joseph shook his head slightly. "It just seems that every time I'm around her, I say stupid shit. It's like being fourteen years old all over again."

"Seriously?"

"The first time I met her, I thought she was about eighteen... twenty tops. And since everybody kept talking about Sam Collins the veterinarian, I was looking around for a man, insulting her when she lets me know *she's* the veterinarian. Then, tonight, I insulted her again. I was surprised to see her walk into the AL meeting. It never dawned on me she'd been in the military. She said she was there because she was a vet, I thought she was confused about veteran and veterinarian. Turns out I'm the one that looked like an idiot."

"Fuckin' hell," Jason laughed, snorting. "You are as bad as a fourteen-year-old."

"Thanks. Thanks a lot."

Jason clapped him on the back and shook his head as Rose started walking toward them again. "I don't know her well, but she seems pretty laid-back. How about just talking to her sometime? Tell her you're sorry for sticking your foot in your mouth and then start over."

"Is that the best advice you got?"

Rose slid back under Jason's arm again, and he

squeezed her shoulder. "Rose will tell you that we didn't get along at first. In fact, she couldn't stand me." She rolled her eyes, and he continued, "But I persisted, and look where we are now."

Jason and Rose walked out of the pub, and Joseph finished his beer. *Jesus... what the hell am I doing here?* Tossing money onto the bar, he walked out into the cool evening. A thought of moving on flashed through his mind but didn't settle inside.

Sighing, he scrubbed his hand over his face and thought about Samantha out in the night working on an injured dog. For a moment, the idea of driving to her clinic to see if she was there and needed any help passed through his mind. *After overhearing those stupid women talk about tattoos and piercings, I'm probably the last person she wants to see.* Sighing once again, he walked down the street toward his apartment over the shop. Alone.

7

On the drive to her clinic, Samantha kept replaying the scene she'd walked in on at the AL meeting. Joseph kneeling next to the elderly veteran in the wheelchair, assisting him with his water while allowing the man to maintain his dignity. She wished it had only been his kindness that she'd noticed, but the way he looked, the way he tucked the single strand of blonde hair behind his ear, and the way his muscles bunched and strained against the worn cotton of his T-shirt... all combined to create a gorgeous package. *Package.* Snorting, she shook her head. "Yeah, girl, when he stood and turned around, you couldn't help but notice his package." It wasn't unusual for her to talk to herself while driving, although singularly focusing on one gorgeous man instead of the upcoming case was not how she usually killed time.

Also hit with the memory of the giggling drunk women in the bar, it was hard not to think of him spending time with a woman's naked breast or vagina exposed to him for an extended period of time while he tattooed or pierced. *Ugh.*

Pushing those thoughts away, she turned her thoughts to the conversation she'd had with Liam after the meeting. She rubbed her hand over her forehead, trying to dislodge the frustration. Liam told her a farmer had called the sheriff's office, swearing he'd seen a wolf. She'd explained that many people could not tell them apart, but that coyotes were naturally in Virginia and wolves were not.

"I showed him pictures of the two, but he swore it was a wolf."

"If it was a coyote, it could be after his cows," she'd warned. "Of course, there could be wolf-hybrid or coyote hybrids which aren't supposed to be on the Virginia Eastern Shore. But that doesn't mean a coyote and dog didn't breed in the wild."

She made a mental note to call the animal shelter and ask if they'd noticed any aggressive animals being brought in.

Pulling into the parking lot, she observed Susan climbing from her vehicle and Nathaniel Tompkins jumping out of his truck and running around to the back. She had managed to call Susan to meet her at the clinic, apologizing that she was calling her instead of Tonya since Susan was single and Tonya had a husband and kids.

With Nathaniel carrying his dog in a bloody blanket, her mind focused, and she opened the clinic, allowing the three of them to rush inside. "Bring him back to the surgical area. We'll need to get x-rays."

Susan grabbed an apron and pulled it over her scrub top. While Nathaniel laid the dog on the table, Susan brought over the digital x-ray equipment. Samantha snapped on a pair of gloves and peeled the blanket away, getting her first look at the injury. Breathing a sigh of relief, she was pleased to see that while the dog's stomach had a large tear, at first glance it did not appear that any of the internal organs were damaged. "Hey, old boy," she crooned, gently rubbing the dog's head.

"We've always had a fence on the south pasture, and I've never seen Toby try to jump over it before. I don't know what he was chasing but it looked like a wolf... big, wild dog... or maybe a coyote. I didn't have a chance to get my gun before Toby took off after it. Poor boy didn't have the height to make it over without getting caught." Nathaniel's voice cracked, and he looked close to tears as he leaned over his dog.

Her head jerked toward Nathaniel. "Have you had other sightings of this wild dog? Or coyotes in your fields?"

"No, never. I mean, we have stray dogs around sometimes, but this one was big. It didn't come after Toby so I can't say it was aggressive, but if it was wild, I don't want it hanging around the barn where my grand-kids play."

Nodding slowly, she offered a tight smile before turning back to the injured animal. The radiographs appeared on the computer screen next to the examining table, and she bent forward to carefully study them. "Nathaniel, we're in luck. I know it looks bad, but I can get this sutured up. Once I get in there, I'll take a closer look, but it doesn't appear that the wire nicked any organs." Looking up at Susan, she said, "I'll start the IV and get him intubated."

Susan nodded and moved to the pharmaceutical closet to get the appropriate drugs while Samantha grabbed what she needed. She deftly managed to get the IV catheter in Toby's front leg and then, after taking the Propofol from Susan, carefully watched as the large dog grew sleepy and stopped whimpering. "Nathaniel, I need you to step out of the surgical room, but if you want to go into that room over there," she jerked her head to the side, "you can watch."

After intubation, she hooked him up to the anesthetic machine before turning that part of the surgical procedure over to Susan. She carefully cleaned the area, moving the torn skin and muscle to the side, examining the complete injuries. "This is not nearly as bad as I was afraid it was going to be."

"Good," Susan agreed. "Do you think you'll be able to send him home with Nathaniel?"

"I'll stay here tonight. I'm sure he's more than capable of administering the pain meds and antibiotics, but I want to keep monitoring him for a few hours. I'll have Nathaniel come back in the morning—well, later this morning." She began suturing, her movements swift and neat. Tying off the last knot, she ordered Susan to turn off the anesthesia. Waiting for just a moment, she pulled out the endotracheal tube.

Looking up, she offered a thumbs up toward Nathaniel and smiled as his shoulders slumped in relief. Once Toby was transferred to a kennel on the floor, resting on a thick blanket, she turned to Susan. "Thank you so much for coming in. I really hated having to ask."

Shrugging, the pretty blonde laughed, "Oh, believe me, I have no social life here. I was glad to be able to help."

She stood at the door to the clinic and watched as Nathaniel pulled out of the parking lot in his truck after promises from her that she'd call if Toby took a turn for the worse. After Liam's questions about the reported wolf sightings, she knew she needed to report this incident to him. *Coyotes? Wild dogs? No way it's a wolf!*

She walked to the door and waved as Susan pulled out after the farmer. A slight noise to the side caused her to jump. Jerking her head around, she was surprised to see a motorcycle parked next to the building. She was even more surprised when Joseph swung his leg over the seat and walked toward her.

His hands held his helmet as he stepped out of the shadows, and the lights from inside the clinic cast illumination over him. Her fingers twitched with the desire to reach up and brush back the lock of hair that was hanging in front of his face. Instead, she gripped the door a little tighter. "Joseph? What are you doing here?"

"I was concerned about you being here so late. I wanted to make sure you got home safely."

"Oh." He stared at his helmet for a few seconds before lifting his gaze to her. It was hard to see clearly, but she could almost swear she saw uncertainty move through his eyes. "It was nice of you to check on me." Her words were rushed as her gaze locked on his lips that curved ever so slightly upward.

"How's the dog?"

"He's fine. In the back, actually. He had a severe laceration, but little muscle involvement and no internal injuries. He's all cleaned up and stitched."

"Good, good." He looked around toward her truck parked at the side of the building and asked, "If you're getting ready to leave, I can wait to make sure your truck starts."

She snorted and shook her head. "Everybody worries about that truck, but it's running fine now." She glanced behind her, then turned back to look up at him. "Um, actually, I'm not going to be leaving, though. It's so late, and I want to keep an eye on Toby. I'll just rest here tonight."

He jerked slightly, blinking as his gaze shifted behind her into the clinic and then returned to her face. "You live here?"

"No, although I keep thinking I'll put a sleeper sofa in the storage room attic to make it easier on nights when I need to stay." She shrugged and shook her head. "But there's always something the clinic needs more than a sleeper sofa, so it hardly makes sense to spend money on that. Anyway, a few blankets on the floor near the kennels will be fine for me to catch a few hours of rest."

A scowl crossed his face. "I hate the idea of you sleeping on the floor, Samantha. It just doesn't seem right. Is there something I can do? I could stay and give you a chance to go home, or…"

She reached out, placing her hand on his arm, feeling the tense muscles cording underneath her fingertips. "That's a nice offer, Joseph, but I assure you, I'm fine. I knew what I was getting into when I became a vet... Well, a veterinarian—" His brows lowered, and she squeezed his arm. "Sorry, it's just that I never really thought about the two meanings of the word. Anyway, it's really the truth. My father and my grandfather were veterinarians, so when I went into the business, I knew it meant long days and sometimes longer nights. Believe me, catching a few hours of sleep on some soft blankets indoors is a lot better than being out in the cold and rain in the middle of the night trying to help a cow give birth. That's probably one of the reasons I didn't go into large animal medicine. That, plus the fact that even though I'm much stronger than I look, it's pretty physically taxing for someone my size."

His gaze dropped to where her fingers rested on his arm, and she almost snatched them back but instead squeezed again. "As far as being a veteran, I confess that I really had no idea what I was getting into then. But long nights in uncomfortable settings was not unusual." His attention had stayed riveted on her, something that sent warmth throughout.

"Well, if you're sure." He sighed heavily. "At least I'll make sure you're locked in safely."

She stepped back and offered a little smile. "Thank you for checking on me. That was really nice."

The door was almost closed between them when he suddenly blurted, "What those women said in the bar... it's not like it sounded."

She tilted her head to the side but remained silent, uncertain what he meant.

Still holding her gaze, he said, "I don't do piercings. It's not something I learned to do or want to do."

She sucked in her lips and nodded.

"I do tattoos. Not like Jason... I'm not an artist. It's just something I picked up when I was in the Navy and was stationed in the Far East for a while. It's not my passion. It's something that I can do to make some money no matter where I am. But when someone's in front of me, it's just skin. It's not... it's not like it sounded."

"What is your passion, Joseph?" She was surprised when the question slipped out, both wanting to know more and feeling afraid to care about knowing more.

He shrugged. "Don't know. Haven't really found it yet. I've never fallen in love with a place or a job or..." He cleared his throat. "I guess that's why I keep moving around. I keep traveling, searching for something that I can't find."

"A true rolling stone."

"Yeah, I guess so." He puffed out a hasty breath and shook his head slightly. "'And they roam the world at will. They range the field and they rove the flood, and they climb the mountain's crest; theirs is the curse of the gypsy blood, and they don't know how to rest.'" He held her gaze and said, "Guess you didn't expect me to quote poetry, did you? It's by Robert Service. He used to travel through Canada, often living in poverty. I guess I always identified with him."

Uncertain she trusted her voice, she stared at the man with the rough clothes, long hair, beard, and tats, quoting poetry. And her heart skipped a beat as she longed to reach out and hold him. Her fingers clenched together, and she swallowed deeply.

Stepping completely into the building, she whispered, "I hope one day you find what you're looking for, Joseph." With that, she offered a little smile before flipping the locks on the door. He stayed where he was, his eyes pinned on her, and she turned and walked to the back, flipping the lights off and setting the alarm. It only took a moment to hear the roar of his motorcycle as it headed out of the parking lot, the sound reverberating into the night as he rode down the road.

She opened the kennel and checked on Toby, pleased to find that there was no bleeding and he appeared to be resting comfortably. She grabbed several clean blankets and made a pad on the floor, using her jacket as a pillow. She lay down, but sleep did not come easily.

She had only been around Joseph a few times, each generally ending in irritation. And yet, tonight, there was something so real and vulnerable as he stood outside, wanting to make sure she was safe and going so far as to explain what she'd overheard in the bar. Rolling to her back, she rested her arm over her forehead and sighed.

There was something about him that reminded her of a skittish animal. No doubt he was an enigma, and for a moment, as she stood at the door staring into his eyes, taking in all the manly beauty, she'd wondered what it would be like to solve the puzzle of him. *But then he'd leave.* At least he'd been honest about being a rolling stone.

Curling on her side, she drew her knees up and felt

her eyes grow heavy as she listened to the steady breathing of the dog... and wondered why Joseph's honesty didn't make her feel any better.

Samantha pulled up to Colt's house, parking her truck next to a multitude of other vehicles. She might have paid more attention to the fact that the other vehicles were much nicer than her truck, but her gaze was stuck on her windshield, peering out at the massive house. "Jeez, my whole camper would probably fit in his guest bathroom!"

Climbing from the truck, she smoothed her hands over her skirt before leaning in to grab her purse and the gift bag sitting on the passenger seat. Colt's wife, Carrie, a waitress in a local diner who seemed to know everyone, was hosting a group baby shower. Staring up at the house, she could now see why Carrie made the offer. She was not only a sweetheart but they definitely had the room. A number of their friends were all pregnant, expecting within the next couple of months, and none wanted anyone to break the bank trying to host individual showers.

Walking inside, she was immediately greeted by familiar faces and wide smiles. The living room flowed into a wide dining room, and just behind was a massive kitchen. Some of the women from the American Legion Auxiliary had provided the food, and the concept was unique. The guests only had to bring one baby gift, place it on a table, and Carrie placed a numbered sticker onto the gift.

When it was time for opening the presents, the five pregnant women were given a number, and they opened the gifts designated for that number. If one of them received a gift they already had, fun trading began. While standing to the side, nibbling the delicious food from her plate, Samantha watched as baby clothes, bedding, diapers, wraps, teething rings, stuffed animals, and a multitude of other gifts began spilling out in piles around each expectant friend.

A sigh escaped her lips as she watched the activities. She wanted what the other women had... husbands that adored them, babies on the way, families in the making. Somehow, it always seemed like there was something else that needed to happen first. Four years of college, another four years of vet med school, another three years of the Army. Now, with two years as a civilian veterinarian under her belt, she was ready for the next big adventure. *To love someone and be loved. But when? And with who?*

As the gift exchange came to a close, she slipped around to the kitchen and noticed two of her friends, Ginny and Belle, moving toward the back door leading to the patio. Deciding that a breath of fresh air would be perfect, she joined them. There, they found another friend, Hannah, enjoying the lighted patio as well. Ginny was a Baytown police officer. Belle was a nurse, married to one of Colt's detectives, and Hannah was the police chief of the small local town of Easton, who'd carried a secret torch for another local police chief.

The four women settled onto the thick, comfortable cushions of the patio furniture. Samantha leaned her head back, admiring the way Carrie had strung lights around the patio and some of the trees, casting a fairy-like glow over the area. For a few minutes, the other three women chatted about being in law enforcement or dating someone in law enforcement.

Belle sighed. "I imagine it's hard being in any relationship nowadays."

Samantha's lack-of-relationship frustration spilled out, and she dragged her hands through her hair. "Hear, hear. It's hard to find time... hard to find the right person... hard to... to... oh, just everything." She hadn't meant to blurt out her feelings and was relieved when someone popped their head out of the kitchen door and let them know the party was breaking up.

Offering thanks and hugs and goodbyes, she soon found herself pulling up in front of her small home. After letting Frodo out for another run, the two were ensconced safely inside the camper. As the large dog turned around in a circle and settled onto the floor with the groan, she smiled indulgently. "If only I can find someone as loyal as you, as easy-going as you, as understanding as you."

Crawling into bed, she listened to Frodo snore and grinned. "Okay, maybe I can find someone who doesn't snore as much as you do." As her eyes closed and sleep began to claim her, Joseph appeared in her mind once again. Somehow, she imagined that if he snored, she wouldn't mind at all.

Joseph looked up from his work on Luke as Zac walked into the tattoo shop, followed closely by some of their friends. Brows raised, he watched as Aiden, Brogan, Scott, Wyatt, and Dylan walked in. Wyatt and Dylan were local police chiefs of small towns north of Baytown. "What the fuck? Was there a meeting planned that I didn't know about?"

"Luke told us he was getting some work done by you, and I thought I'd come in and take a look at some of Jason's new designs," Brogan said. "Plus, Ginny's at the baby shower tonight."

Joseph nodded, remembering Jason mentioning that with a bunch of their friends expecting, Rose was at a group baby shower. He had no idea what happened at a shower but figured they'd all get gifts. It dawned on him that Brogan and Aiden's wives were pregnant. Glancing toward Zac, he noticed his friend's shit-eating grin and wondered if he'd be announcing impending fatherhood sometime soon.

Jason, sitting at the counter, turned his sketchbook around so that Brogan could view it.

Aiden peered over his brother's shoulder and said, "When Brogan said he was getting more, I thought about it, too."

"I don't know why you're looking at this notebook," Brogan quipped. "You just want to get your wife's name tattooed over your heart."

"You can't tell me you don't have Ginny tattooed somewhere!"

The others rolled their eyes as the two brothers traded barbs.

"The work Jason did around my stump was so much better than anything I've ever had," Scott said, settling into one of the chairs, patting his prosthesis. "Lizzie wanted to know if you could tattoo an alpaca."

That question had the others stop and stare, wide-eyed. Scott laughed and shook his head. "Damn... wish I had a camera on your faces. Don't worry, guys. She hates needles, so while she might be curious, you'd never actually have to try to tattoo one."

"Thank fuck," Joseph cursed under his breath, thinking of the alpaca carving on Samantha's Hoofs and Paws sign. Turning his focus back to Luke, he wiped the excess ink and continued the pattern. It was easy. A friend's name with Never Forget tattooed underneath. "Almost finished," he said, covering the skin with an antibiotic ointment and a sterile bandage. Rolling his chair away from the table, he turned and gathered the materials to be thrown away. Snapping off his gloves, he shoved them into the bag before tossing it into the garbage. Wiping down his station, he stretched his back and rolled his shoulders.

Luke was standing at the front counter, swiping his credit card with Jason. Looking up, he caught Joseph's eyes and thanked him. "I really appreciate you getting me in. I've been thinking about it for a while, and today was the third anniversary, so I decided it was time." He shrugged and ducked his head. "As far as tats go, I guess it seemed pretty cheesy."

"It's never cheesy to memorialize someone who meant something to you," Joseph said.

"Fuck, yeah," Brogan said. "Every one of us lost someone over there." He glanced toward Aiden and sighed. "In fact, most of you newcomers don't know but one of our close friends was killed in the service.... hell, he'd been engaged to our sister, Katelyn."

"Fuck, that's hard," Joseph murmured under his breath.

"Sam's comments about the dogs at the last AL meeting made me remember a dog assigned to us for a while," Aiden said. "It was fuckin' amazing watching the handler and the dog together. That dog could sniff out and avoid IEDs. Saved my ass a couple of times."

"I didn't even realize the military had veterinarians," Joseph admitted. "It never dawned on me who would take care of and treat the dogs that were used over there."

Luke leaned forward, resting his forearms on his knees. "I was thinking about talking to Sam."

Joseph swung his attention around to Luke, curious about why the jail medic needed to talk to the veterinarian. "Why do you need to talk to Sam?" He winced at his sharp tone and turned back to his station, putting away a few more items. The back of his neck felt hot, but he refused to turn around to see if the others noticed his discomfort.

"Some of the prisoners have PTSD. I know there are dog programs where prisoners can help train dogs until they can get adopted out. I have no idea what it would take to do something like that, but it's been on my mind.

When Sam mentioned the local shelter, I wondered if the prisoners could help. She might have some ideas or maybe resources to take a look at," Luke explained. "I guess I'd better start with Colt first, though, to see if it's something he'd allow."

Nodding, Dylan said, "Put something together, and I'll bring it up at our next Law Enforcement Leaders meeting. I know Liam has been talking to Sam about some strange sightings lately so we might call her in."

"What sightings?" Joseph asked, forcing his voice to remain neutral.

"A couple of farmers have called in to complain about a wild dog in the area. Well, one said it was a wolf, but that can't be right."

"Coyotes?" Zac asked. "I know the Eastern Shore has had a few sightings that probably came down from Maryland."

"Don't know. Just know that we don't want anyone hurt either by the dogs or by some fool hunter trying to take them out."

"And Sam?" Joseph pressed, ignoring Jason's smile directed at him.

"As the only vet around, she may have heard something or had a client mention a sighting. Anyway, Liam said that she'd keep an eye out for any news."

Wyatt grinned. "Sam's amazing. Tiny, but tough as nails. And she's fuckin' gorgeous." He stood and stretched, cracking his back. "I'm heading out. See y'all at the next AL baseball game."

He was quickly followed by many of the others, leaving Joseph with Jason, Zac, and Dylan.

"From your expression, I thought you might plant your fist in the middle of Wyatt's face," Jason said, grinning toward Joseph.

"Don't know what you're talking about."

"Sam is a really great woman. You ought to ask her out." Zac's comment was accompanied with a wide smile, but Joseph only scowled.

Before giving him a chance to respond, Dylan held his gaze. "Just seems like the two of you are always going at it. Instead of fussing, you might want to try something else."

"I don't know," Jason grinned. "Makeup sex is great."

The others laughed, and Joseph shook his head. "Christ, shut up." Thoughts of holding Samantha close, tilting her face up to his, and kissing those beautiful lips had crossed his mind more times than he wanted to admit even to himself. And he sure as hell wouldn't admit it to his friends. "Don't know that a woman like her needs anyone like me."

"What the hell does that mean?" Zac's brow lowered.

Joseph shrugged. "You know me… never stay in one place for too long. Makes no sense to start something only to have it end badly when I decide it's time to leave."

"You plan on leaving?" Jason asked, still sitting on the stool behind the counter but turning to face him.

His breath caught in his throat, realizing the implications of his comment considering he worked for Jason and paid rent on Jason's apartment. "No, no, man. Not now. I just mean… sometime."

"So just because you think that sometime in the

future you might want to leave Baytown, you decide it's not worth getting to know a really great woman?" Zac shook his head and said, "Sounds to me like you're just trying to protect yourself, not her."

A heavy sigh left his lungs, and he bit back the urge to argue and deny. Finally, he hefted his shoulders and shook his head slowly. "I don't know. I'm not sure anyone's right for me or I'm right for them." He stood, hoping the others would take the hint and follow his lead. They did, and soon Dylan and Zac headed out of the shop.

Just before Jason left as well, he stopped with his hand on the door handle and looked over his shoulder. "No one has a crystal ball, Joseph. No one can look into the future and see what's going to happen. But if you close yourself off to the possibility of a relationship just because you *think* you'll leave one day, then you could be kissing something really wonderful goodbye. Stop running away. Man, of anyone I know, you deserve a chance to love someone." With that, he pushed through the door, letting it close behind him.

Joseph stared at the empty shop, Jason's words on repeat in his mind. *You deserve a chance to love someone.*

Swallowing deeply, he shook his head. *Love someone? Samantha? Hell, I can barely bring myself to talk to her.*

Flipping the lock, he turned out the lights before walking back through the shop, up the stairs, and into his apartment. Thoughts of Samantha filled his mind. She was so different from the debutantes his parents tried to push his way when he was younger. Or the women who hung out in bars near Navy bases. She was unlike anyone he'd ever met, but as he learned more, everything about her called to him.

Sleep was elusive as he tossed and turned, wondering when he would see her again. And wondering if Jason was right. *Do I dare open myself up to love someone?*

8

Samantha walked toward an examination room, hearing an ungodly yowl coming from within. Glancing down at her tablet, she grinned as she opened the door and walked into the room. "Hey, Hannah. Percy."

Hannah's cat emitted another long, drawn-out meow, effectively summing up his feelings on being dragged into the vet's office.

"I should just make a house call and save you the discontent." Samantha efficiently pulled the big cat from his carrier and placed him on the examining table.

"I'm sorry he's such a grouch," Hannah moaned.

Samantha ran her hands along the healthy feline, murmuring softly to him. He never purred, but he did calm. "Cats generally hate to be in carriers, and they always hate the vet. Don't worry, I don't take this personally."

Susan stepped into the room with the vaccinations and held Percy as Samantha readied the injections. Glancing up at Hannah as she finished, she said, "I saw you and Dylan at The Diner the other day." She watched as pink hit Hannah's cheeks. "And, if Carrie's information is right, it's not the first time you two have sat closely on the same side of the booth."

Hannah rolled her eyes. "Yes, we've shared a booth... just like in middle school. There. Satisfied?"

With her hands still stroking the beautiful cat, Samantha shook her head. "Hardly! I want details. After all, I have to live my love life vicariously through my friends."

"Well, you wouldn't have to if you'd give Joseph a chance."

Shocked, Samantha blinked. "Jo... Joseph? What on earth are you talking about?"

"Oh, come on... you have to know he's interested."

"You're crazy." Samantha tried to keep her tone neutral, but it sounded wistful even to her own ears. She focused on Percy, not wanting to meet Hannah's gaze.

"What makes you think I'm crazy? I saw the way he looked at you at the AL meeting. But maybe you're not interested—"

Unable to stop, she blurted, "We're complete opposites. As closed off as he is, who knows what he's thinking? And God knows I don't have time for his brand of complicated even if I was interested!"

"Complicated?"

Samantha's lips were pressed together as she continued to rub the beautiful feline, now noting that Percy was purring. "He's quiet... broody. Not rude, but not overly friendly." Snorting, she added, "I have no idea if he's got baggage or just introverted. But my life doesn't offer any time to help someone sort out their shit when I work all day, am on-call most nights, and can barely take care of my own life. I'm afraid *complicated* just doesn't work for me."

Wishing she had kept her mouth shut, she was almost glad when Percy decided he'd had enough and emitted another loud meow. That seemed to jolt Hannah out of her questions and her focus back onto her cat. Percy readily re-entered the carrier, and Hannah carried it out the door. Samantha waved goodbye with a wide smile that drooped as soon as her friend was out of sight. The entire conversation about Joseph had shocked her. Yes, the handsome, taciturn man intrigued her, but interested in her? *Sure, he came to the clinic to check on me, but that doesn't indicate interest. Not for a drifter.*

"They're ready for you in room three," Susan called out, walking past the exam room door.

She glanced down at her tablet to see who her next patient was, plastered another smile onto her face, and walked into the hallway, Joseph still on her mind. *I wish I had time for his brand of complicated.*

"Dammit!" Samantha cursed, fighting the urge to slam her fist down on the steering wheel. She had just entered the small town of Seaside when her truck lurched to the side. "This better not be a flat tire!" She cut the engine and pulled to the side of the road.

Hustling around to the passenger side, she stared in dismay at the front tire losing air. *Oh, shit... I don't have a spare.* She leaned forward, slightly banging her forehead onto the side of her truck window. *I just need a break.*

She was still standing there a moment later considering banging her head harder when flashing lights pulled up behind her. Twisting her head around, she watched as Dylan climbed out of the Seaside Police Chief SUV and walked toward her.

"Sam, when are you gonna put this thing out of its misery?"

Throwing a narrow-eyed, pinched-mouth expression his way, she plopped her hands onto her hips and shook her head. "As long as I can keep it running, it's better than having to fork over money for a new one."

He glanced down at the tire. "Well, at least it's just a flat tire. I can get your spare on."

Heaving a great sigh, she felt the heat of embarrassment hit her face and hated having to admit the truth. "I... I don't have one. I took it out to make more room to haul things and forgot to put it back in." She watched his brows lift and opened her mouth to tell him to keep his opinions to himself, but he just chuckled.

"Have you called for anyone yet?"

She shook her head and started to lean into the truck to grab her phone, but he beat her to it. She listened as he said, "Hey, it's Dylan. Can you send someone with a tow truck? Looks like Sam needs some more help." He grinned while still holding the phone to his ear. "Yeah, that'll be fine."

She crossed her arms over her chest, wondering if

the scowl on her face was going to be permanently etched. "You called Jason?"

"I don't know why you're grumpy. Jason has the best garage in the area."

"I was going to call someone from just up the road. Now you've got me being towed all the way back to Baytown."

"Not if the person can fix it here."

"Oh. Will they have the right size tire?"

"I don't know," Dylan said as he walked over next to her. He went back to his SUV and leaned in for a moment, shutting the door with his shoulder as he turned around. Walking back to her, he had two water bottles in his hands, reaching one out toward her.

She murmured her appreciation, and they chatted for a while until the rumble of a large truck could be heard rolling down the road toward them. Unable to see who was driving, she lifted her hand to shade her eyes and spied Joseph sitting in the driver's seat.

Once more she hid the body shivers as she enjoyed the visual of watching Joseph climb down from the driver's seat in all his rough, hot, gorgeous-bod, masculine beauty. Glancing to the inside of her truck, she spied her sunglasses and inwardly cursed that she didn't have them on her face, hiding the way her eyes followed his movements.

He walked over, inclined his head toward her, and his voice rumbled as deep as his truck. "Samantha." Shifting his gaze toward Dylan, he offered a chin lift before he turned and glanced down at her flat tire.

She winced, wishing that his glance could stay on her and didn't have to focus on her truck again.

As though hearing her thoughts, Dylan chuckled and walked back to his vehicle. "I'll leave y'all to it," he said, offering a wave before he climbed into his SUV and pulled out onto the road.

"I'm surprised Dylan didn't offer to change your tire."

Joseph's deep voice held disapproval, and she pinched her lips together, remaining quiet for a moment. Finally, not having any choice, she grumbled, "I don't have a spare with me."

His reflector-sunglasses kept his expression guarded from her, but she squirmed under his perusal. Finally, all her frustration exploded, and she waved her arms around wildly. "I know, I know! I know exactly what you're going to say! I should always have a spare! Especially when I go out by myself at night! I know! Well, guess what? I can't always remember everything! And you know what? Most of the time I'm fine with everything I'm trying to do! There's just something about you… something about you that gets me flustered and makes me feel stupid! You can't change my tire because I don't have a fuckin' spare! So, just tow me and deal with it!"

She immediately felt ridiculous having lost her cool but refused to look away. His face had been carved in stone as she ranted, but now the corners of his lips twitched upward. Uncertain if she was hallucinating, she lifted her hand to shade her eyes again. Yes… Joseph smiled, and her heart stumbled. *Christ, he's beautiful.*

Every time she'd seen him he was gorgeous, but right now, right here, right in front of her, his smile threatened to capture her breath. And steal her heart.

She opened her mouth to speak, croaking instead. Clearing her throat, a blush heated her cheeks, and she mumbled, "Sorry. I shouldn't have taken my frustrations out on you."

"Never be sorry for saying what's on your mind."

His words were soft and deep, and they curved around her like arms hugging her tightly. Whatever quip was on her tongue faded away, and she nodded slowly. They continued to hold each other's gazes, and unable to think of anything to say, she finally glanced toward her truck and said, "I guess the sooner we go, the sooner I can get going."

Without saying a word, he nodded, turned, and walked over to his truck to maneuver it into place. While she stood to the side, he hooked up her vehicle. Before she had a chance to get to the passenger side of his truck, he was there, his hand on the door, pulling it open. She smiled at the repeat of the gallant gesture, reminiscent of her father always opening the door for her mother.

Climbing inside, she glanced down at her clothes. Her blue jeans had seen better days, and upon closer investigation of her big rubber boots, she realized there may have been a bit of blood and fecal matter smeared on one of them. Her green T-shirt was emblazoned with the logo Hoofs and Paws across her chest. She dropped her chin and stared at her hands, her unpainted nails trimmed short. The way she looked, if

Joseph was being gallant, it must be a habit… sure as hell not because she looked like someone he would want to impress.

He climbed into the driver seat and looked over, not starting the engine. Uncertain why he was staring, she cocked her head to the side. "Is something wrong?"

"Buckle up."

Jerking slightly, she grabbed the seat belt and pulled it across her, clicking the latch in place. He started the engine and the growl of the large truck vibrated through her as he pulled onto the road.

"So… um, do you think it'll take long to get my tire fixed?"

"Not sure. If he's got the right kind, it shouldn't take long. If not, then it might be tomorrow before he gets it."

"Oh. Um… should I have you drop me off at—"

"Let's see what he's got first. I can always take you home if he needs to keep it for a day."

It was on the tip of her tongue to refuse, but the thought that he would drop her off, even if it was out of his way, sent a tiny spiral of pleasure through her. Sucking in her lips, she nodded. "Thanks." She wished she could think of something more to say than the single-word answer, but a side glance exposed his lips quirked upward again.

As they pulled into Jason's garage, she couldn't help but smile when Jason walked out, his hands planted on his hips as he stared at the two of them, shaking his head. She climbed down from the tow truck and immediately walked over, her hands up. "I know, I know. I didn't have a spare when I had a flat tire."

Jason looked at her truck as Joseph lowered it to the ground. "I've got one that will work, but I'm not letting you get out of here without having a spare. I can get it tomorrow."

"But Jason, I need—"

"What you need, Sam, is to make sure you have a spare!"

Considering she'd been stuck on the side of the road, she could hardly argue with his logic. "That's true, but I've got to get home." Even though she couldn't see him, she heard Joseph's heavy footsteps as he approached, but the way her skin tingled as he neared, she would've known it was him anyway.

"I've got her. I'll get her home."

She observed Jason and Joseph staring at each other, neither speaking, but man-words seemed to dart through the air between them. Not understanding their silent messages, she was about to interrupt when Jason grinned widely and nodded. Looking down at her, he said, "Looks like you got a ride." Turning, he walked back into the garage, leaving the two of them standing on the pavement.

"You ready?" Joseph asked, his sunglasses back on his face, hiding his eyes.

"Yeah… um… I guess." Staring up at him, her heart pounded as her mind wondered what on earth she was ready for.

9

Joseph held Samantha's gaze for another moment before he turned and walked toward his motorcycle. Her eyes widened as a jolt of excitement hit her. She'd never been on a motorcycle but had always wanted to. Bouncing on her toes, she followed him, not hiding her eagerness. He turned and looked down, then grinned. Christ, he was beautiful when he smiled.

"Hang on." He left her standing, and her gaze trailed after him as he went inside the shop and returned with another helmet. "You can use Rose's. Jason won't let her on his bike while she's pregnant."

"I've never ridden but always wanted to." She placed the helmet over her head and lifted her chin, feeling like a child standing still as he adjusted the strap, making sure it was snug. With his hand on her lower back, he guided her toward the bike. She tried to ignore his fingers, but each tip was a warm brand through her shirt. Clearing her throat, she refocused. "Um... what should I do? Do I get on first?"

His deep chuckle sounded out. "Nah. Wait till I get on, then swing your leg around and settle behind me. You'll need to scoot up close and wrap your arms around my waist tightly. Then move with me and hang on for the ride."

She watched as he swung a denim-clad leg over the seat, his heavy boots resting on the asphalt. Standing next to the large motorcycle was a reminder just how short she was. Placing her hand on his shoulder, she managed to get her foot over the seat, then shimmied her body until she was nestled behind him. Her knees were pressed against his thighs, her crotch against his ass, and her breasts against his back as her arms encircled him, holding tightly to his muscular abs. She had always thought riding a motorcycle with someone would be sexy, but with their bodies pressed together and the engine rumbling under her ass, her mind shot straight to pure sex with Joseph. Her arms jerked at the thought, but before she had a chance to rethink the ride, they lurched out onto the street. Even going down the road out of town slowly, the wind in her face caused her to gasp, and she tightened her grip.

As soon as they made it to the highway, they roared up to speed, and she laughed out loud, loving every moment. She wanted to scream for him to go faster but knew the Sheriff's department kept a close watch on the highway cutting through the Eastern Shore. The green fields flew by in a blur, and for a moment, the idea of traveling the country on the back of a motorcycle—Joseph's motorcycle—rushed into her mind, and her arms tightened again.

Noticing where they were as she got her bearings, she yelled, "Take the next left at the light," and he nodded. She leaned into the turn as he pulled off the main road. "Stay on this road for five miles."

He nodded again, and she watched the trees and farmland glide by, less of a blur now that they were traveling slower. She'd been down this road every day for several years but couldn't imagine enjoying it more than she was right now. As they neared her place, she called out, "Go past the farm and take a right. I need to let my dog have a run."

In just another moment, the bike slowed as it rumbled down her gravel and oyster shell drive. Her camper came into sight, and she hoped Frodo wasn't frightened by the noise of the motorcycle. As soon as Joseph stopped and cut the engine, she hopped off awkwardly, her heel catching on the seat, causing her to stagger. He jerked his arm out and steadied her, a slight smile playing about his lips. Laughing, she said, "The trials and tribulations of being short!" Unsnapping the strap on her helmet, she handed it to him and turned, jogging toward the dog pen.

"Hey, boy!" She greeted Frodo as he frolicked around her, excited as always for her to come home. He sniffed her hands and pants as she rubbed him down, then loped along until he came to the bike, offering a deep baying bark before giving Joseph the same sniff-treatment. Seemingly satisfied that he had catalogued all the different smells, he galloped down the path toward the beach.

She walked over to Joseph as he pulled off his helmet

and smiled up at him. "I really appreciate you coming to get me. And for towing my truck. And for bringing me here." With a self-deprecating shake of her head, she added, "It seems like you're always catching me at my worst. I'm really not such a mess. I'm just... I'm just..."

"Busier than one person should be," he finished for her.

Shoving her fingers into her front pockets to halt the desire to reach up and brush his hair out of his eyes, she nodded. Hearing Frodo baying in the distance, she glanced toward the sand dune and hesitated.

"You need to go check on him?"

She shifted her gaze back to him and nodded. "Um... if you don't have to rush back, we could take a walk on the beach. He won't run off, but I do need to keep an eye on him."

"Yeah. I got nowhere I need to be."

Her breath had halted but rushed out as a smile crossed his face when he answered. They fell into step next to each other, walking past the scrub brush and over the dune, coming out onto the beach. Frodo was frolicking at the edge of the water, and she clapped her hands. "Frodo! What have you got, boy?"

"This view is amazing." Joseph stood with his hands on his hips, looking out over the Bay.

"Yeah, it's pretty special. I love being out here and wish I had more time just to do nothing but walk on the beach."

"We've got time now."

She nodded, nibbling on the corner of her bottom lip. Joseph seemed more at ease now. She'd actually witnessed him smiling several times this afternoon. She glanced down at his boots and said, "We can't walk on the beach in boots."

"Is that a rule I don't know about?"

He was still smiling, and she laughed. "Yes... it's one of my rules. As long as the weather permits, bare toes are a requirement. In the winter, of course, boots are acceptable."

"Well, I don't want to be a rule breaker."

He bent and untied his laces, toeing off his heavy boots and dropping his socks inside while she did the same thing. Standing, her gaze slid from his windblown hair down his muscular frame, ending at his pale, bare feet at the bottom of his jeans. Sucking in a ragged breath, she wasn't sure she'd ever seen anything sexier. And that included him on his motorcycle.

"No one ever comes out here, so we can leave them right here." Forcing her mind back to the task at hand, she dropped her boots to the sand, noting the nasty smears. Blushing, she lifted her gaze to see him staring at her. "I'm sorry."

His chin jerked back slightly as he cocked his head to the side. "Sorry? For what?"

"My job can get pretty... um... messy. I never think about it anymore, but I was on your bike with boots that weren't very sanitary."

His gaze left her face and dropped to her boots. A snort erupted before turning into laughter. She had no idea what he found funny, but the beautiful sound shot right through her.

"Samantha, my bike's been through sand, dirt, mud.

Hell, there's nothing you could get on it that can't be washed off."

Still blushing, she stared at her boots, still examining them. "Yeah, but this is probably some blood and maybe a bit of—" His hand landed on her shoulder, and all her attention swung back to him.

"Seriously, Samantha, stop worrying. There's not one thing about you that I don't like. Even your work boots."

"Oh," she muttered, now blushing for an entirely different reason. They turned in unison and fell into step as they wandered along the shore. Frodo alternated between chasing crabs, sniffing every scent he could gather, and loping along with them.

"How long have you been out here? Or were you raised here?"

"No, I was raised in the western part of the state, near Blacksburg. My grandfather was a country veterinarian. He saw some small animals but worked mostly farms, especially with their cows." A bubble of laughter came forth. "That old truck that you keep rescuing was my grandfather's. I remember riding with him as he bumped along backcountry roads to farms in that old truck."

"It means something to you."

Joseph's statement was simple, but her heart squeezed at the memories. "Yeah... it does. He was a good man... a good vet... kind and loving to two-legged friends as well as all four-legged ones. It's like his soul is in that old truck as well as a lot of memories."

She sent out a ragged breath then continued. "My

father followed in his footsteps and went to the Virginia School of Veterinary Medicine in Blacksburg and joined his practice. For a while, he did mostly farm animals but now has a few younger vets that do that while he sees the small animals in-office. I, of course, took up the family mantle, but I had a different path to take."

"The Army."

Nodding, she said, "I love the mountains around that part of Virginia. But, I suppose, like so many young people, I felt the need to forge my own career. The Army gave me a way to settle all my vet school debts, perform service, and I felt like I was doing something important. The IED dogs saved so many lives, and if I could keep them healthy and safe, I felt like I was saving lives, too."

"You absolutely did."

They were quiet for another moment, the sounds of the Bay filling the silence. She felt his gaze on her, and she turned to see him peering closely.

He reached over and tucked a windblown strand of hair behind her ear, and it struck her how often she'd wanted to do the same thing to him but had been afraid.

"So, how did you end up out here?"

Still in her trance, staring at him, she startled when he spoke. Blinking, she looked toward Frodo to give herself something else to look at.

"My mom was raised in Virginia Beach, and I loved to visit my grandparents when I was a kid. I'd often look across the Chesapeake Bay and wonder what was on the other side of the long bridge. My grandmother would tease me and say it was 'the land beyond'. They're gone now, but when I got out of the Army, I took a trip to the place of my wonderful childhood memories and sat in a little bar overlooking the water. On a whim, I drove over the bridge to see *the land beyond* for myself and was sold. The draw to the Eastern Shore had been strong, and considering North Heron County was one of the poorest counties in Virginia, I knew my services would be needed. The only vet in the area wasn't much older than me but had run his clinic for almost ten years. He gave me the freedom to work in the clinic and take trips out to some of the area farms to work with their smaller animals as well."

"That sounds like what I did. Went to a little bar on the Bay and looked out at the bridge. I had two Navy buddies, Zac and Jason, that had written to me and told me about this place. Decided the time was right for a visit."

"Where did you serve?"

"Zac and I were firemen aboard an aircraft carrier that was running drills in the Orient. Then we both landed on the Abraham Lincoln carrier and spent time in the Middle East. That was where we met Jason."

They had turned and started back along the beach, the sun moving across the sky. Frodo galloped over, and she laughed as he sniffed Joseph's pants once again. As though both having the same thought, they plopped their butts down onto the sand, allowing Frodo to lay near their feet.

"What about you?" he asked.

"Afghanistan." She opened her mouth to say more, to give details, then decided against it. Some of her memories were held close to her heart. She swallowed deeply, wondering why her service time was so hard to talk about. Not that she wouldn't share when the time was right or the listener was right. Glancing to the side, she noted the strong lines of his face as Joseph stared out over the water. It struck her that the listener felt right, but it definitely wasn't the time. Heavy stories were best shared by people that would help carry the burden, not walk away.

They continued to sit quietly for a few moments, the gulls laughing in the distance and the herons walking on stilt legs as they hunted for their evening meal of crabs.

"Can I ask you something?"

She resisted the urge to quip that he just had asked a question and nodded instead.

"I saw Liam talking to you after the AL meeting and heard that he's asked about some wild dogs around... maybe wolves or hybrids?"

Her forehead scrunched. "I know some of the local farmers have claimed to see something around, but there are no wolves in the Eastern Shore. They aren't indigenous. Now, wild dogs? If they mean un-owned, running-loose dogs, that's possible. But from what I've been told, it's not like a pack has been seen. So, I don't think there's anything to worry about. Well, I wouldn't want an unvaccinated dog around children or other animals, but as to wolves and coyotes, we're safe."

"Good," he mumbled, looking down at his hands.

Sucking in her lips, she wondered if there was something else on his mind.

"Liam seems like a nice guy," he ventured.

"Yeah…" she agreed. "I don't know him well, but he seems nice enough."

"He's single."

She sniggered. "Are you interested?"

His head jerked around, his eyes wide. "No!" He hesitated, then dropped his eyes to her upturned lips and scowled. "I just wondered if you were."

Her mirth eased as she witnessed the intensity of his gaze. Placing her hand on his arm again, she shook her head. "No, Joseph. Liam is a nice guy, but I'm not interested in him in any other way than friendship."

He ducked his head and grinned. They continued to sit in silence for a few more minutes until Frodo came back over and looked at her with his soulful eyes. "I guess I'd better feed him." They stood, dusted the sand off their butts, grabbed their boots, and walked back toward the camper. "I really appreciate you bringing me here." She glanced toward the door before swinging her gaze back to him. "Would you like to come in? I know there's beer in the fridge."

He narrowed his eyes for a second, his head swinging around as though looking for something. "Um… sure. Don't reckon I'll turn down a free beer."

They walked toward the camper, and she pulled a key out of her bag. Turning the lock, she swung the door open, giving Frodo a chance to bound inside first. Stepping in, she moved to the refrigerator and pulled out a beer. "I'll call someone to get a ride into town when my truck is ready tomorrow."

As he followed her inside, he said, "I'll take you

home tonight and will pick you up—" His words halted as his gaze shot around the interior of the camper.

Her brow lowered as she cocked her head to the side. "Home? But you did bring me home."

His gaze continued to scan the small space before landing back on her. "You *live* here? I thought this was just a place where you checked on the dog."

"Frodo is my dog. This," she said, swinging her hand out, "is my home."

"You live in a *camper*?"

Trying to ignore the incredulity in his voice as well as assumed derision, she propped her hands on her hips and stared up at him, eyes glaring. "I don't live in a mansion, Joseph. I work all the time and most of my money goes right back into the business or one of the area shelters. Hell, I've forgiven more fees from people that can't pay, but I've got to make sure my staff is paid. I'm sorry my accommodations don't meet your approval!" She plopped down onto the small sofa, blinking to battle the gathering of moisture in her eyes, hating that she even felt like crying.

Joseph stood inside the camper, not knowing where to look first. Frodo jumped up to the bunk over the driver's seat, so that's where his gaze first landed. The area was long enough for two narrow mattresses, and from the looks of it, one was where Frodo made himself comfortable. Directly in front of him was a section that pushed out, housing the two-seater dinette set and sofa, both with overhead cabinets. Samantha had plopped onto the edge of the sofa, and he forced his gaze not to settle on her but to continue taking in the space. On the opposite side were more overhead cabinets, a counter with a tiny sink, microwave, two-burner stovetop, and a mini-fridge.

A cabinet with a small flatscreen TV faced the sofa, and directly in the back, he spied the bed and minuscule closet. A door was closed, but he'd been in enough campers in his travels to know the shower, toilet, and sink were there. The entire area was neat and yet with touches of color creating warmth.

Now, he dropped his gaze to her and wished he could wipe away the frustrated expression on her face. A small shelf over the TV caught his attention, and he stepped forward to inspect the small statuettes. Gandolf. Gimli the Dwarf. Legolas the Elf. Frodo and Samwise the Hobbits. *Frodo and Sam. Fuck me.*

Feeling the heat of her glare on his neck, he turned. His heart squeezed as he watched the myriad of emotions cross her open face. The tinge of embarrassed blush. The indignant fire in her eyes. The defense in her crossed-arm posture.

"You're the first person who's been in here. Thanks for reminding me why I don't invite others."

Her words were snapped, but he recognized the loneliness in her tone. "I've stayed in a lot of campers." His statement had the desired effect as she sat erect, curiosity now in her eyes. "This is a nice one."

She hesitated, then said, "If you're making fun of—"

"Not at all." He shook his head for emphasis. "I'm serious. I've traveled around a lot. Didn't always want to stay in a hotel, so I'd look for campgrounds that had campers to rent for a few nights, a few weeks, even occasionally, a few months." He reluctantly shifted his gaze from her face to scan the room again. "Stayed in some decent ones and a few that were downright shitty. This one is real nice."

"So, why did you act the way you did when you found I live here?"

"Seriously, Samantha?"

She jumped to her feet, her hands spread out to the side. "Yes, Joseph. I don't know you well enough to read your mind, so I have no idea what you're thinking."

Frodo, reacting to the tone in Samantha's voice, lifted his head, a warning growl rumbling from his chest. Samantha looked over and sighed. "Frodo. I'm fine." With that, the large dog laid his head back down on his paws but kept his eyes on the couple.

Joseph only had to take one step forward and was directly in her space, looking down once more, seeing how she'd tuck perfectly underneath his chin. She tilted her head back to hold his gaze. "You're a woman. Alone. Living way out here with no neighbors around. Your camper's nice, but it wouldn't take much for someone to bust in."

"I know how to take care of myself. I was in the Army, remember? And yes… I have a gun in here."

Now it was his turn to sigh, but before he had a chance to speak, she jumped in.

"I'm not stupid… I know that someone my size would have a hard time with an intruder, but between Frodo and the locked doors and windows, I would have the upper hand before anyone made it in here. Plus, I'm out here where no one knows this place. The only one who knows is the old farmer who sold me this land and my staff."

He nodded but watched her carefully. Her body was strung tight, her lips pinched. The odds of him convincing her she was unsafe were minimal right now. And he really didn't want to get kicked out. "Okay."

Her eyes were still narrowed as though she was trying to figure him out. He almost chuckled. Many had tried but few succeeded. *But her... yeah, she just might do it.*

Shoving his hand through his hair, he thought over his words carefully. "I admit I was surprised but didn't expect you to live in a mansion. I'm sorry, though. I didn't mean to make you feel self-conscious. Hell, I've had enough people look at my life and wonder what the fuck I was doing. I should know better than to do that to someone else."

His apology or his explanation must have hit the target because the tension in her shoulders left and her lips curved slightly. She stepped around him and grabbed the beer she'd placed on the counter. Handing it to him, she said, "With everything else, I forgot to give you your drink."

She grabbed one for herself and walked over to the dinette table, sliding onto the booth, nodding toward the other side in invitation. An invitation he wasn't about to decline.

They drank in silence for a moment. He wanted to know more about her but wanted to avoid landmines. Something she'd said a moment earlier slammed into him, and he blurted, "You said you forgive fees when someone can't pay."

Her gaze jumped to his, then back down to her hands clasped around the beer bottle, a tinge of blush staining her cheeks. "Forget that. I shouldn't have said anything."

"Come on, Samantha. Don't shut down on me now. What did you mean?"

Sucking in a deep breath before letting it out slowly,

she stared at her beer bottle a moment before lifting her gaze up to him. "North Heron is a very poor county. When people are in Baytown, or Easton, or Seaside, they can forget that. Especially Baytown. Little shops selling quaint merchandise. Restaurants. The public beach. Most of the town is adorable rental houses that fill up during the warm weather with families itching for a chance to see small-town life, fabulous beaches, and a place for their kids to run around." She lifted her gaze back to his. "But beyond that, it's rural. The cement factory shut down. Some of the farms have gone under. It'll never be a vacation metropolis because of the environmental protections. Everything that makes it perfect to visit or for those of us that love it here also make it economically depressed."

Understanding dawned on him. "And that affects your business."

She hefted her shoulders in a half-hearted shrug. "Yes. I'm sure Jason gets a lot of business from travelers, vacationers and people who have car trouble while driving through the area. But, I'll bet, for the people that live around here, he's probably done work for free as well."

"Embarrassed to say I haven't thought about that, but I'm sure you're right." He shifted in his seat, realizing that while the tattoo shop wasn't open often, the ones that came in could pay. It had never dawned on him how Jason might run the garage. Focusing his attention back on the beautiful woman sitting across from him, he asked, "And your clinic?"

"When I first came to the Eastern Shore, it was in

answer to an advertisement for a veterinarian to join a small practice. The building was decent, the money flow was okay, and we had two techs that worked for us. But it didn't take long to realize that we had a lot of clients who simply didn't have the money to pay their bills in full. I know it frustrated the vet I worked with, but he let some people pay in installments, and even sometimes forgave part of the debt. When he left, I maintained the same practice." Shrugging, "What else would we do?"

"And your staff?"

"To run a practice like ours, especially now that I'm the only fully licensed veterinarian, I need a good staff. I have one vet tech, one vet assistant, and the office manager. I've got a veterinarian intern which is as good as another veterinarian, and hopefully, he'll want to stay when he graduates with what I can pay."

"And so, you make sure everyone else is taken care of, including the animals and your clients, but what about you?"

She snorted and rolled her eyes. "It's not like I'm living in a hovel! I saved up money and bought this land from the farmer next door. But that didn't leave any money left over to build a home. I had enough money for this camper and got a really good deal. It was practically new and was left at one of the area campgrounds when the owners just abandoned it after not being able to make their payments. The campground sold it to me, I drove it out here, and figured it was good enough to live in for a couple of years until I had saved for a down payment."

"There's no denying this land is amazing."

She didn't respond but took another sip of her beer and nodded slowly. They continued to drink in silence for a few more minutes, but soon, the sound of Frodo's snores reverberated through the camper, causing both of them to chuckle.

"Frodo?"

She blinked, fiddling with the label on her beer. "I suppose you're asking about his name and the statues I collect."

He nodded, thrilled that she was still talking to him. He found he wanted to learn more. Everything. He hadn't been this interested in a woman in... hell, he'd never been this interested. He couldn't ignore the attraction, but it was more than physical. Everything about her called to him, leaving him both breathless and with an ache in his chest. He usually had to tell his dick to behave when he was around her, but now, all he wanted to do was hold her close. She was an enigma, and he wanted to peel back the layers.

"I like Tolkien's Hobbit and Lord of the Rings."

"Lots of people like those. But it's kind of unusual for a dog's name." Frodo groaned, and he glanced up at the dog, seeing him still asleep, dreaming peacefully. A slight giggle had him swing his gaze around, finding Samantha smiling at Frodo before looking back at him. Her smile caused his heart to squeeze again with her beauty while feeling relieved that she was smiling at him.

"There are volumes and volumes of people analyzing Tolkien's work. How his friends and his time in the war shaped the author that he became. But for me, it was always so simple. Yes, there was duty and honor. Sacrifice and fighting for what's right. But mostly, it was about true friendship. And that was never more exemplified than between Frodo and Sam."

"Have you always gone by Sam?"

Her shoulders hefted. "Sometimes my family calls me Samantha, but often it gets shortened to Sam. In college and vet school, I was known as Sam." She held his gaze for a long moment then tilted her head to the side. "You always call me Samantha."

"To me, you are Samantha. It's a beautiful name for a beautiful woman."

Her fingers halted in the middle of a beer label rip and she stared, not breathing. His gaze never left hers as his hand reached across the table and wrapped around her fingers. "Breathe."

Her breath rushed out, and she blinked. He wanted to pull her to a stand, wrap his arms around her, and kiss her slightly opened lips. He did the first, then battled to not fulfill his wishes. *She deserves so much more.*

With them now both standing, his hands still holding hers and her face tilted up to his, he blurted, "Did you like the ride on my bike?"

Her smile widened, and she nodded.

"Then I'll come pick you up tomorrow evening and take you into Baytown. You can get your truck, but I'll take you to dinner first."

Now it was his time to hold his breath, wondering what she'd say. And just like the Samantha he was getting to know, she said what was on her mind with no hesitation.

"I'd like that. I'd like that a lot." Her admission was open. No games. No playing coy. It dawned on him that while she might come off as prickly at times, she simply was who she was—a lot like him. She said what she thought and felt but was never rude. And her big heart... *no, not going there.*

Now his smile matched hers, and as he gave her hand a squeeze and turned to leave, Frodo lifted his head, saw that all was right with the world, groaned, and flopped to the side. Chuckling, Joseph walked outside and started toward his bike.

"Joseph!"

Turning at the sound of Samantha's voice, he waited as she stood in the doorway of her camper. The light from inside illuminated her profile, casting an other-worldly glow about her.

"J.R.R. Tolkien wrote in The Fellowship of the Ring something I thought you should hear. 'Not all those who wander are lost.'" She shrugged but held his gaze. "It makes me think of you."

He stared, transfixed by her beauty framed in the light and her words that surrounded him. He tried to swallow past the lump in his throat, offering a chin lift, his silent good night, before turning once again and jogging to his bike.

Throwing his leg over the seat, he fastened his helmet and started the engine. He'd always loved the feel of the machine underneath him, the power so connected to his body's movements. But as he watched her wave while she stood in the door of her camper home, all he could think of was how his bike now seemed lonely without her sitting behind him. *Not all those who wander are lost.* He already knew he was falling under her spell, but with those words, he wasn't sure how to keep from drowning.

Taking off down the gravel drive, he sighed. In the past, no matter where he landed, he always had one foot out the door. For the first time, the urge to pack up and leave hadn't struck.

He headed back to town and pulled into the garage just as Jason was beginning to shut the shop down. Glancing over at Samantha's truck, he thought for a moment, having not considered that she had an emotional attachment to the old hunk of junk. "Hey, Jason, tell Troy to do what he can to really get it going. The works. Make it like new as much as he can. I'll cover the cost."

Jason lifted a brow and grinned. Chuckling, he said, "You just might stick around after all."

Flipping him off, he pulled around to the back and parked at the bottom of the steps leading to his apartment. Climbing the stairs, he let himself in, placing the helmets on the counter.

Grabbing another beer, he opened the paper sack on the counter. He'd stopped at a fast-food place on the highway heading into town, grabbing a couple of burgers and fries. Not bothering with a plate, he sat at the counter and wolfed down his food.

He looked around, scanning the space. He hadn't bothered decorating, not unusual for him, but couldn't help but compare it to Samantha's small camper. Hers was neat and yet he'd seen a few family pictures pinned to the refrigerator. The sofa had two pillows in swirls of blue, green, and yellow. Her bed covering was blue and green. Curtains in the same colors hung over the windows. *Hell, even her dog's blanket was bright blue.*

She essentially lived in less than two-hundred-fifty square feet. He, on the other hand, was living in a large, two-bedroom apartment with a full kitchen and dining area, large bathroom, and living room with a wide picture window that overlooked the town. Snorting, he shook his head as he walked over to the refrigerator. *And I'm supposed to be the one who travels light.*

He later sat on the sofa with a book in his lap, but the words blurred on the pages. Finally admitting his thoughts were on Samantha and not the story, he snapped it shut and tossed it to the coffee table. Dragging his hand through his hair, he sighed heavily. *She makes me want to take a chance... but am I worth a chance for her?*

Annette picked Samantha up the next morning and they drove to the clinic together. She stifled a yawn. Sleep had not come easily after Joseph left with his delicious woodsy scent still wafting throughout her home. She didn't know what it was about him that made him more interesting with every encounter. There was something mysterious about the normally quiet man, and the fact that he had now given her glimpses into the man he was made her want to continue delving deeper.

"Sam?"

Jerking her head to the side, she rushed, "Sorry! Trouble sleeping last night. What did you say?"

Annette laughed, shaking her head. "I'm glad it's not a surgery day for you, or you'd be falling asleep over the patients! Anyway, I only asked if you were ready for me to sign off on the orders. We're getting a little low on several things."

She opened her mouth to reply, then pretended to yawn again in an effort to gain a moment to try to think of an answer. She'd been trying to keep an eye on the pharmaceutical stock, fearful that something may have gone missing. The canine vaccinations were still off by a few even with the new orders that had come in. Glancing to the side, she hated to keep Annette in the dark considering Annette had been the administrator for a long time. *Susan? Tonya? Brentley?* They were all employees that she trusted and liked. *Is it just miscounting? Clerical error?* While neither of those would make her happy, at the same time, it would be much better than thinking somebody had stolen drugs. *Stolen... shit.* That was the first time she'd allowed herself to think of the possibility. *But it's vaccines... not pain meds or something worth stealing to put on the black market.*

Scrubbing her hand over her face, she knew she had to give Annette an answer. "Things have been so nuts lately I didn't look over the order very carefully. I promise to get that done so you can order before I have to go to the meeting with the local law enforcement."

"What's it about?"

Shrugging, she said, "I'm not sure. Liam said that they needed to talk to me. Since Hannah is picking me up and will drop me off at home, I won't need you to wait on me. You can make the pharmaceutical order before you leave today." Her response seemed to appease Annette, and they chatted amiably the rest of the way to the clinic.

An hour later, she smiled at the little boy who rushed into the examination room with his father, an excited German shepherd puppy bounding around, straining on his leash. "Oh, what do we have here?" she asked.

"We got a new puppy!" the little boy called out loudly, his hand rubbing the puppy's head.

His dad chuckled while shushing his son. "Jonny, you don't gotta shout the house down. Use your inside voice."

"Sorry," Jonny whispered. "His name is Bosco."

"Well, let's take a look at him," she said, kneeling onto the floor, her hands moving over the wiggling dog. The puppy was adorable, and she could not help but laugh at the enthusiastic antics as it jumped around. She examined the ears, eyes, mouth, teeth, and then moved to its body, checking its bones and fur. "He's got a nice double coat. Where did you get Bosco?"

"We found him," Jonny's dad replied. "He looks like a purebred."

Her gaze shot up, seeing the pride on the man's face. She knew that purebred German shepherds could go from as low as five hundred dollars to two thousand.

Before she had a chance to say anything else, Jonny's dad added, "He'd been running through our fields for a couple of days, and I thought he must belong to someone. Then Jonny fed him, and he ate like he was starved. Been with us for the past week."

"Oh… um…"

"I know, Doc Collins. You're going to ask why we didn't try to find an owner, but we did. I made some calls, put up some flyers, but nothing. No one's claimed him. Someone told me that there was a fancy big-dog breeder about forty miles at the north end of Acawmacke County. I made a call to check if they'd lost a puppy."

"What did they say?"

He rubbed the whiskers on his chin and scrunched his nose. "I think I insulted them. Told me they'd never be so careless as to lose a puppy."

"Who was the breeder?"

"Let's see... Bender. That was the name. Bender."

Standing, she made notations in Bosco's chart, twisting her head around as Susan walked in to assist. Looking back toward Mr. Tolson, she continued, "I'm going to scan him to see if he has a chip. That would make sense if he was someone's pet."

She ran the chip reader over the wiggling dog from nose tip to tail, trying to ignore the way Jonny's face held worry. Nothing. Turning back to them, she shrugged. "Well, if someone did lose him, they didn't have an identifier chip inserted. If he was from a breeder, he certainly would."

Taking the papers from Susan that Mr. Tolson had given when he first came in, she glanced through them. "I estimate him to be about nine weeks old, and with no background information, we'll give him vaccinations. And then you can come in four weeks after that."

Susan held the puppy while Samantha administered the injections. With a final rub down, she said goodbye to the Tolsons. As soon as they left the room to settle their account with Annette, she turned to her assistant. "Have you ever heard of Bender breeders?"

Shaking her head, Susan looked up from the papers

she was filling out. Catching Samantha's gaze, she cocked her head to the side. "Suspicious?"

"I don't know," she said, shrugging. "Bosco seemed active, alert, happy to play with Jonny. The next time I go to the shelter, I think I'll ask them about this breeder. Bosco seemed purebred, although... well..." Giving her head a shake, she continued, "There are people charging a lot of money for them when they're nothing more than puppy mills. If their business isn't legitimate, it might be why they lied and said the dog wasn't theirs. Better to take the loss than have someone snooping into their business."

Before she had a chance to ponder breeders anymore, she was called into the next exam room. By the end of the day, she finally had a chance to settle into the chair in her office and pulled up her computer. A quick Internet search gave evidence to a website for Bender's Breeding in Acawmacke County. She was surprised, expecting to find no Internet footprint. The website had several pictures of German shepherds, both puppies and adults.

The site and the breeders looked legitimate. Nibbling on her bottom lip, she leaned back in her chair and huffed. *Why does it bother me that they look legitimate?* Maybe it was because the website said they'd been in business for a number of years but she'd never heard of them. She didn't recall Tom ever mentioning them, either.

The Tolson's puppy had looked fine, happy and healthy. She couldn't tell by observation or physical examination if it was purebred, but she hoped they had facilities that kept up with their pets and not let one escape.

Her phone rang, dragging her attention from her internet search to the office phone. Picking it up, Annette announced, "You have a call on line two."

Clicking the appropriate line, she answered. "Doctor Collins."

"Sam? This is Luke. I don't know if this is a bad time, and if it is you can let me know and I'll set up a time to come in—"

"No, Luke, this is fine."

"I haven't been by the shelter that you mentioned working with, but I've had an idea about seeing if we could start a program where some of the prisoners help take care of some of the dogs. I've heard of programs similar to this, but I have no idea how it would be set up."

"Well, I've never thought about that. Are you thinking about the dogs actually living in the jail?"

"Honestly, Sam, I don't know what I'm thinking. I just thought that maybe the prisoners and the local shelter could help each other. They need volunteers and the prisoners need a chance to do something worthwhile."

What he was suggesting caught her imagination, "I know the shelter is always looking for help. I don't know how we could bring together the prisoners and the shelter, but it seems like we could come up with something."

"That's what I was thinking," Luke said. "I just didn't know who to call first."

"How about I talk to the shelter supervisor? I was going to stop by in the next couple of days to talk to her about a few things anyway. I can easily see what she thinks."

"That sounds good. I also talked to Colt the other day. He's got questions, obviously, but said that he'd like to know what we can come up with for a proposal."

"I'll talk to the shelter supervisor and get back with you."

Disconnecting, she opened the spreadsheet on her computer she'd started the other day. When Tom had been in charge of the clinic, he'd insisted on making sure the veterinary records were computerized, going so far as to utilize new software. While she'd been trained on their program, there were aspects that she had not paid close attention to, such as the ability to keep track of the exact doses of vaccinations and medications prescribed and what had been ordered.

Just as she suspected, the number of vaccinations left in their refrigerated storage container was less than what they should have compared to the inoculations they had given. Without knowing whether the error was in the initial order or sloppy record-keeping, she printed off the spreadsheet, determined to keep a closer eye on the medication during the next month.

Looking up at the rap on the doorframe, she clicked the mouse to clear the screen as Annette walked in with order forms for her to sign.

"I know you wanted to take a look at things before you left for your meeting. I'd like to get this order sent off before we leave today," Annette said.

Taking the papers, she scanned them before signing. Looking up, she caught Annette's furrowed brow.

"Is everything okay?"

Sucking in her lips, she sighed, "It just doesn't seem like the vaccinations we ordered the last time have lasted as long as I expected them to."

Annette slid into the chair across from Samantha's desk and nodded slowly. "I noticed that, also. I just have no idea why."

"Is everyone documenting the way they're supposed to?"

Annette shifted in her seat as though uncomfortable. "Look, Samantha, I've been thinking about this, and I'm not comfortable trying to pinpoint the discrepancy right now. I remember the last time we received a shipment of vaccinations, and I'm embarrassed to admit that I didn't count everything against the invoice. We've never had a problem before, but that's no excuse. On top of that, I haven't been checking behind Brentley to make sure he's entering everything into the computer. I can't imagine that Susan or Tonya have changed what they're doing, but I thought once we get this order in, I'll pay closer attention."

Samantha lifted her hands and placated, "Hey, I'm not throwing around accusations. If anyone knows how crazy things have been lately, it's me. I find it strange that none of our other drugs seem to be missing or short, but it's not like vaccinations are high on a black market list." She rolled her shoulders, shifting her neck back and forth to ease the tension. Looking back down at the papers, she signed the forms and pushed them across the desk toward Annette. "I agree, let's just keep a closer eye on things going forward."

Annette nodded her agreement and smiled. "Was there anything else?"

"Yeah. Have you heard of Bender Breeders?"

"Big dogs, I think. I'm pretty sure they're north, near the Maryland line." Annette cocked her head to the side and scrunched her brow. "Are you thinking of taking them on as clients?"

"Oh, hell no! They'd never ask, and I don't have time to deal with a breeder who expects house calls."

"Not to mention I'll bet they're picky like Hazel Woods and her little show dogs she breeds."

Samantha grinned. "You're probably right." She looked out the front window and spied the Easton Police Chief vehicle pull into the parking lot. "Looks like my ride is here."

"Enjoy your evening," Annette called out as she left the office.

As Annette hurried back to the front, a smile crossed Samantha's lips as she thought about Joseph picking her up. *I wonder if we'll be on the back of his bike...* Suddenly, that thought made her wonder about what to wear since they were going to dinner. Grabbing her cell phone, she sent a quick text.

What should I wear? Are we going on your bike?

It only took a minute for his reply to come back.

Wear whatever you want. And if you want on the back of my bike, that's where you'll be.

Excitement lurched through her at the thought of riding with him again.

Absolutely. I'll dress accordingly!

Pick you up at 6

Shoving her phone into her bag, she was anxious to get the meeting over with so she had time to get ready for her date. Grinning widely, she hurried out to the parking lot.

Samantha looked around the table at the others she'd gotten to know over the past couple of years, not only through their jobs but the American Legion. The gathering was ensconced in a utilitarian conference room at the Acawmacke Sheriff's Office. Liam had invited her to the Law Enforcement Leaders meeting, and around the table were Hannah, Dylan, Colt, Mitch, and Wyatt. He'd explained that the various police chiefs and two Eastern Shore sheriffs got together monthly to discuss any items that would be of interest to all of them.

"We know your time is valuable, Sam," Liam began. "We just need your expertise."

"Whatever you need, just ask."

"What can you tell us about wolf-dog hybrids?"

Jerking slightly, her brows snapped together. "Well, they aren't allowed in North Heron or Acawmacke Counties, but I'm sure you already knew that. They are regulated as exotic animals, and in Virginia, each locality can determine what they will allow." Giving her head a little shake, she added, "Of course, as law enforcement, you already knew that. I'm sorry, what exactly are you looking for?"

"Honestly, anything you can tell us about possible wolf breeding. And please, don't assume we know anything about the subject other than just the local laws."

"Oh, okay." She nodded, gathering her thoughts. "Well, wolves and dogs are canines. They are inter-fertile, which means that they can breed. It's possible to occur in the wild, but it's not as common as you might think. In fact, because of the territorial nature of wolves, they protect their ranges from intruding canines such as dogs, coyotes, and other wolves. But they can also be commercially bred in areas that allow that."

"So, where legally allowed, someone can keep a wolf to specifically breed with dogs?" Hannah asked.

Shaking her head, Samantha replied, "No. Well, I should say no one should. Usually, someone has a dam or a sire that is a wolf-dog hybrid that they breed with the dog."

"Which would just make a more diluted wolf-dog hybrid?" Hannah asked, her confusion evident in her furrowed brow.

"Essentially, yes, but then for someone buying a wolf-hybrid, it doesn't have to be fifty percent wolf and fifty percent dog. In fact, that would *not* be preferable. Too unpredictable."

"I hate to ask a stupid question," Dylan said, leaning

forward, "but why the fuck would anyone want to breed a dog with a wild animal?"

"There are those that believe you can get the best genetic mix from both animals, but there are a lot of misconceptions out there. The topic is greatly contested among those who breed and those who want them regulated." She pulled out her phone and quickly searched. Glancing up, she said, "Since I don't deal with exotic animals, I've got some information here that hopefully will make some sense. For example, some people feel that a wolf-hybrid will make a better guard dog, but the fact is that wolves are shy by nature. Another myth is that they might live longer than a dog, but the truth is their lifecycle is virtually the same. Another myth is that they're healthier than dogs, less prone to disease, but that also isn't true."

"What about the unpredictable behavior you mentioned?" Mitch asked.

"Full-blooded wolves constantly explore their environment because they are so territorial, and this exploration often takes place with their teeth and paws. So, if you have a hybrid that is more wolf than dog, they'll explore the house in a way that the owner probably doesn't want. They'll rip off cabinet doors to see what is behind them. They have a desire to roam, and in the wild, wolves can travel thirty miles a day. They also have a predatory nature… so cats, other dogs, or even children can be in danger." She sighed and shook her head. "Again, let me say that for every negative you can read about wolf-hybrids, you will find those that defend the legitimate breeding as gaining the best animal possible and get angry at any naysayers."

That was met with silence for a moment as the others processed her words. She waited to see what else they needed from her.

"Obviously, we don't have any breeders in the area, but do regular dog vaccinations work on wolves?" Colt finally asked.

"There is no approved rabies vaccination for wolf-dogs. Legitimate breeders have to give them, and rabies vaccinations can only be given by a veterinarian. Because breeders are not using a full-blooded wolf as one of the parents, the hybrids they're selling are going to be over fifty percent dog, so they would have a better chance for the vaccinations to be effective." She clicked further on the site she was looking at. "I am seeing where some vets do not treat hybrids because of liability reasons and that the owners have to acknowledge that they understand the rabies vaccination cannot be relied upon to deliver protection against rabies in a wolf-dog hybrid."

"You mentioned some people think you get the best genetics of both, but what if you don't?" Mitch asked, leaning forward with his forearms on the table. "Could you get a more aggressive animal?"

She nodded slowly, carefully looking at the concerned faces of her friends in law enforcement. "The problem comes with the challenges of the unknown behavior. They may be canines, but there is a diversity of genetic composition, even within one litter. So, the puppies could all look very different, and they could act very differently. Wolves and dogs do not mature at the same rate. Wolves are even more territorial than dogs, especially to protect their food source. Dogs, through domestication over centuries, have lost some of that instinct. A wolf reaches sexual maturity much later than a dog, but with the interbreeding, the coinciding behavioral changes can be hard to predict."

"Same with coyotes, right?" Liam asked.

"Fuckin' hell!" Dylan cursed. "Coyotes, too?"

"Now, this is an area I really don't know anything about," Samantha admitted. She tapped through a few more veterinarian sites. "Coydogs were deliberately bred in ancient Mexico. But they are not playful or outgoing, and definitely not a good choice for a pet. Their mating cycles are even more off than a wolf-dog, so they are much more uncommon."

"So, why breed wolves and dogs?"

Before she had a chance to answer, Wyatt spoke up. "Because to people who think they're getting the best, they'll fight to keep their right to do this." He looked over at Samantha and lifted his brow. "Right?"

She nodded, her nose scrunching slightly. "For legitimate and regulated breeders, they'll work with veterinarians and complete DNA testing on their animals. And yes, they truly feel that the beauty of the wild animal paired with the domestication makes the perfect pet for the discerning owner."

The group became quiet, and curiosity swept through her. "I know if this is dealing with an active investigation there's little you can tell me, but why all these questions? Please, tell me we don't have wolf-dogs illegally here on the Eastern Shore." Her attention was drawn to Liam since he was hosting the meeting of law enforcement leaders.

"We don't have anything concrete, but at these meetings, we discuss things that come up that might have ramifications. There is a major investigation going on in Norfolk of dogfighting. As soon as they shut down one area or ring, another one crops up. The investigation has taken them out of some of the warehouse areas in Norfolk where the dogfighting had been occurring to more rural areas in Chesapeake. One of the things that they have found is some hybrids—specifically wolf-hybrid dogs—that are being used in the fighting. On the outside, they look mostly like German shepherds, but their aggression is incredibly high. This was only discovered when they found an illegal breeder."

The air left her lungs in a rush, and she rubbed her forehead. "What people do to animals... Jesus, it makes me so angry." A thought hit her, and she jerked her head around quickly. "Oh, my God. Is that happening here?" She caught the side glances between the others and her heart pounded.

Liam's jaw clenched, and he said, "One of the illegal breeders said his dog came from over the bridge. He didn't know who bred the dog or where he came from. He just knew he paid a lot of money to get a wolf-dog."

"We don't have any evidence, and we haven't heard anything," Colt added. "But in discussing how we needed to stay vigilant, we wanted to have your professional input."

"There are only a couple of registered breeders on

the Eastern Shore. One of them I've met. Hazel Woods. She's been breeding little dogs for a long time. I think she's even had a couple of champion show dogs in the toy categories."

"Do you provide services to her?"

Samantha snorted and shook her head. "No, and believe me, it's no offense. The few times I've met her, she's been very nice, and if there was an emergency, I think she'd call me. But she gets top dollar for her little precious dogs and she has a veterinarian in Virginia Beach that specializes in toy dogs for people with a... um... discerning pocketbook."

The others laughed, and Hannah rolled her eyes. "I suppose you mean she forks over a fuck-ton of money."

Joining in the laughter, Samantha said, "Like I said, I'm glad she does. I have my hands full in dealing with the wonderful average pets and small farm animals. I wouldn't even have time to take her on as a client."

Liam rubbed his chin and held her gaze. "What about Bender's Breeders?"

"Jim Bender? I don't service him as a client. My guess is that he also uses a specialized veterinarian."

"I've met him," Liam said. "We've never had any complaints about his breeding business. I think he may have even sold some of his dogs for police or military."

Sam nodded. "There's a lot of people who have dogs to sell that aren't breeders, of course. Commercial breeders have to be licensed and regis-tered. There's a whole list of rules they have to follow and laws that regulate what they can and can't sell. But you all know that in a rural area like our two counties, there's a lot of farmers who have dogs that run loose in their yards or barns, have litters of puppies, and if they can make a few bucks by selling the puppies, then they do. I see that all the time. Or they end up at the shelter to be adopted."

As the meeting came to an end, she placed her hands on the table and pushed to a stand. "Is there anything special you want me to keep an eye on?"

"Now that you know what we're looking into, just let us know if anything comes across your radar. Anything at all that might point to someone illegally raising wolf hybrids here on the shore," Liam said.

The others stood as well, thanking her for coming as she said her goodbyes.

Thirty minutes later, Hannah dropped her off at her camper, and she waved goodbye. Greeting Frodo, she hurried him through his run before placing his food on the floor. Taking a quick shower, she stood at the mirror, swiping her hand over the condensation. She pulled out her small bag of rarely-used makeup and applied blush, eye shadow, and mascara with a light hand.

She eschewed the idea of a dress and pulled on dark jeans, pairing them with a jade-green wrap-around shirt. After drying her hair, she wondered what to do with it since she'd be wearing a helmet. Finally, deciding that simple was best, she pulled the front away from her face with a clip and left the length to hang down her back.

She had just slid her feet into ankle boots when she heard the roar of a motorcycle approach. The sound made her heart beat faster, and she sucked in a deep breath before letting it out slowly, willing her body to calm. Frodo was pawing at the door, and she peeked out before throwing it open, laughing as Frodo bounded around Joseph's legs, cataloguing all the scents.

Joseph didn't bother pulling off his helmet before leaning down and rubbing his hands over the large dog's head, scratching behind his ears. She stood and stared, struck dumb with the realization that Joseph had never looked more sexy than at that moment, straddling his motorcycle, his dark boots planted on the light oyster shell drive, a wide smile on his face, and scrubbing his hands over her beloved dog. The idea of those hands doing the same to her flashed through her mind, and her breath caught in her throat.

Joseph turned his gaze to her and cocked his head to the side. She jerked out of her drooling, lust-induced zombie stance and offered a goofy wave. Even though his eyes were hidden behind his sunglasses, his wide smile gave evidence he surmised the trail her thoughts had jogged down.

Clapping her hands, she called for Frodo, and he dutifully returned to her. She led him around to the pen and fastened him in. By the time she'd walked back to the camper door, Joseph was waiting on her, Rose's helmet in his hand. She feasted her gaze on him, noting the light blue button-up shirt underneath his jacket and dark jeans. With his sunglasses no longer shading his eyes, she warmed under his perusal.

He leaned forward and placed his hand on her waist, and she looked up, readying for—and hoping for—their first kiss. Instead, he veered to the side and kissed her cheek, close to her ear.

"You look beautiful, Samantha," he whispered.

She felt his words move through her, their simple sincerity causing a smile to spread across her face.

"You ready to ride?"

A multitude of thoughts rushed through her head at the idea of riding Joseph, and the heat of a blush moved from her chest to her forehead. She began to think he was a mind reader when another wide grin from him indicated he guessed exactly what she was thinking.

"Absolutely." Determined to recapture some of her dignity, she turned quickly and grabbed her cross-body bag. Locking the front door, she faced him with what she hoped was an *'I'm cool'* expression.

He was still grinning as he took her hand and led her over to his bike. She fastened Rose's helmet on securely, and with a little more finesse than the first time, she climbed onto the seat, wrapping her arms around his waist and pressing tightly to his back.

For a split second, she wondered if she'd enjoy the ride as much as she'd looked forward to it, but just like the first time, it surpassed her imagining. With the wind whipping her hair behind her back, the sight of the rural farmland rushing by, and the feel of his body so intimately held by her, she couldn't imagine anything better... *well, other than being held by him.*

13

Turning at the intersection that led into Baytown, Joseph could not help but compare this trip to the one he'd made a few months ago. Then, alone, with no other thought than to connect with a couple of old Navy buddies. Now, with Samantha's breasts pressed against his back, her legs against his thighs, her arms wrapped around his waist, her fingers linked and yet perilously close to his crotch, he fought to keep his mind on driving and not running off the road. And yet it was her joyous laughter that made his heart beat faster. For once glad that the town's speed limit was greatly reduced, he slowed, wanting to prolong her enjoyment.

Parking outside the Seafood Shack, his abs tightened as she slowly dragged her fingers along his muscles before placing her hands on his shoulders for leverage as she climbed off his bike. He secured their helmets, and with his hand resting on her lower back, guided her toward the door.

"I've only been here a couple of times," she admitted.

"The food is good, but it can get crowded on the weekends. They've got a deck at the back. Is it okay if we eat out there?"

"Sure."

She smiled up at him as they walked toward the hostess counter. Without thinking, his hand slid from her back to grasp her fingers as they followed the hostess through the restaurant toward the back deck. As soon as their fingers touched, he felt a jolt and almost dropped her hand, both in surprise and uncertainty, but she held fast. She was looking straight ahead, but he watched her lips curve as their fingers linked together.

A tall, two-seater table at the end of the deck gave them a perfect view of the Baytown Harbor. Making sure she was settled first, he scooted his seat closer before sitting. It didn't take long for their beer to arrive, shortly followed by the appetizer selection. He dove into the onion rings while she scooped cheesy crab dip onto her pita chip. His chewing came to a halt at the sound of her moan of delight. Her eyes were closed, and her face appeared orgasmically pleased as she chewed and swallowed.

"Oh, that was amazing," she groaned, her eyes popping open.

The sound coming from her had shot straight through him, ending up at his cock. Glad that his hard-on was hidden, he nonetheless made sure his napkin was on his lap. Swallowing his own bite, he grunted, "Yeah."

She narrowed her eyes and pretend-glared. "No way are you going to revert back to single word answers,

Joseph Hernandez. When we first met, I wasn't sure you could speak in a complete sentence."

Chuckling, he shrugged. "Never been much of a talker. At least, not until recently."

"And what's happened recently?" She was munching on another chip but held his gaze and leaned closer, her eyes pinned on him. And if he wasn't mistaken, a hopeful gleam showed in her gaze.

"I figure you can guess, Samantha. I'm not much of a talker if I don't have anything to say or anyone to say it to. With you around, it's different."

His answer appeared to satisfy her, and she smiled before snagging one of the onion rings. Groaning again, she said, "Oh, I've got the perfect combination!"

He watched in fascination as she scooped up cheesy crab dip with the onion ring before popping it into her mouth. Before he had a chance to respond, she repeated her actions, only this time holding the tasty morsel to his lips. Without hesitation, he opened his mouth and took the bite from her fingers, gliding his tongue over the tips. Her eyes widened, and she laughed.

"Well, I was just going to give you something to nibble on, but it seems like my fingers may have done the trick."

He chuckled before chewing. "Damn, that's good!"

"Told you it was!"

His attention was riveted on her and wasn't shaken when she held his gaze and leaned closer.

"Tell me something about yourself, Joseph."

He generally avoided situations where personal questions would be asked but knew when he asked her to dinner that he was opening himself up to them getting to know each other better. He shifted, uncertain what to say or what she expected. His gaze dropped as she placed her hand on his arm, squeezing gently.

"It doesn't have to be deep or dark or secret... I just like hearing you talk."

Surprised, he stared but found nothing but sincerity looking back at him. He couldn't remember the last time somebody just wanted him to talk for the sake of talking. In fact, he felt sure that had never happened. But when Samantha offered him the freedom to say anything, the awkwardness fell away.

"I'm from California originally."

"Ooh, Northern California? I can see you riding along the coastline and going through the vast forests. Or maybe you were a surfer teen in Southern California?"

Chuckling, he shook his head. "No, Silicon Valley." He watched as her brow lowered, seeing her surprise so clearly written on her face. He shrugged, uncertain what to say, but the tug to talk to her was strong. "My grandfather worked for IBM in the post-WWII days. Money was there to be made for people who were smart and driven. My dad stayed in the area after graduating from Stanford and got on with one of the gaming start-ups. He worked for them for a while until creating his own business."

As he talked, his gaze had drifted toward the water but now was drawn back to her, curious and yet dreading her reaction. In the past, he'd found people were either shocked that he'd come from that background, or the speculative gleam of family money loomed in their eyes. He didn't realize he was holding his breath as he stared at her until she dipped another onion ring into the crab dip and licked her lips.

"Isn't it funny how different people are drawn to different things?"

He blinked slowly. Then he opened his mouth before shutting it, not saying anything. Finally, he mumbled, "What?"

"Like, your family is very into technology, I'm assuming studying a lot of math and computer science. My family was into biology and anatomy." She licked her lips again, her brows lowering. "Not that we didn't have to learn physics and math, but chemistry and biology were more our specialties. But it sounds like your family was immersed in computers."

"Yeah, I guess we were. I never really thought of it like that."

Continuing to hold his gaze, she asked, "And you never wanted to follow in their footsteps?"

"It's what *they* wanted."

"Yeah, I can see that. I'm sure they hated that you left California. I followed my family's footsteps as far as career, but, as you know, followed my own path." By now, their appetizers were finished, and she pushed the plate back. "And the Navy? Was that your calling?"

"Probably more like the ultimate rebellion." The words leaving his lips surprised him. Not what the words were but more the fact that he'd actually said them aloud. A first date should be about trying to impress the person you're with, and he had no doubt that opening up to Samantha might have the opposite effect. Her hand landed on his arm again, and he looked at her small, capable fingers resting on his tatted skin. Incongruent, and yet her comforting touch looked perfect. Without thinking, he continued, the words tumbling forth.

"My grandfather went to Berkeley. My father graduated from Stanford. Growing up, I was expected to excel in math and science to prepare for a software engineering degree. School was easy for me, and when I graduated, I started my freshman year at Stanford in their engineering program a year early. Two years later, I was halfway done and had a 4.0 GPA. The next two years were planned out, would've been a cakewalk, and a job in my dad's company guaranteed."

Her fingers were gently rubbing over his arm, easing the tension that had built. He lifted his gaze, seeing the same ease in her eyes.

"But that wasn't what you wanted, was it?" Her voice was soft, and surprisingly, held no condemnation.

He snorted. "I was nineteen years old and didn't have a fuckin' clue what I wanted to do with my life. But I knew I didn't want to live my parents' life."

"And what was their life like?"

His jaw tightened. "My dad worked all the time and demanded the same from everyone who worked for him. He was never satisfied with the amount of money he made but constantly wanted more. It was a competitive business, and he was determined to come out on top. My mom had been smart; they met in college. But he wanted a trophy wife, and she enjoyed filling that role. She was a good mom when I was a kid, but as I got older, my memories of her are mostly of the martini glass in her hand and trying to ignore the way she slipped into the pool house with one of the gardeners, pool boys, or delivery men."

He sighed heavily, not able to remember the last time he'd talked this much to anyone besides the drunken night with Zac and Jason. The feel of Samantha's fingers on his arm continued to calm him while making it easy to open up. "I'd feel sorry for Dad except for the fact that he was banging a number of the young women that worked in his company. It's like one day I woke up and simply knew that was not the life for me. I went down to the beach, sat alone drinking beer, and watched as a few Navy ships moved out of the harbor. The idea of doing something so completely opposite of how I'd been raised appealed to me. Probably the stupidest reason in the world for joining the Navy, but it's what I needed. I slept on the beach that night, sobered up, and the next day walked into the recruiting station."

Her fingers squeezed, and he heard the sharp intake of her breath. Lifting his gaze, he watched her blink away the moisture that had gathered in her eyes as she said, "I think that's the bravest thing I've ever heard."

The sounds of other patrons' conversations mixed with the background music coming from the restaurant's bar floated all around, but Joseph was sure he could hear his own heartbeat roaring in his ears. Uncertain what to say, he waited while she continued.

"To have a secure future laid out for you but feeling

as though you would sell your soul if you gave into that... wow, Joseph, how brave of you to strike out on your own."

They stayed silent, unspoken words passing between them until jumping in surprise when the server brought their dinners. Relief poured over him, needing to step back from his personal episode of fuckin' true confessions. Easing off the heavy conversation, they dug into their food. She reached over and speared some of his crispy clam strips after plopping one of her fried shrimp onto his plate. They continued to share their seafood, watching as the sun slipped lower into the horizon.

"I never get tired of the sunsets here," she said, laying her fork down and patting her belly. Grinning, she added, "This is the best. Good food, good conversation, good company."

Her words wrapped around him, easing into the crevices of the cold wall he'd spent years building. "Yeah." He couldn't think of anything else to say but she appeared unconcerned. He'd wanted their date to go well but had no idea what to expect.

After paying their bill, it felt natural to link fingers with her again, guiding her around the side of the restaurant toward the harbor. They walked along the water, chatting about the fishing boats that were coming in with their catch and wondering about the voyages of some of the privately-owned sailboats.

The sun had set, and he wrapped his arm around her, tucking her in tightly as they made their way back to the parking lot. Standing next to his bike, he cupped her face with both of his hands, his thumb sweeping over the apples of her cheeks. His chest ached with want but he hesitated, fearful of her not feeling the same overwhelming desire. Her gaze dropped to his mouth as her lips opened slightly. He accepted what he hoped was a silent invitation, need overtaking fear. Bending, he kissed her. The feel of her lips nearly caused his knees to buckle, and he tightened his hold on her to steady his legs.

She yielded immediately, and the tingle that met his own lips zipped straight through him, striking his heart as well as zinging to his cock. Her hands clung to his shoulders, her fingers digging in as the kiss flamed. What started as a simple touch of lips became a tongues-tangling, noses-bumping, fingers-grasping, lungs-bursting kiss. Finally, he lifted his head, clutching her closely to his chest as he sucked in gulps of air to clear his mind.

"We keep going like this, I'm going to forget where we are and create a public spectacle right here next to my bike."

Her arms tightened around his waist. "We keep going like this, I'm gonna let you."

A chuckle erupted, and he pulled her back slightly so that he could peer down into her face.

"I don't want the date to end," she confessed with her usual no-bullshit honesty.

"My apartment is only a few blocks away. Next to Jason's garage, where your truck is parked."

Her lips begin to curve. "That still seems a long way off."

His chuckle was replaced with laughter. He turned and unlocked their helmets, handing her Rose's. "Then we best get going." This time, with Samantha on the back of his bike, her hands once again driving him to distraction, all he could think about was getting them to his place. Parking in the alley, he held out his hand, assisting her off. Swinging his leg over the seat, he reached out to take the helmet and his gaze landed on her upturned face. Her eyes were bright in the street-light reflection and her lips were curved. And her trust in him was palpable.

He sucked in a quick breath, afraid he wasn't worthy of that trust... but wished he was.

14

Samantha had noticed a specter of doubt seemed to move through Joseph's eyes as they stood in the alley, but she'd launched herself at him, laughing as their lips melded together once again. With her legs wrapped around his waist and his arms holding her tight, he carried her easily up the stairs to his apartment, only fumbling for a moment with the key in the door lock.

Once inside, he whirled around and pressed her back against the door, their bodies aligned from shoulder to hips. His erection was impressive, and a desperate need to see all of him coursed through her. It had been a long time since she'd had sex... too long. But she had no doubt what she felt for Joseph was the beginning of something real. That and the total package he came wrapped up in only made her fingers tear at the buttons on his shirt even faster.

She managed to get several buttons undone by the time he turned and made their way past the kitchen counter. He started toward the sofa, then changed directions before halting as though he couldn't make up his mind which way to go. Wanting to remove all doubt, she clutched his face with her hands, nuzzled his nose, and ordered, "Bed."

She grinned against his lips as he turned toward the short hall between the living room and the kitchen counter. He bent and, as she felt her ass hit the mattress, unlatched her legs. Expecting him to press forward, she was surprised cool air passed between them as he stood.

He stepped back, scrubbing his hand over his face, dragging in a deep breath. Letting it out slowly, his hands landed on his hips, his chin dropped, and he stared at the floor.

Uncertain what was happening, she remained still, watching him fight an inner battle that she was witness to but not privy to. Swallowing deeply, she finally whispered his name. "Joseph. What's wrong?" He lifted his gaze to hers, and she reached out her hand, praying he wouldn't reject her.

He stepped forward, surprising her once again when he dropped his knees to the floor and took her hands in his, continuing to hold her gaze. "I can't do this without being honest with you."

She opened her mouth, then snapped it shut, her thoughts tumultuous. Swallowing deeply, she nodded. "Okay, I respect that. So, be honest."

"I... I told you I traveled a lot. It's more than just traveling. I just don't feel at home anywhere long enough to put down roots."

"A rolling stone. I remember."

"I told you I left home... left California. It just wasn't

the life for me. But my family kept expecting me to come back when I got out of the Navy. I went back once to visit, but my parents' lifestyle and expectations were even less than what I wanted. So, I looked for something else."

She had no idea why he felt compelled to tell her this before they slept together, but it was obvious the confession was important to him. Now, it was her turn to drag in a ragged breath and nod with encouragement.

"I bought my bike and took off. Headed east. For months, I traveled through the Midwest and eventually ended up in Texas. It didn't feel right to just travel and spend money, so I got a job on an oil field. Hard, dirty work, but I felt useful. My paycheck was earned because I put my back into the job, not because I was working for my dad. But after about eight months, the urge to roam came over me again, so I turned in my notice and hit the road. Traveled along the Gulf and ended up working on a shrimp boat off the coast of Louisiana. Again, hard work, but I earned an honest paycheck. After a while, I left there and traveled up through the South. Orchard in Georgia. Ended up working in a whiskey distillery in Tennessee."

"Wow, that's quite a resume."

"'Fraid it's not the kind of resume that would impress most people."

Understanding slowly dawned, and she grasped his hands tighter. "Is that what you're concerned about? What will or won't impress me?"

"Partially. According to some, finishing my engineering degree would have made me a success. Being a rambler just made me a loser."

She assumed he was referring to his parents. She couldn't imagine the life he'd lived for the past several years. Money must have been tight, but he'd worked everywhere he lived. Moving slightly to make sure she was in her line of vision, she said, "I can tell you right now that doesn't matter to me at all. I might have a doctorate degree, but I spend my days up to my elbows in animal blood and poop, hoping there will be enough money to keep the clinic running."

Her words had the desired effect as his lips quirked upward for a moment before somberness returned. She sucked in her lips, feeling like there was more. "You said partially. What else are you concerned about?"

He glanced to the side, his gaze not seeming to focus on anything in particular, and she gave him that play. Whatever was on his mind needed to come out in its own time.

Finally, he looked back at her and inclined his head toward the bed she was sitting on. "I'm concerned about this. What we're about to do. Us. This attraction between us."

"Okay..."

"Samantha, I like you a lot. I don't see you as just a warm, willing body. But I also don't want to take advantage of you. I don't know what my plans are. I don't know where home is. I'm renting an apartment from a buddy. The same buddy that I'm working for. My housing is transient. My job is transient."

More understanding slid through her, now feeling

colder than she had before. Nodding slowly, she said, "I see. What you're telling me is there are no promises between us. What we have is for right now." He held her gaze but didn't speak, and she looked to the side, her thoughts whirling in her head. She thought of the time spent in her clinic. She thought of the fun times spent with friends. Then she thought of her little camper where she always went home alone. She thought of Joseph's honesty as he was making sure she knew that being around next year, next month, next week... hell, even tomorrow wasn't a guarantee.

Her eyes found his again, and she drowned in the warm intensity of his gaze. *I just don't want to be alone tonight.*

He cocked his head slightly and asked, "Are you sure?"

Realizing she'd spoken her thoughts aloud, she nodded. "Whatever this is, whatever we have, I'm here for right now." Not wanting to give him a chance to pull away, she leaned forward, erasing the space between them.

As soon as her lips landed on his, all hesitation disappeared. He stood but their lips stayed attached, and as he moved forward, she was pressed against the mattress onto her back. His body settled on top of hers, his heavy weight held off her chest by his forearms planted on either side of her torso. His hips were nestled between her thighs, his erection pressing against her core, and the weight felt comforting.

"Christ, I'm too heavy," he mumbled, starting to slide to the side.

Clinging to his shoulders, she held him in place. "No, please. I love the feel of you right where you are."

Her body began to burn, the heat trapped by their clothing. His kisses stole her senses, but she knew she wanted more. Her hands slid from around his neck, over his shoulders, to his chest where her fingers continued to unbutton his shirt. The last buttons were captured between their bodies, but she tried to drag the material over his shoulders and down his arms, none-theless.

Once more, the air between them felt cold as he sat up quickly, ass to heels between her thighs. She started to protest but caught his grin as he finished unbut-toning his shirt and jerked it off. Like a feast laid out before her, she didn't know where to look first. His thick, wavy hair that was falling about his strong jaw. His hazel eyes that stayed on her. The corded muscles of his arms, chest, and abs. The tattoos that snaked over his body. He was like a work of art, one that she could stare at forever and always find a different nuance.

"God, Joseph… you are so beautiful." Her words were spoken with soft reverence.

He blinked and swallowed deeply. "You keep staring at me like that and this won't last very long."

"And how am I staring at you?"

"Like an onion ring going into the cheesy crab dip."

A bark of laughter erupted, and her hands covered her face. "That's embarrassing! But so true!"

His hands grasped her wrists and gently pulled them away from her face, bringing them toward his lips. He kissed and licked her fingertips before nipping one. "You even taste good."

The feel of his tongue swirling around her fingers sent another shockwave of need to her core. Glancing at his naked torso, she said, "I feel overdressed."

"Then I'd better do something about that." His hands reached to the knot at her waist where the wraparound shirt was tied. He pushed the two sides apart, exposing her flesh-colored satin bra. She thought he'd immediately go for the clasp, but instead, he bent forward again, his lips trailing kisses along the mounds over the lacy edges before latching onto a nipple through the material. The slow seduction was winding her tighter, and her hips shifted upward, seeking friction.

Just when she thought she would cry with want, he flipped the clasp and pulled open the sides of her bra, releasing her breasts as her nipples pebbled in the cool air. He latched onto one, pulling it deeply into his mouth, while his fingers rolled the other. After driving her wild as he moved between breasts, he finally shifted off the bed, standing between her knees as they dangled over the edge of the mattress.

Gliding his hand down her calf, he unzipped her ankle boots and pulled them off, dropping them onto the floor. Next, he unzipped her pants, and as she squirmed under his perusal, he slid them over her hips, snagging her panties along the way.

His hands moved to his own boots as he unlaced and then toed off first one and then the other. It didn't take him long to unfasten his jeans and shuck them and his boxers to the floor where the belt buckle clanged on the wood.

She leaned up on her elbows and stared at his naked body, gloriously on display for her. The top half, which had already met her perusal, was still just as fine, but his trim hips, muscular legs, and long, thick cock had her breath catching in her throat. She tried to shimmy out of her shirt and bra, her movements jerky with her body half-reclining on the bed. While she floundered in contortions, finally getting the offending material off, he jerked open the small drawer of the nightstand and pulled out a condom.

It had been a long time since she'd had sex but seeing the readily available condom made it obvious that he had not gone so long without a partner. Refusing to think of who he might have brought to his apartment, she dropped to her back again and scooted further up on the mattress.

His hands snatched out, his fingers wrapping around her ankle. "No way."

Lowering her brows, she offered him a questioning gaze.

"Most men keep condoms around so they have 'em when they need them. But I saw the look on your face. Samantha, you're the first woman that's been in this apartment with me. In fact, you're the first woman I've been with in a while."

Her lips made an 'O' but she remained silent, surprised he had caught the quick doubting expression that had crossed her face and at the admission he readily offered. He gently pulled on her ankle, sliding her back to the edge of the mattress. "This is right where I want you." Dropping to his knees again, he kissed the inside of her thighs before licking her folds.

She moaned, her hands reaching down, her fingers clutching his hair. He chuckled, and she felt the reverberations from his lips through her core to deep inside.

"This, babe, is better than any dip," he said, thrusting his tongue inside.

Her hips jerked upward, and with her thighs over his shoulders, he held her in place with his large hands wrapped around her waist. The coil inside tightened, and she wasn't surprised when she flew apart as soon as he sucked on her clit. Barely aware of her short fingernails dragging along his scalp, her thighs shook with exertion as her release rocked through her body.

"I guess you can tell it's been a while for me, too," she said, panting, her voice raspy to her own ears.

He stood and crawled over her body, his hands now underneath her armpits as he shifted her upward so that she was completely reclining on the mattress. Latching onto her lips, she tasted her essence on his tongue and moaned once again.

She kept her eyes pinned on him, and he brushed her hair away from her face. "Going down on you was a dream, but I figured it was also a necessity. I needed to make sure you came first because when I sink inside your body, I might just blow right away."

She attempted a sexy laugh, but it came out more as a snort. That only made her giggle more, and he threw his head back, laughter erupting. She watched as his eyes twinkled and his chest heaved, thinking he was the most beautiful man she'd ever seen. Not grumpy but reserved. Kind but in an understated way. Smart but not in your face. And when he called her babe, it sounded almost as good as when he called her Samantha.

I wish we could be more... but he's a rolling stone. Her heart squeezed but she kept her smile beaming up at him, never wanting him to regret giving her this night.

They kissed, lips devouring and tongues tangling as his hand reverently glided over her body. He explored every curve, driving her wild with his caresses. Electricity zapped through her body, and she almost wept with relief when she heard the foil packet rip open. She watched as he rolled the condom over his impressive erection before shifting between her thighs again.

He entered her slowly, hesitation in his movements. Her hands had held onto his shoulders, but now, she moved them around to his hips, pulling him closer.

"I don't want to hurt you, babe."

"Only if you stop, Joseph."

He pushed deeper, his cock filling and stretching her. With her heels on his ass, she lifted her hips, meeting his thrust. Their eyes stayed locked on each other as he moved, alternating between slow, dragging his cock along her slick inner core, and then hard and fast. She thought her orgasm from his mouth on her clit had been amazing, but it was nothing compared to the tight feeling inside just before she came. Finally, her body shuddered, and she squeezed her eyes tight, crying out his name. The tremors flew from her core along every nerve of her body until finally, she felt boneless lying on the mattress.

She opened her eyes just in time to see thick, corded muscles of his neck strain as his own release poured from him, his thrusts continuing until he finally shoved his face against her neck, gasping as his chest heaved from dragging ragged breaths into his body.

She held him tight, loving the feel of his heavy weight on her. She closed her eyes again, wanting to memorize every sensation. The feel of his thick hair against her shoulder. The warm puffs of his breath against her neck. The scent of their combined arousal as well as his earthy, masculine smell. The feel of his chest rising and falling as it pressed against her breasts. His heavy thighs, tangled with hers, the hairs tickling her skin. Their heartbeats synchronizing.

She felt tears sting the backs of her eyes as she smoothed her hands over his sweat-slicked skin. *He's leaving. Maybe not now. Maybe not for months. But he was honest when he told me the desire to roam always came. He's not mine. At least not forever.* Sadness threatened to overwhelm her at the realization that she wanted more time to see what could happen between them. *But what if I felt more... gave my heart to him... and he left?*

15

Once again Joseph woke, and the early morning sun was already streaking through the window, casting pale light across the bed. Like so many mornings since he'd been in Baytown, he woke surprised that he had slept all night. Only this morning, he jerked his head to the side as he instantly realized he was alone. A different kind of alone than usual. This kind of alone came from having gone to sleep with his body curled around a warm, soft, female body... Samantha. And she was no longer in bed with him.

Sitting up, he scrubbed his hand over his face as he listened for sounds from the bathroom. Quiet. He jerked his gaze down to the floor where their clothes had been tossed. Empty. He tossed back the covers and stalked into the living area. Vacant.

A piece of paper on the counter caught his attention, and he snatched it up.

Joseph, thank you so much for dinner. I had a wonderful time... the ride, the dinner, and the time spent in your apart-

ment with you. I woke early as is my habit and needed to get back to Frodo. Thank you also for being honest with me. I wish you the very best in your stay at Baytown and in your travels beyond. Samantha

He read the words on the page multiple times, trying to read between the lines, looking for hidden meanings, searching for a clue as to what her thoughts were. The note was so polite... so fuckin' sterile. But just like Samantha, there was no bullshit. She was ever practical, and even if she'd wanted to still be with him in the morning, she needed to get back to her dog. She also took the time to write the note instead of just sneaking out. *That must mean something, right?*

His gaze swept around the room as though she might suddenly be standing right behind him. He'd told her the truth about not bringing women into the apartment. She was the first. He reached up, his palm rubbing against his chest as his heart squeezed. *She could have been the last.*

That thought slammed into him, causing the air to rush from his lungs. There was no doubt what he felt for Samantha was more than what he'd felt for any other woman. She was real. Honest. Smart. Loyal. Hard-working. And so fuckin' beautiful. *And I let her walk away. No, I fuckin' chased her away with my talk of leaving. But that's best, right?*

He looked back down at the note still in his hand, still trying to divine more of her thoughts. *If I hadn't confessed to roaming, would she still be here? Was it just the need to get back to her dog that had her leave?*

No answers came from the words written on the

page, but he carried the note with him as he walked back into his bedroom. Laying it carefully on the top of the dresser, his fingers rested over the words for just a few seconds before heading into the bathroom. He stared at the reflection in the mirror, something he rarely did. *"God, Joseph... you are so beautiful."* Her words resonated through him as though she were standing close by. Giving his head a shake, he showered, then dressed in the bedroom, his eyes continually darting to the rumpled sheets on the bed. He walked over with the intent to pull them off and throw them in the laundry. While he'd never had another woman in this apartment, the habit of washing his sheets after a one-night romp had started years before. But as he bent over the bed, the delicate scent of her shampoo wafted past, mixed with the earthy scent of their time together. Instead of jerking off his sheets, he smoothed his hand over them before pulling up the covers. She might not have stayed the morning with her beautiful, naked body cuddled up to his, but he didn't want to wash her away.

He walked back into the kitchen, but instead of going to the refrigerator, he stood in the middle of the space and looked around. The apartment might have only been temporary, but the desire to leave had not struck. The wool sweater-itchy feeling of having spent too much time in one place had not begun.

Making his way across the living room, he looked down at the street below. From this angle, he could see the corner where Jason's garage was located, the tow truck parked just outside. Of course, Samantha's truck was no longer in the garage lot since she took it when she left. Sweet Rose Ice Cream Shop was just across the street, and he knew Jason and Rose were in the apartment above. The town had not woken yet, the streets clear. Not much going on. And still, the need to leave did not fill him.

Having not pondered that until now, his inquisitive mind began to search out the reason why. Always before when he'd landed somewhere, he'd had no previous friendships to draw upon. In Baytown, the whole reason for coming was to reconnect with Jason and Zac.

Now, he'd made more connections in a few months than he had in his past wanderings. The American Legion and the youth ball games they coached. Finn's Pub and the antics of the MacFarlanes. The police were never people he sought out, and yet here, he counted numerous local law enforcement and their spouses as friends. He'd met the childhood friends of Zac, the original Baytown Boys, and their families, witnessing the type of family dynamics he knew existed but had not experienced.

No answers came forth, but the desire to see Samantha again soon overrode his normal reticence. *But how do I move forward when I have no idea what the future holds?* Knowing he wouldn't find the answers while standing in the middle of his living room, he headed to Stuart's for breakfast.

He walked in, not surprised to see the morning crowd having not arrived yet. He passed a booth with a couple sitting side-by-side, glancing back as his name was called. Seeing Zac and Maddie, he turned and greeted them, shocked to see them out so early. "Hey, are you two okay?"

"Yeah, we're fine. Sit down, join us," Zac said, Maddie nodding enthusiastically in agreement. Their empty plates were still on the table and it appeared they were just finishing their drinks.

Sliding onto the bench seat opposite, he waved toward Doneeta, who hustled over to pour a cup of coffee and take his order.

"Twice a month I work a nighttime shift at a suicide hotline center in Virginia Beach," Maddie explained, stifling a yawn. "Zac doesn't want me to drive back across the bridge by myself, so he takes me and then picks me up. We started hitting the diner for breakfast before going home. Doneeta knows to give me the decaf tea since I'll be going to bed right afterwards."

Since he'd been in town, he'd had dinner with Jason and Rose numerous times because they were directly across the street, but he'd also spent some time with Zac and Maddie.

Zac stared at him with suspicion. "You're up awfully early."

Hefting his shoulders in a shrug, he took another sip of the hot brew. "Just woke up and couldn't go back to sleep."

"With Maddie gone last evening, I stopped for takeout at The Seafood Shack."

Zac's words hung in the air, but Joseph refused to take the bait, instead focusing on his cup of coffee and wishing Doneeta would hurry with his breakfast.

"I haven't even had a chance to tell Maddie this shit,

but I caught a glimpse of you and Sam sitting together on the deck."

Realizing Zac wasn't going to give up, he lifted his gaze and speared his friend with what he hoped was a shut-the-fuck-up glare. Zac's wide grin gave evidence that his hopes were not going to be realized.

"Zac, sweetheart, maybe Joseph doesn't want to talk about his date with Sam," Maddie said, placing her hand on Zac's arm before turning her wide eyes toward Joseph.

An awkward silence descended upon the three, and finally, Joseph shook his head and grumbled. "Fuck." Ignoring Zac's bark of laughter, he glanced toward Maddie. "Sorry."

Maddie's smile was sincere, and she shook her head. "It's fine, Joseph. And honestly, you don't have to talk about Samantha."

"I'm just glad he got his head out of his ass," Zac said. "She's a great woman."

"I never said she wasn't," Joseph huffed, leaning back in the booth. "She's wonderful. It's just... I don't know. She deserves a lot more than what I've got to offer."

Zac rolled his eyes while throwing his hands up into the air, but it was Maddie's reaction that caught his attention. She cocked her head to the side, her gaze boring deep inside. "Why do you think you don't have enough to offer?"

"She deserves a man who can offer a future. Who knows where I'll be when I decide I've had enough of Baytown?"

Zac blinked in surprise, his body jerking back as

though he'd been hit. "You're leaving? But… but you just got here!"

"No, man, I'm not leaving. It's just that… hell," he swiped his hand over his face and glanced at Maddie, who was now staring at him as though looking even deeper inside. "I never stay anywhere for very long. No roots, you know?"

"Maybe you've just never found what you're looking for," she said, her voice soft, filled with understanding. "That's something the two of us understand all about."

He blew out a breath and remembered what Zac had told him about her. Maddie had been raised in Baytown until her mother finally got tired of her alcoholic husband and left, taking Maddie with her. It was only when her father died and Maddie came back to town to clear out his house that she found Zac and they fell in love. In many ways, her story paralleled Zac's, with his alcoholic father and mother who abandoned them.

He licked his lips, unable to turn away from her kind expression but grateful when she tugged on Zac's arm.

"Sweetie, I'm falling asleep, so you'd better take me home." Zac and Maddie slid out of the booth, and Zac pulled out money to cover their breakfast. Turning back to Joseph, he said, "You've got money. Why the fuck don't you put it to good use? Look around, man. Make a change, don't run away."

Maddie cocked her head to the side and placed her hand on his arm. "Joseph, I don't know what Zac is referring to, but I'd hate for you to miss out on the chance to love someone because you're uncertain of the future." She offered a sweet smile and a wave goodbye before walking out with Zac.

Love someone. A chance to love someone. Those words should have scared him or sent him scrambling to his bike to get the hell out of town. But instead, the image of Samantha filled his mind. Her smile. Her warm eyes. Her laughter as she called out to Frodo loping along the dune. Placing her hand on the deceased goats, taking a moment to deal with grief over a lost animal. The way she talked about her family. The feel of her hands clutching him as they connected in the most intimate way possible. The sound of her voice as she whispered, "Whatever this is, whatever we have, I'm here for right now."

I'm here for right now. Fuck, that should have thrilled him, but the truth was he wanted more. *But to ask her for more, I've got to be willing to give more. To ask her to take a chance on me, I've got to be worth that chance.*

His thoughts were interrupted as Doneeta brought his breakfast, but as he ate alone, his thoughts turned over Zac and Jason's advice. The last bites of his breakfast tasted like cardboard, and he pushed his plate away. Tossing down a wad of cash, he headed back to his place before work. Rounding the corner, he jogged past his bike to the bottom of the outside stairs. A tiny sound caused his feet to stumble on the bottom step as he jerked around to look down. Not seeing anything, he held perfectly still, wondering if he would hear it again. A movement by the front tire caught his attention and he sucked in a hasty breath as eyes from two miniature balls of fur looked up at him.

Two kittens, smaller than anything he'd ever seen, cried out, their meows barely more than little squeaks. His head swung back and forth, looking up and down the alley as though he expected to see someone there, searching for their lost kittens. His next thought was wondering if there were more. He scooped the two into his large hands and searched the area, not discovering any others nor finding a mama cat. He had no idea how old they were or what had happened. *Did their mama have them in the alley and then die?* He knew little about cats but could tell they weren't newborns. *Did someone abandon them here?* That thought made his blood boil, but as their tiny claws dug into his wrist, he knew he needed to take care of their needs first. And while he might not know what their needs were, he knew who would.

He looked down at the two bundles of mewling fur. Ever since he'd woken alone he wanted to go to Samantha but was afraid of what she thought after their night together. Holding the kittens up directly in front of his face, he grinned as one reached out their paw and swiped at him. "You, little tigers, are exactly the excuse I need."

He shot a look at his motorcycle before turning and jogging back toward Jason's Garage. Jason was just opening the front door, and he called out, "Hey, can I take the tow truck?"

Jason turned around with a smile on his face, then his gaze dropped to what Joseph had in his hands. "What the hell have you got there?"

"Kittens." He held them up for Jason to see.

"You got kittens?"

"They were in the alley, hiding near my bike. Someone must've dumped them in the alley."

A dark look crossed Jason's face as he reached out and rubbed the kittens' heads. "Some people are assholes." He lifted his gaze to Joseph and said, "You can take the tow truck if you need it."

"I don't know how old they are or what I need to do for them, so I thought I'd take them to Samantha. I sure as hell can't take them on my bike."

A slow smile curved Jason's lips, and Joseph looked down at the kittens in his hands, trying to avoid making eye contact. *Hell, I was doing the same thing this morning with Zac.*

"So, the man who always has one foot out the door went on a date that didn't seem to have an end and is now adopting two kittens."

Ignoring the part about the kittens, his gaze shot up to Jason's. "How do you know about the date?" Lowering his brow, he narrowed his eyes. "Fuckin' hell, were you spying out your window?"

Throwing his hands up between them, Jason laughed. "No. But I admit that Rose has trouble sleeping through the night with the baby pressing on her bladder and she gets up and walks around some. When she came back to bed, she commented that Samantha's truck was still parked at the garage." He inclined his head toward the empty space and added, "But I notice it's gone this morning."

"Christ, between you and Zac and everyone else in

this town, how does anyone have any secrets? Y'all are worse than a bunch of gossipin' old ladies!"

Jason threw his head back and laughed. "I think we're all just pulling for you to stick around, Joseph. Anyway, go take those two fluff-butts to Samantha."

He walked over to a cardboard box just inside the garage bay door and checked to make sure it was clean. Placing the two kittens inside, he gently set it on the truck seat. Tossing a wave toward Jason, he pulled out of the parking lot, careful with his turns, not wanting to jostle the box.

Sucking in a deep breath as he neared the vet clinic, he hoped Samantha would not mind the impromptu visit. Glancing down at the sound of rustling and mewing coming from the inside of the box, he blew out a long breath, "I may have fucked things up last night, but you two are my way back in. Now, if I can just not fuck things up again."

16

On the drive home in the faint daylight of early morning, Samantha tried to keep her mind off what she had left lying in the bed. The gorgeous man who had thoroughly made love to her... no, not made love. It was sex. Fabulous, toe-curling, bone-melting, electric-filled, singing-to-the-rafters sex. Her body ached in a few places that had been dormant for a while, and she wouldn't mind a repeat performance, but... *I know me, and I know my heart would start to fall for the man who has one foot out the door.*

She inhaled deeply, and as she let it out slowly noticed a faint whiff of fresh pine scent. As the sun rose, allowing her a closer investigation, she spied that the inside of her truck was clean. Floor mats vacuumed, dust wiped off the dashboard, windows clear. *Why did Jason have my car detailed? And what is it going to cost?* She hoped the cost would fit her pocketbook, but that thought left her mind as she pulled into her driveway and heard the familiar baying of Frodo.

As tired as she was, a smile still slipped across her face. She walked over the dune, giving him a chance to run and gallop along the shoreline even though she was exhausted. Finally, with a wide yawn splitting her face, she called him back and led them both into the camper.

As he gobbled the food from his dish, she glanced toward her bed, the pull to climb in and sleep almost overwhelming. *Couldn't I just call in sick for one day?* Knowing the answer when she was the only licensed veterinarian on staff at the moment, she headed into her minuscule bathroom to shower and start the day.

An hour later, after opening the clinic with Annette and Tonya, she sat in her office to place a call. Glad when Jason answered, she said, "You weren't open when I got my truck this morning... uh... last night. It would help if I had an idea of how much the towing, the detailing, and all that work is going to cost." As she said the words, she winced, wondering what the final bill would be.

Jason quoted a price much lower than she anticipated. "There's no way that's right. It's got to cost more than that."

"That's just for the towing to the shop."

"Okay..." she replied, drawing the word out. "But what about the rest of the work?"

"No charge for that, Sam."

His voice sounded strange, but she couldn't figure out why without being able to see him. It almost sounded like he was trying to keep from laughing. But maybe he mixed her bill up with someone else's and was trying to figure out why her estimate was so low. "Um...

I think you need to relook at that, Jason. The work that's been done is more than that."

"Sam, don't look a gift horse in the mouth."

"Huh? What gift horse?"

"He'll probably hate that I told you this, but it was Joseph."

"What was Joseph?"

"He wanted to make sure your vehicle was safe. So, he told Troy to do the work on it and he covered the cost. Look, Sam, I've really got to go. Come by anytime and you can pay up. No rush." With that, Jason disconnected.

She stared at her phone for a few seconds, her mind playing catch-up with what Jason had said. *Joseph wanted my vehicle safe? He covered the cost? If I'm pinching pennies, he must surely be also.* She rubbed her hand over her forehead, and not for the first time wished she had a best girlfriend to talk over the muddled messages floating in her head.

"Dr. Collins, you've got a drop-in. A man found two kittens and is in exam room two."

Glad for the interruption, she nodded toward Tonya and walked down the hall. Entering, her gaze landed on the familiar face, the lips curving as his eyes found her. Blinking, she cocked her head to the side, staring at the man she had left in bed just a couple of hours ago. "Joseph?" Before he had a chance to respond, he lifted his arms, and there, nestled in his large hands, were two tiny kittens. She sucked in a gasp so quickly her throat constricted. It didn't matter how many animals she treated, worked with, cured, kept healthy… there was something so intrinsically precious about a kitten.

She rushed forward, scooping first one and then the other out of his hands, bringing them closer, her practiced eye checking for fleas. Seeing they were clean, she pressed them against her chest, their fur tickling her neck. She immediately heard the faint, rumbling purrs and smiled widely, her gaze jumping up to him. "I just left you! Where did you find them?"

"They were in the alley, right under my bike. Normally, I wouldn't even be out there in the mornings. But I woke up alone, and hated staying in my place by myself—"

Another gasp escaped, this one less painful but just as surprised.

He blushed and shrugged. "I get it. You needed to get back to Frodo, and we hadn't exactly decided…" He scrubbed his fingers through his hair, pulling the long locks back from his face as he seemed to search for the right words. "Anyway, I walked to the diner for breakfast, and when I came back, they were there."

She wondered what he'd been about to say about the two of them but focused on the kittens instead. "Oh, it's a miracle you found them."

"I don't know anything about cats. I looked around for more, but it was only these two. Then I looked around for a mama cat but didn't see one." He shrugged and said, "I've got no idea how old they are or what they need, but I knew you'd help me."

"Okay, let's get these two checked out, and then you'll have a better idea of what you should do."

She could not help but laugh at the antics of the two kittens as they tumbled over each other, swatted at her fingers with their tiny claws, and meowed. "The one with more gray is a little boy, and the one with the white face is a girl."

"What do I feed them?"

"We've got kitten food in the front lobby you can purchase. I know you can get kitten food in the grocery store, but what we have is formulated for their age and needs. It's a little bit more expensive—"

"Doesn't matter. I want to get what they need."

She hesitated, chewing on the corner of her bottom lip. "Joseph... um... you don't have to keep them. You... you could take them to the shelter." As soon as those words left her mouth, she knew she couldn't part with them. If he didn't want them, she did. It would be ridiculous to try to have two growing kittens along with Frodo in her camper, but somehow, knowing Joseph had rescued them made them all the more precious.

"No." He spoke definitively while shaking his head. "I want to keep them, but I need your help. I don't know what to do for them."

She slowly lowered her arms, placing the kittens onto the examining table, keeping them safely tucked into her hands. "Joseph," she began, shaking her head. "You need to think about what's best for them. They won't fit into your bike's saddlebags when you decide to hit the road. Is it fair to make them love you when you won't be around?" As soon as the words left her mouth, she knew they were not only about the kittens but herself. She sighed and dropped her gaze to the table.

Not giving him a chance to speak, she clicked into professional mode.

Checking their teeth, she determined that they had probably just been weaned, therefore felt certain they'd had no vaccinations. She called for Tonya to bring what they needed, and while waiting, her heart melted at the way Joseph carefully cuddled each one, playing with them while making sure they didn't get too close to the edge of the examination table. She even heard his sharp hiss each time a kitten was vaccinated as though he was the one getting the shot.

After Tonya left the room, she scooped up the closest one, and he did the same with the other. He walked around to her side of the room and stood directly in front of her with little space between them other than for the kittens to be able to rub against each other. She lifted her gaze, finding his eyes pinned on her. Unspoken longing blanketed the room, blocking out everything other than the desire to lean into him. He bent, and with her face upturned, he kissed her lips lightly. Warning bells be damned, she wanted this man and knew there was no way she could protect her heart. She leaned forward but he suddenly shifted back, and she halted.

"I... I... uh... I'd better be going. I'll get them home," he said, his voice gruff.

Jerking slightly, she nodded, plastering a smile—or what she thought might be a smile—onto her face. "Yes, sure. Um, you can check out at the front." Her emotions tumultuous, she swallowed hard, blinking to keep the tears that threatened from falling. As he stalked out after the kittens had been gently replaced into the cardboard box, she watched as his tall, muscular body walked away. And she doubted her sanity for having agreed to one night with him. Dropping her forehead against the door frame, she sighed.

"Dr. Collins, patient in exam room four."

Squaring her shoulders, she lifted her head. "Got it," she called out, shoving her feelings to the side.

Joseph swiped his hand over his face while standing in his living room, staring out the window. He'd wandered the apartment, twitchy, as though his body was too big for his skin. Samantha's words rang through his head. *What is best for them? They won't fit into your bike's saddlebags. Is it fair to make them love you when you won't be around?*

After he'd left the clinic, he'd come back to town and carried the kittens, a litter box, and the bag of food up to his apartment. They'd pressed their faces into the bowls, eating greedily. Making sure they had water and nothing they could get hurt on, he let them explore the living room before they curled up tightly together, taking a nap. Two tiny little balls of fur that were totally dependent on him. And no desire to flee set in. Instead, he was filled with a desire to stay.

Sighing, he dropped his chin and stared at his boots for a moment, wondering what the hell he was doing. Suddenly, he turned, and after a quick check to make sure the kittens were still sleeping and safe, he headed out to his bike. Roaring out of town, it only took fifteen minutes to make it to the Eastern Shore Animal Shelter.

He parked his bike but sat with his long legs on either side, his booted feet resting on the concrete as he looked up at the building. Samantha had mentioned the shelter's needs in her talk at the AL meeting. When he had paid at the reception desk for the kitten's clinic visit, he'd noticed a sign on the wall reminding clients of the need for food donations for the animal shelter. The nondescript brick building was set on a side road with green farmland all around. The sounds of dogs barking could be heard in the distance. Swinging his leg around, he secured his bike and helmet, then headed inside.

The reception area looked very much like the vet clinic, only there was no bustling of employees. A bell sat on the rather plain desk, and he rang it, the ding causing the barking in the back to increase. It only took a moment for a spry, gray-haired woman to pop in from the back. Jeans with water sprinkles on the front, feet in rubber boots much like what Samantha wore, and a long-sleeve T-shirt completed her outfit. Her gaze was sharp, and she smiled as she looked at him.

"Welcome to the shelter. What can I do for you?"

"I saw the sign." He winced as a look of confusion passed over her face. "Sorry, a sign at the vet clinic. It said you could use donations."

Her eyes sparked with recognition, and she nodded, smiling widely. "Oh, Sam's place. God bless her for putting a sign in her reception area. Lord knows that sweet girl is the best! Believe me, we can use anything we can get. Food, old towels, newspaper, money. Hell, just this morning the printer in the office crapped out on me!" She shook her head and laughed. "Of course, with all these animals around, that's probably the least offensive thing that's crapped on me!"

His lips twitched. "I'm sure, ma'am."

She waved her hand dismissively. "I appreciate the respectful salutation, but around here, I'm just known as Betty."

"Nice to meet you, Betty. I'm Joseph." He looked around, suddenly uncertain. "Um... I'd like to help. I guess... I'm not really sure what you need."

Betty waved her hands around. "We work on a shoe-string budget, and I rely mostly on volunteers. My husband retired a couple of years ago, and he helps out, too. We're run by grants, donations, and a whole lot of prayers, and if you came here to donate anything, I'll consider it an answer to a prayer!" Another sigh escaped her lips, and when she looked up at him, a specter of sadness passed through her eyes. "I'll tell you something that I haven't even told Sam yet, and that is this shelter may have to close."

His body jerked slightly. "Close?"

Betty's name was called from the back, and she said, "That's my husband. Come on with me, and we can talk while we check on the animals. I've got a volunteer who's coming in a few minutes, and she can watch the front."

He nodded and fell in step right behind her as they moved through a doorway and down the hall, passing several doors. He peeked through an open doorway to the right, seeing a storeroom with bags and cans of food on the shelves. To the left, he heard meowing and through that door could see a large, clean room with crates. Some were empty, but others were filled with cats and kittens.

Continuing to follow her, they came to a much larger room in the back where clean kennels held a variety of dogs and puppies, each with their own fenced run that gave them exercise and sunshine. A gray-haired man dressed in a similar way to Betty was just turning off the hose.

"Sid, this is Joseph. He came by to make a donation. This is my husband, Sid. All-around handyman and excellent kennel washer!" She clapped her husband on the back, her wide smile still present on her face.

The two men shook hands, and Joseph recognized his face. "It's nice to meet you. I believe I've seen you at the American Legion." His gaze dropped to the embroidered Navy insignia on Sid's shirt. "Navy, sir?"

Glancing at his own shirt, Sid smiled as he nodded. "Many years ago, but yes." He looked up and held Joseph's gaze. "Were you in the service?"

"Served in the Navy also."

Interrupting, Betty said, "Joseph, we were just heading back to the house for a coffee break. We live just behind the shelter. We'd love to have you join us." He opened his mouth to politely decline when she added, "We don't often get a chance to have visitors."

"I'd be honored, thank you." She still hadn't told him what she meant by the shelter closing and hoped the topic could come up. He followed them out the back and down the short lane to a small, two-story brick home. The grass was neatly trimmed and flowers were planted along the front. A large tree provided shade for the front porch. As soon as he entered the house, the scent of vanilla struck him, jolting his mind back to a memory long buried.

"I made some banana bread yesterday, and Sid always says it's better the second day after the flavors have had a chance to mix together. I'll fix a fresh pot of coffee," Betty said.

It didn't take long for the coffee to be poured and the thick slices of banana bread to be served on plates around the kitchen table. They chatted for a few minutes, and he wasn't surprised to find out that they had also come to The Eastern Shore after Sid's last assignment in Norfolk.

Finally, in a lull in the conversation, he asked, "You mentioned about the shelter closing?"

Betty and Sid shared a look and both sighed. "We're going to have to relocate very soon. Our son-in-law has become quite ill, and our daughter and grandchildren need help. They have a large house in North Carolina that includes an in-law suite. We hate leaving this area and the shelter that we worked so hard to establish. But..."

"I understand." He hesitated, a multitude of thoughts striking him one right after the other. "What... what would it take for the shelter to keep running?"

Betty snorted and Sid laughed. "Probably somebody just as crazy as we are!"

Joseph's lips curved, and he leaned back in his seat.

"Sid handles the books, which aren't overly complicated, although we do receive money from grants, local sources, and donations, as I said earlier. He also helps out with some of the daily care. I work most every day and run a group of volunteers that help. Sam Collins donates her time checking out and inoculating the animals that come through. It's a lot of work, not a lot of glory, but as we say, when we go to bed at night, we feel as though we've done a little bit of good in the world."

"I'd say the two of you have done a lot more than just a little bit of good, but I understand your sentiment."

As Sid and Betty continued to talk, a tiny seed planted deep inside Joseph's chest. The seed of an idea that no matter how much he tried to squash it, it began to grow. An hour later, he shook hands with the older couple. Climbing onto his bike, he headed home, anxious to check on the kittens. One there, he pulled out his phone. "Jason? Got something I want to talk to you about."

17

Joseph parked outside Zac and Maddie's house, seeing Jason's vehicle already in the drive. Maddie flung open the door before he had a chance to knock, and a grin slipped across his face as he bent and kissed her on the cheek.

"Don't worry about me and Rose being here," she assured. "We know you want to talk to Jason and Zac, and we'll just be in the kitchen."

"No, no, it's fine." Stepping inside their house, he spied Zac, Jason, and Rose in the living room.

Rose smiled her greeting and turned to Jason. "Babe, help me up, and I'll sit with Maddie in the kitchen for a while—"

"No," Joseph repeated, his hands in front of him. "Please, I'd like for you to stay. I could probably benefit from your input as well."

Seeing the curious expressions and side glances moving between the others, he accepted the beer Zac handed to him and settled into one of the comfortable chairs. Maddie moved to sit next to Zac, and the attention he always shunned landed on him.

He puffed out his cheeks as he blew out a breath, his thoughts jumbled as he now sat staring at his friends.

"Did I ever tell you how Jason and Joseph and I became friends?" Zac asked, looking toward Maddie.

Joseph smiled, recognizing his friend taking some of the pressure off by diverting the attention for a moment. Maddie turned toward Zac and shook her head. Jason was also grinning as Rose shifted her attention toward Zac as well.

"Joseph and I were both assigned to the same ship as firemen. Our duties weren't like what a civilian firefighter does. Certainly, we were trained to put out fires, but we also worked with a lot of the machinery. We were certified as Damage Controlmen and almost always had the same shift. Jason joined us not long afterwards, but he'd gone through the mechanical apprenticeship. We got to know each other about the same as you do most of the other people around, but it was one night... one very drunken night—"

Maddie laughed, rolled her eyes, and Rose snorted, but Zac continued.

"We spilled our guts over way too much alcohol." Shrugging, he grinned. "But that solidified a friendship."

Jason leaned back with his long legs in front of him, his arm around Rose. Joseph waited to see if Zac was going to continue the story but realized that Zac had simply opened up the conversation.

Nodding, Joseph agreed, "Yeah, that crazy-ass night is what really made us friends and not just shipmates.

Jason had gotten back from bereavement leave, and Zac and I found him drinking alone. We didn't figure anybody should have to do that." He held Jason's gaze. "As much as you were hurting, and still do, I was always envious of the relationship you had with your parents. You didn't want to go into the same restaurant business as your parents, so you became a mechanic and then joined the Navy. And I remember you telling us that they were proud of you."

Turning his attention to Zac, he sighed. "I know your dad's alcoholism split your parents' marriage apart and made things really hard on you. You talked about the other men in Baytown, your friends' dads stepping up and stepping in. So, in a crazy, fu— um... messed up way, I was envious of that, too. I told them about my family, and while it might seem nuts, it was Zac and Jason who ended up thinking they had it better than me. Even though I had both parents, they disowned me as soon as they found out I went to the Navy."

Rose's face fell, and Maddie immediately rushed, "Oh, Joseph, I'm so sorry."

He waved away her concern and shrugged. "I never wanted to go back to California after I got out of the Navy. I went once, but there was nothing there for me except my parents' continued judgement of how I turned my back on their lifestyle, my *potential* as they liked to call it, my duty to join Dad's company and make something of my life. I loved how I got to travel with the Navy, and once out, I didn't stay anywhere very long. I'd travel to a different state, find a job, live in a temporary place, and then move on when the notion hit me. For a long time, I thought I was just being free. But I think I've been searching and just haven't found what I was looking for."

The others nodded, but Maddie smiled as well. "You're very self-aware. I wish some of my counselees had your understanding."

Zac leaned forward, one arm around his wife and the other resting on his knee. "So, Joseph, what are you looking for?"

"A reason to stay." He shook his head slightly, surprised at the words that came bolting from his lips without the cautious consideration he usually gave. "I… I guess it's really that simple. I just never found a place that felt like home."

"And now?" Jason prodded.

He rubbed his chin, the scruff of his beard abrasive against his fingers. "I don't know. I mean, I don't have a desire to leave. That's what I can't figure out."

"It scares the shit out of you, doesn't it?"

He barked out a laugh, appreciating Zac's ability to cut to the heart of the matter. "I used to get your emails about Baytown. How it was a great place to live. How it was a welcoming place for vets who didn't have a good place to land when their service was over. It all seemed like such bullshit."

"I can imagine that coming from your background it did seem like bullshit," Rose agreed. "But I'm curious. How does it seem now?"

"People are nice. I've got a way to make money and a place to live. Although both of those feel temporary, I know there's more I can do here."

"And…" Maddie prodded.

He dragged in a deep breath and let it out slowly. "Yeah… Samantha. She makes me want more." The others remained quiet and he pulled his thoughts together. "I like her too much to hurt her if I pull up stakes and leave." He heaved a sigh. "But if I'm too chickenshit to stay, then I'm missing out on something amazing. I always thought that I was in charge of my life —not living in fear by going where I wanted when I wanted. But the truth is that I've been afraid of really living. Letting someone in."

"I told you earlier that living in fear will keep you from experiencing all that life has to offer," Jason reminded.

"Ask yourself where would you be if you don't make this life change? If you keep roaming," Maddie said, her voice soft.

The idea that he wouldn't be in Baytown and wouldn't be with Samantha made his chest hurt and he reached up, rubbing his fist over the ache.

"When we're afraid, we pull back from life. When we're in love, we open to all that life has to offer with passion, excitement, and acceptance." The others jerked their gazes to Rose, who blushed. "Sorry," she gushed. "I always loved that quote by John Lennon. It reminds me how afraid I was to move here when I did."

"You and John Lennon are right," he chuckled. As his mirth ended, he sighed again and leaned forward. "There's something that Zac and Jason know that no one else does. They've kept my personal business to themselves but… well, the truth of the matter is that my grandfather left me a rather large sum of money. It's just been sitting in the bank and in investments, getting bigger until I figured out what I wanted to do."

"And have you?" Jason's eyes were bright as he stared back at Joseph.

He grinned before plunging ahead. "Did you know the animal shelter is about to close?" Knowing he had their full attention, he gave voice to the tumultuous thoughts and plans running through his mind.

Later, he headed back to his apartment, excited to see the kittens again. And plan his next move. Not to leave... but to stay.

Samantha stirred the small pot of tomato soup on her stovetop, then stepped one foot over to where the bread, cheese, and butter sat on the counter. She liked to cook, and in the past year had managed to become quite proficient at whipping up meals that were delicious but didn't require a lot of prep space. Sometimes, like tonight, a grilled cheese sandwich and tomato soup were all she could manage.

She rubbed her hand over her forehead, trying to dislodge her tension. She had called the shelter earlier to ask Betty about more rumors of wolf-hybrids in the area, but the shelter's answering machine announced that a change in management was taking place and the shelter was closed for the week. When she asked her employees, Annette said she'd heard that Betty and Sid needed to take a trip to see relatives, but she'd been assured that the animals were cared for.

Stirring the soup absentmindedly, she felt bone-weary loneliness settle in. It had been a week since she'd seen Joseph. Well, six days, eight hours, and about forty-two minutes. *But who's counting?* How many times had she picked up her phone to send a text or see if he had sent one? She wondered if he kept the kittens or had given them to the shelter before it closed. The ridiculous notion had run through her mind that if her truck was not running so reliably now, she would have an excuse to see him when he came to tow her.

They'd spent a night together… a beautiful night. She'd tried to protect her heart by not falling for someone who wouldn't stick around, but now she wondered if their night together was a mistake. If she hadn't, then she wouldn't have the memory of his body pressed to hers, his kisses taking her breath away, and the luscious feel of him moving deep inside of her. But then her heart wouldn't have hurt so much for the past six days, eight hours, and now forty-three minutes.

Frodo lifted his head from his cushioned bed over the cab, eyes alert as he twisted his head toward the front of her property. "What's up, boy?"

After a moment, she heard the crunch of tires over the drive. She leaned to the side, following Frodo's line of sight, and looked out the front window, having not closed the curtains yet. A large SUV was approaching, one she didn't recognize. Glancing down, she flipped off the stovetop, wiped her hands on a dishtowel, and patted her thigh, calling Frodo to her.

She opened the door, allowing her large dog to bound out ahead of her. She followed, her gaze pinned on the approaching vehicle. Huge, black, and shiny, it looked new. And as it came closer, she recognized Joseph behind the wheel as he parked next to her truck. A smile was on his face, and she matched it with one of her own as she walked closer. Frodo sniffed each tire as he moved about the vehicle, ending up at the driver's side door as Joseph threw it open and stepped out. Before she had a chance to greet him, he opened the back door and reached inside, pulling out a small pet carrier.

"Oh, Joseph, you kept them!" Clapping her hands, she rushed forward, nearly tripping over Frodo as he caught the scent of what was in the carrier. Hushing her dog while calling him back, she made it to Joseph, peering first into his face before peeking into the carrier to see the two little kittens' wide eyes staring back at her. Sticking her finger through the hole, she laughed as they batted at her.

Turning her attention back to him, she asked, "What on earth is going on?"

"I wanted to see you but didn't want to leave them alone."

"Oh," she said, jerking her chin back slightly, surprised and yet inwardly thrilled. Her brow scrunched as she looked past the carrier in his hand over to the vehicle that managed to dwarf her old truck. "Whose SUV is that?"

"Mine."

His simple, one-word answer caused her to swing

her head back around toward him, her brows now raised. He chuckled, and as always, the sound reverberated through her. She wanted to ask more questions, but Frodo let out a deep bay, his nose planted against the carrier, and she knew the kittens would be frightened. "Um... do you want to come in? I'm just fixing grilled cheese and tomato soup. It's not fancy, but I have enough for two."

"Yeah, I'd like that."

Patting her palm against her thigh again, she called Frodo to her and led the way. At the door, she twisted her head around and hesitated. "Oh, I'd better put him in his pen so the kittens won't be frightened."

"Nah, he'll be okay. They need to start getting used to each other anyway."

Sucking in her lips, she continued to hesitate until he inclined his head toward the door, indicating they should go in. Jerking out of her trance, she threw open the door, ordered Frodo up to his bed, then led the new entourage inside. She was filled with questions, but after six days, eight hours, and forty-six minutes, she didn't want to jinx his surprise appearance by showing her curiosity.

Popping open another can of tomato soup, she poured it into her pan and lit her stovetop again. Buttering the bottom of her cast-iron skillet, she soon had three grilled cheese sandwiches and two bowls of soup prepared.

While fixing the simple meal, she'd continually glanced to the side and watched as Joseph had placed the carrier on the table, keeping the door latched while poking his fingers through the holes. She could not help but smile as he cooed and talked to the kittens. "I hate to interrupt the three of you."

He set the carrier on the floor as she walked over with their bowls of soup. Offering him a plate with two sandwiches, pickles, and chips, she grabbed her dinner and slid into the opposite seat. Frodo lifted his head from his cushioned perch and offered sad eyes toward the couple sitting at the table before looking down at the carrier on the floor. Finally, assured that all was copacetic in his world, Frodo flopped over with a groan, going back to sleep.

Finishing her soup, she began pulling apart her sandwich into smaller bites, curiosity building with every moment. Finally, she shifted in her seat, propped her elbows on the table, rested her chin in her hands, and huffed. "Are you going to tell me what's going on?"

His gaze darted to hers and a light tinge of pink hit his cheeks. Clearing his throat, he said, "I'm making some changes."

Brows lifted, she waited. He swallowed his last bite, took a drink of beer, and held her gaze. For the first time, she noticed a specter of nervousness move through his eyes. She reached over and placed her hand on his arm, hoping whatever strength he needed would be passed between them.

"I'm keeping the kittens."

"O… kay." It was a strange beginning, but she could see there was much more on his mind. She kept her hand on his arm, gently rubbing the corded muscles.

"The SUV out there is mine."

Her fingers flexed involuntarily, and her gaze jumped to the window at the side of her camper where the big, new, shiny, black SUV was parked. She remembered her words to him about not being able to carry the kittens on his bike. "O… kay," she repeated, then brought her gaze back to him. "You bought an SUV so you'd have a way to carry the kittens?" He chuckled again, but this time, instead of a deep caress, the sound was more like a sand burr stuck in her foot. Glaring, she said, "Joseph, I want you to feel free to tell me whatever is on your mind, but honest to God, I'm confused right now!"

"Yeah, I guess I'm not making any sense." He scratched his hand through his beard, then stood, collecting their plates and bowls, taking them to the small sink.

She continued to watch him in silence. How many times had she sat at the shelter or even in the field, waiting patiently for an animal to finally trust that she was not going to hurt them? So she remained still, understanding that whatever was on his mind, he had not found the right words yet. Begging, nagging, or pleading wouldn't do any good and might serve to push the words further away from being spoken.

He finished rinsing the dishes, then turned. "Can we sit on the sofa?"

She nodded, inwardly relieved that he wanted to sit close to her. Sliding out of the booth, she walked the few feet to the small sofa and sat, making room for his much larger body to settle next to hers. She shifted slightly so that she was facing him. Her knees were drawn up, resting on his thigh, and he reclined, placing his arm on the back of the sofa, his fingers skimming her shoulder.

"I told you about my grandfather, but I never told you about my grandmother."

Shocked at his opening, she was instantly interested and focused all her attention directly toward him, shaking her head.

"I never knew my mom's parents since they died when I was just a baby. But my dad's parents were really cool. I told you my grandfather worked for IBM and was super smart, but he was a lot of fun. Whenever we visited, he didn't ask about my grades or how I was doing in school. He asked about my friends. He asked what I liked to do. We'd go out in the backyard and throw a football. My grandmother was the same way. She cared more about if I was happy than constantly grilling me to do better. She loved to bake, and their house always smelled like vanilla. At Christmas, she'd make an applesauce cake."

At those words, he swallowed deeply, and Samantha leaned in slightly, seeing his memories rip through him.

"That was always what Christmas meant to me," he said, letting out a heavy sigh. "I don't remember the expensive presents. The ones my parents dangled in front of me if I did what they wanted. What I remember was my grandmother's applesauce cake."

"Oh, Joseph." Her hands reached out and grasped the one that was lying in his lap, linking fingers with him.

"She died of cancer when I was a senior in high school. Looking back, I can see that was a time when everything changed for me. She was a great balance between my father's expectations and my mother's decline into alcohol and neglect. Her death devastated my grandfather, and he slowly pulled into himself, passing away several years later, about the time I joined the Navy."

Samantha wanted to rush in and offer condolences and platitudes but remained quiet, knowing no words would fully soothe his grief.

"I know, though, without a doubt, they would've been proud of me no matter what I did. While my dad was amassing as large a fortune as he could, moving us to a huge house in a gated country club community, my grandparents still lived in the same house for forty years even though my grandfather had done very well at IBM. Their house felt more like a home to me than anything my parents had."

The shadows began creeping throughout the camper as the sun settled lower in the sky. Frodo's light snores created a soft background noise, and the quiet from inside the carrier gave evidence that the kittens were sleeping. With her gaze on his profile, she lifted her hand and placed her palm along his jaw, gently rubbing her thumb over his beard. The touch was soft, but he turned his face toward her, his eyes warm as they scanned over her face.

"We never took vacations when I was growing up except to exclusive golf or ski resorts in California. Dad would network with his cronies and Mom would hang at the bar. I finally got a chance to travel with my four years in the Navy. When I got out, going back to California to finish school and work for my dad was not what I wanted, so I roamed. Traveled. Every place I landed, I knew it was temporary. Or maybe I set it up that way. Simple employment, one that was easy to leave when I wanted. Temporary housing, not wanting to be tied into a lease. The friends I made, I kept on the outskirts of my life, making it easier to leave them as well."'

As he held her gaze, he mimicked her actions by lifting his hand and cupping her cheek. She closed her eyes for a moment and leaned into his warm palm, the feel of his thumb sweeping over her cheek comforting. Finally, opening her eyes, she held his gaze, hoping and yet fearful of what was coming next.

"Zac and then Jason used to tell me about Baytown, and I thought they were full of shit. No place could be that good. No place could ever compete with my grandmother's house for feeling like home. Yet here I am. And I don't want to leave."

I don't want to leave. Her breath caught in her throat. "You make it sound like you have to leave. Like you're being forced to leave."

He shook his head slowly, a sad smile crossing his lips. "No, it's just that leaving was what I expected to do. I think perhaps it was fear. Fear that I might actually find a place that felt like home. That I might actually want to stay somewhere. That I'd find a place that was just as good as my grandmother's house."

"I understand what you're saying, Joseph, but I'm not tying in the new vehicle or the kittens or why you're here with what you're telling me."

He leaned forward and rested his forehead against hers. "What I'm trying to say is that I don't want just one night with you, Samantha."

His warm breath puffed against her face, and she closed her eyes, drawing in a ragged breath.

"I didn't just wake up lonely after the night we shared and realize that I wanted more. It's something that's been building inside of me, but the past week brought it all to the forefront. Yes, I hated that you were gone when I woke, but then I ran into Zac and Maddie at Stuart's, and it felt so fuckin' good to have breakfast with an old friend. Then Maddie made a comment about hating for me to not allow myself to lo—to be with someone because I was afraid of the future. Jesus, then there were the kittens. And all I could think about was wanting to take care of them. I was desperate to see you, but I also wanted you to see them and tell me that they were okay. And while it might seem whacked, I wanted to buy a vehicle that was safe but also comfortable for us. Babe, having you on the back of my bike is a dream, and it's still parked at my place. But I needed a vehicle for all the other times in my life when it isn't enough.

"I thought roaming was who I was. But I know that I was just searching. Not always looking to leave a place, but once I discovered it wasn't really home, I left. But Baytown is different. You're different. I don't have a crystal ball and can't see into the future, but I don't have one foot out the door, Samantha. I want to take a chance on building a life here, but I need to know if you can take a chance on me."

She gasped, tears springing to her eyes. Her head nodded in a jerky motion as she swallowed deeply. "Yes," she cried, her fingers clutching the soft material of his T-shirt. There was more she wanted to ask, more she wanted to say, but the words were caught behind the lump in her throat. He wrapped his arms around her, and she swung her leg over, straddling his lap. Clutching his cheeks with her hands, she settled her lips over his.

1 8

Joseph couldn't believe she was in his arms. It had been a week since they'd fallen asleep in his bed, limbs tangled together, his sheets wrapped around their bodies. He'd convinced himself that his stupidity might have cost him any chance he had with her, but now, with her lips pressed against his mouth, her tongue gliding over his, he cast off all thoughts other than how she felt at that second.

Standing, with her legs wrapped around his waist, he easily carried her in front of him for the few steps to the bed, dragging his lips from hers in order to see what he was dealing with once there. The queen-sized mattress filled the space with only room for a nightstand and wall cabinets on one side. Deciding caution was best, he hefted her slightly to show his intention, then slowly let her legs drift lower until her feet rested on the floor. Her bed was made, the colorful bedspread neatly tucked. The backs of her legs were against the mattress. She smiled as she started to sit down.

He held her steady with one hand and bent past her to grab the bed covers with the other hand. Giving a jerk, he pulled them down, exposing the soft, pale blue sheets.

She twisted her head to follow his movements before giving her attention back to him, her brow scrunched. Not giving her time to ask why, he grinned. "When we fall asleep again, I want the sheets tangled around us."

Her eyes brightened as her lips curved, but she didn't trust her voice to speak.

"Tangled in the sheets with you was the best feeling I've had in my whole life."

She inhaled sharply as her eyes now widened. Bending again, he slipped his hands to the bottom of her shirt and his fingertips glided along her smooth, warm skin. Trailing kisses along her forehead to her jaw, he continued the downward path until he could feel her fluttering pulse at the base of her neck. His fingertips continued their own trail upward, skimming the silk of her bra before discovering the tight bud of her pebbled nipple. She moaned and pressed her body against his, her hands sliding around his waist until there was nothing between them, and his cock swelled with desire.

Wanting to be rid of the offensive material keeping his gaze from her, he leaned back and swept her shirt upward, forcing her hands straight into the air as he pulled it up and off, dropping it onto what little floor space was available next to the mattress. He unhooked her bra, freeing her breasts, cupping them as he circled her nipples with his thumbs.

Her hands moved to his shirt, her fingers skimming over his abs before circling his own nipples, eliciting a growl before he reached to his back and jerked his shirt over his head, letting it pile on top of hers. Thrilled she was in stretchy yoga pants, he hooked his thumbs into the waistband and skimmed them over her ass and hips, down her thighs, catching her panties along the way.

Her hands held onto his shoulders, and she lifted her feet one at a time as he bent to slide the pants completely off. With his head so low, he suckled first one breast and then the other, the scent of her arousal wafting in the small room. His cock was already straining at his zipper, and he was afraid he'd barely last. Calling upon all his discipline, he forced his mind back to her pleasure.

Now, completely naked, she sat on the edge of the bed, leaned back, and scooted so that her entire body was reclined, and every luscious inch was exposed for his perusal and pleasure. He worked quickly, uncertain how he managed to get his jeans unzipped and shucked over his aching cock, snagging a condom from his pocket while he removed his shoes, jeans, boxers, and socks added them to the pile of discarded clothes.

Her gaze had held his but now scanned down his body, stopping on his impressive erection as he fisted his shaft. "I'm hanging on by a thread, Samantha."

"Then I suggest you come on over and take care of business," she quipped, her arms lifted toward him.

"I want to make sure that you're—"

"Honey, you take care of yourself, and I promise I'm going to be right there with you."

Grinning, he ripped open the foil and rolled the condom on. He climbed onto the mattress, looming over her, and she lifted her knees, opening her thighs wide. His cock was aching, but the sight was too tempting to resist. Shifting slightly, he licked her slowly, tasting her essence. She was primed, ready to detonate, which made his ego swell as much as his erection. Tonguing her while his fingers teased her nipples, he sucked on her clit and she cried out, her body exploding in quivers that reverberated straight through him.

Foregoing any thoughts of finesse, he shifted over her body, lining up his tip at her entrance. Hesitating for only a second, he waited till her eyes lifted to his and her lips curved before plunging deep inside her warm core. A long hiss was emitted as his teeth clenched together. His upper body was suspended over her chest with his weight on his forearms, but his hands clutched her head, his fingers buried in her silky hair and his thumbs moving over her cheeks.

Thrusting hard and deep, he maintained enough sanity to worry that he might be hurting her, but she only clung tighter and lifted her hips to meet his movements in a rhythm as old as time. Their bodies generated heat in the tiny space, but instead of roasting in an oven, it simply felt as though the two of them were cocooned in their own little world.

Just as he suspected, he was not going to last long. "I'm going to come, Samantha."

"O… kay," she replied, the single word forced from her lips by his thrusts.

"Want you to come again, babe," he groaned.

Her short fingernails dug into his shoulders, and her heels pressed against his ass. "O… kay," she repeated.

Unable to stop the tidal wave, his fingers fisted in her hair at either side of her face as every muscle in his body tensed. Just as his release hit him, she cried out, and her slick inner muscles squeezed against his sensitive cock. Barely able to drag breath into his lungs, he continued to plunge slowly until every ounce of energy was depleted.

Shoving his hands under her back, he rolled to the side so she was lying on top, their sweat-soaked bodies pressed tightly together. A moment later, he was still sucking in deep breaths when she tried to roll off of him, mumbling, "Too heavy."

His arms tightened, holding her in place, grunting, "Uh-uh."

She stopped moving and dropped her cheek to his chest. They lay for a long time until slowly their bodies cooled and his cock slid from her warmth. He hated to move but had no choice. Shifting her to the side, he slid his feet to the floor and went into the bathroom. True to what he suspected of most campers, every inch of space was used. The toilet was in one corner with a minuscule sink opposite and a shower that encompassed only about four-square feet. Quickly taking care of business, he stepped out and looked toward the bed, surprised to see it empty.

Hearing a noise behind him, he jerked around and

saw her standing in his T-shirt, bent over to peer into the kitten carrier. Her naked ass was peeking from underneath the hem of his shirt, and his cock twitched at the sight. "Jesus, babe. One look at you, and I'm ready to go again."

She twisted her head around, her smile wide. "I heard them stirring around."

He moved behind her and leaned over. The position was suggestive, and his body was primed, but he stuck his finger into the carrier and the kittens began to tumble around, meowing. Now, when she turned her head toward him, her mouth was right next to his.

"Can we let them out?" Her breath puffed against his face.

"Sure. Frodo wants to know who's invaded his space."

"He's a gentle giant. He's been around kittens and will be sweet with them."

He petted Frodo's large head as Samantha opened the cat carrier, scooping up the tiny bundles. Nuzzling them, she cooed. The dog, now interested, jumped down from his bed, making the camper feel even smaller. Joseph hovered, nervous, ready to snatch the kittens out of Samantha's hands if Frodo made a false move toward them. Instead, the dog sniffed first one and then the other, nuzzling them as well. "You're right. He seems to like them."

"I told you so. I promise he's not going to make them his next meal."

"Speaking of meals, I've got some kitten food and a litter box in the truck. I can get it if you don't mind them eating here." Shaking his head, he added, "I guess I should have asked if I was welcome when I said earlier that I wanted the sheets tangled around us."

Samantha stood and faced him, her gaze starting at the top of his head and moving all the way down, resting on his groin. Lifting an eyebrow, she grinned. "You'd better want to spend the night, and of course, I don't mind the kittens. But you might want to put some clothes on first. I don't have neighbors, but what I'm looking at right now is all for me!"

"Smartass," he grumbled, turning to grab his jeans off the floor and jerking them on commando. He jogged out to his truck and grabbed a bag of kitten food. Stepping into the camper, he noted the kittens were already exploring while Frodo lay on the floor, allowing them to clamber over him.

Samantha took the food from him and placed some in a saucer. "I love them so much. It's the hardest thing about being a vet—I want to keep all the animals!" Looking up, she asked, "What did you name them?"

He hesitated, a slight grin hitting his face. Scrubbing his hand over his hair, pulling it away from his forehead, he held her gaze. "The girl is Merry, and the boy is Pip."

She gasped, eyes wide. "You named them from The Lord of the Rings?" He nodded, hoping she didn't mind. She jumped up, startling the kittens as she launched at him, throwing her arms around him. "Oh, I love it!"

Samantha woke slowly. Her mind was still sleep-groggy, but she was instantly struck with the heavy warmth that surrounded her. It only took a second to realize a very masculine and muscular thigh was between hers and arms curved around her torso. Twisting her head slightly, she watched Joseph sleep. He'd wrapped her up in his body and the sheets when they'd fallen asleep. He looked younger, his face relaxed in slumber. Her fingers itched to smooth over the tiny lines emanating from his eyes, but she didn't want to wake him.

When he'd arrived the previous evening, she'd been shocked to see him climb down from a new SUV. She'd been equally shocked to see him with the kittens. Pip and Merry. Her lips curved as she remembered the blush tinge his face when she realized the significance of their names.

They'd made love again before drifting off to sleep. Now, the early morning light interrupted the dreams of the night before, and she wondered about everything he'd told her. The desire to make Baytown his home. Putting down roots. No longer roaming. *But can I trust him with my heart?* She winced at the thought. *I do trust him. But if the urge to roam hits him again, will I become as temporary as everything else in his past?* She knew life held no guarantees but hated the doubts that crowded in. The sounds of mewling cut into her thoughts and she shifted to slide out of the bed.

Joseph's arms tightened around her as his eyes blinked open. His lips curved as he pulled her closer. "Been dreaming of this."

"Dreaming of what?"

"Dreaming of waking up with you, tangled in the sheets." He kissed her and she melted into him.

The desire to stay in bed was strong, letting the warmth between them spark into a flame, but the sounds of tiny meows increased, mixed with Frodo's snuffling. "As much as I would love to keep doing exactly what we're doing now, the animals are calling." Since she was closest to the edge of the bed, she slipped out first. She grabbed her clothes and hurried into the bathroom. By the time she stepped into the main room of the camper, Joseph was already placing food down for the kittens. The sight caused her feet to stutter to a halt, seeing him standing shirtless, the top button of his jeans undone, and his hair tousled from sleep. *And my hands running through it.*

Forcing her attention away so she wouldn't want to drag him back to bed, she glanced to see the front door was open, and Frodo had disappeared.

"I told him not to go far. I'll go check on him in a minute," Joseph said.

Grinning, she shook her head. "I'll do that." She stepped out into the fresh air, spying Frodo as he bounded around, taking care of his business, and with nose to the ground, checking out the critters who'd passed by during the night. She started to put him in his pen, but he headed back into the camper, immediately going over to the kittens. She stepped into the camper behind him and laughed. "I think he's decided that babysitting Pip and Merry is his favorite job."

They soon sat down to coffee and bowls of cereal. She held up the bowl and slurped the milk. Setting it back on the table, she noticed his eyes on her. Ducking her head, she blushed. "Sorry... I guess my table manners are lacking considering I share my space with Frodo."

He stood and leaned over the table, barely giving her a chance to swipe at her milk mustache before he kissed her.

They sipped their coffee in silence, both keeping an eye on Frodo as he adapted to his kitten-sitting duties with great dignity. Thoughts began swirling through Samantha's mind, and she chewed on her bottom lip. Joseph stopped the motion when he reached over and gently pressed his thumb against the abraded flesh.

"What's on your mind, Samantha?"

It was on the tip of her tongue to deny that her thoughts were as tangled as the bedsheets, but she knew if she didn't give voice to her concerns, it would be hard to accept Joseph fully into her life. She sucked in a deep breath, let it out slowly, then lifted her gaze to his face. "I loved that you shared about your grandmother. And I loved what you've spent time thinking about... why you made the choices you did. And I loved what we shared last night. It just seems that you made a lot of changes in a week, and I suppose I'm... well... I'm..."

"Doubting my sincerity?"

A touch of sadness seeped through his words, and she shook her head. "I never doubt your sincerity. I guess I just wonder what happens next. "

He clasped his hands together on top of the table and sighed. "I didn't finish telling you everything I meant to tell you when I came over yesterday. I wasn't sure how things stood with us, and I wanted to make that right. I didn't come over here with the intention of seducing you or spending the night, but I can't deny that this isn't exactly where I want to be right now."

He stood and took her hand, drawing her out of the bench. "Let's take our coffee and walk to the beach. Frodo can have his run, and I'll put the kittens into their carrier to take a nap."

She nodded, and soon, they had walked over the dune and wandered along the shore, the early morning breeze blowing tendrils of hair out of her hastily made ponytail. They wandered silently for a few minutes, then he stopped and stared out over the bay.

"I gave my notice to Jason. I can still work a couple of weekend nights per month at the tattoo shop, but I won't be driving the tow truck anymore."

She blinked and jerked slightly but remained silent. His gaze was still on the water.

"I stopped by the shelter after I left your office last week. Your words struck a chord with me. About the kittens and was it fair to want to keep them if I was only going to end up leaving—"

"I shouldn't have said that, Joseph," she said, her hands snatching out to land on his arm. "It may have been well-intended, but it came out judgmental."

He turned and faced her, covering her hand with his own. His gaze was intense as he peered down at her. "No, it wasn't judgmental. You're right. Absolutely right. I sat in the tow truck outside the shelter, just thinking. For the first time, I felt like I was somewhere where I had friends. Old friends and new friends. And I thought about the kittens in my apartment, how they had looked up at me with those big eyes in those tiny little faces, I knew I didn't want to give them up. It wasn't just them. It was you."

She sucked in her lips, pressing down. She wanted to pepper him with questions but stayed quiet. He glanced out toward the water and then directed his attention back to her face.

"Everything about you called to me. You are everything good in this world, Samantha. Caring, dedicated, smart, selfless. You are the antithesis of everything my parents are and what I want to be. I want more time with you. I... I want everything with you."

Her breath rushed out, but she continued to remain silent.

"Sitting outside the shelter, thinking of you, I finally acknowledged that the desire to roam alone had left. I almost drove away but decided to go into the shelter to check it out." He shrugged, still holding her gaze. "I know places like that run on shoestring budgets, and I wondered if they could use some help."

"Oh, Joseph, I'm sure Betty would have appreciated it, but I just heard from Annette that she and her husband may have to move away. I have no idea what's going to happen to the shelter now." She watched as his lips curved slowly until a wide smile settled across his face. Sucking in a quick breath, she cocked her head to the side, her unspoken question filling the space between them.

"You're looking at the shelter's new director."

Her fingers gave an involuntary flex, and her mouth dropped open. "You... you're... what?"

He started to sit and tugged on her hands, and she fell to the sand next to him. "I know it's a lot of changes all at once, but I'm serious when I say I found a place to put down roots."

Her brow furrowed, uncertainty crowding out the excitement she saw on his face.

"I can see in your expression that you're not sure," he said, offering a rueful snort. "I can't blame you."

"No, Joseph, it's not that I'm unsure. Well, not completely unsure. It's just... you're right. It is a lot of changes." She dropped her gaze to their clasped hands and sighed. "Tell me about the shelter."

"I liked what I saw, but when I met Betty and Sid, we talked about the Navy, and they invited me into their house. I swear, it smelled just like my grandmother's kitchen, and I felt right at home. They told me about needing to move to North Carolina but were trying to figure out what to do with the shelter. Samantha, I walked out of there, and it was as though everything was so clear. Somewhere that needed me. Really needed me."

"I understand the desire to help, and I understand that without working for Jason you'll have time. But... um... you'll need to apply for grants and funding and—"

He smiled. "I can handle that. Plus... well, there's something I never told you."

Uncertainty moved through his eyes, but she remained focused on his smile.

"I have money."

She blinked, then lifted her brows. "Money?"

"Yeah, money."

"Um… okay."

He swallowed and pushed back the lock of hair that always fell into his eyes. "My parents may have cut me off, but my grandparents left everything to me."

"So, you're… well off?"

A deep, rueful chuckle erupted, and he blew out a long breath. "Yeah, babe. I'm well off. So well off that I never really needed to work, but I did, wanting to pay my own way. I lived off what I earned, just letting their money sit in investments. I figured one day I'd know what to spend it on. Now, I have the shelter to make improvements on, and… well, I'm sure other things will come up."

"So, you're going to take over running the animal shelter." Her words may have been a statement, but she was still trying to wrap her mind around all that he had told her.

He twisted to shift his body closer, lifting a hand to slide along her face, his fingers tangling in her wind-blown hair as his palm cupped her cheek. "A place to stay. A job that makes a difference. Friends I can count on. Animals that needed me. But, Samantha, the shelter is a bonus, not the only thing tying me to this place."

He swept his thumb over her cheek as though to gain her attention, but it hadn't wavered. She squeezed his leg, swallowing deeply. "What's tying you here, Joseph?" she whispered, her words almost lost in the Bay's breeze.

"You."

His one-word answer threatened to steal her breath, and she pinned him with her stare. "Me?"

"Most of all, I want to stay for you." A slow smile curved her lips at the same time a tear slipped down her cheek. He leaned forward and kissed it away, repeating his words as a whisper against her soft skin. "I want to stay for you."

"Babe, I don't like the idea of you going there by yourself."

Samantha loved the way 'babe' fell off Joseph's lips. For many men, 'babe' was a throwaway, but with him, she felt the endearment soothe over her. From Joseph, the word had a claiming effect but in a good way. In the way a man speaks to a woman he cares for.

The first time he'd said it was when they were making love and his body was slowly rocking into hers, his hands were cupping her cheeks, and his intense gaze was peering into her eyes. She knew she had his attention and his devotion. The one word was spoken with such reverence, she had to battle to keep a tear from escaping. Since then, he'd used it more often, but each time, as the word rumbled from his chest to reverberate into her heart, she loved the way it sounded.

"Babe?"

He was standing at her tiny stove stirring the beef stew, but his eyes were on her. Blinking, she realized her fanciful thoughts had sidetracked their conversation. She rushed, "Sorry. Um... you said you didn't like me going there?"

"Where's your head at?"

Blinking again, she said, "It's back at you calling me babe."

His brows lifted for a second before he tilted his head to the side. "Do you not like it? I don't mean it to be patroniz—"

"I love it."

He held her gaze, staring. Slowly, he smiled. She blurted, "I know for some men it's a throwaway name, but with you, it sounds..."

"Special."

Her eyes widened. "What?"

"Special. You, that is. I've never been the kind of man who called women 'babe' just because I didn't remember their name. I've always had a knack for remembering names. As soon as you told me your name was Samantha, I thought it was beautiful and suited you perfectly. But 'babe' works for you as well. Just for you."

Smiling, she looked down at the bowl of stew he'd placed in front of her, the comforting scent of beef and vegetables filling the camper. Just as she was about to take a bite, she looked up suddenly. "Wait, what was it you said? You didn't want me to go by myself." In the talk of 'babe', she'd ignored their previous conversation where she told him she wanted to check out Bender's Breeders.

He slid into the bench seat across from her. "It might not be safe."

"Bender's Breeders is a reputable breeder facility. I'll be perfectly safe there. They would hardly want to draw suspicion upon themselves."

"Then why go at all? It's in Liam's County, let him check it out."

"Liam can't just show up and start poking around on privately-owned land without probable cause. Plus, there's no reason why I shouldn't go. I'm one of the few vets on the Eastern Shore, and I'd love to see his facility."

"Then I'll go with you."

"Okay."

Now it was his turn to blink, his brow lowered as he stared. "Okay? That's it?"

"If it's important to you that you come with me, then yeah... okay."

"Easy."

His deep-voiced word moved through her, and she smiled, shaking her head. "I swear, Joseph, sometimes I think you communicate more in one word than most people do blabbering all day."

He leaned over and kissed her lightly before sitting back down in his seat and picking up his spoon. They ate in companionable silence for a few minutes, but she had no doubt his mind was working. She was proven right when he pushed his empty bowl back and rubbed his chin.

"What are Liam and the others most worried about? Someone illegally breeding? Selling dogs for illegal fighting? Someone with a full-blooded wolf to breed?"

Wiping her mouth with her napkin, she shook her

head slowly. "I don't know... I suppose all three. Wow, I can't imagine someone with a full-blooded wolf kept for breeding."

"What if one of the dogs got away? I was thinking of that farmer who thought he saw a wolf."

"Oh, I'd think whoever is breeding wolf-dogs would be very careful to not have one get out. I'm sure they're getting top-dollar for the pups and to lose one would be like losing several thousand dollars."

He suddenly jumped and widened his eyes. He reached under the table and snagged Pip as he climbed up Joseph's jeans. "Damn, little man, you've got sharp claws!"

Laughing, Samantha reached over and plucked Merry from the floor just as she was about to follow in her brother's path up Joseph's leg.

After the kittens were fed and placed back in the carrier for the evening, Frodo jumped up onto his bed, and the camper secure, they showered separately due to lack of space and then climbed into bed.

Laying in the afterglow of sex, she snuggled against his chest as his hand drifted over her back.

"I had something I wanted to ask you about, but we started talking about the dogs."

She felt the rumble of his words through her cheek and smiled. "What is it?"

"The camper."

Sucking in her lips, she was uncertain what he meant with those two words. It struck her that, unlike earlier, sometimes she needed more to discern what he was trying to convey. She lifted her head off his chest and stared down at his face where she saw concern move through his eyes. "My camper? What about my camper?"

"I was thinking that maybe it's not big enough…"

His voice trailed off at the end as though he was uncertain about saying more. She shifted upward, her forearms now on his chest. "Not big enough? I thought you liked my home."

His arms banded around her middle, and he squeezed. "I love your home—"

"I thought you didn't mind it being a camper."

"Babe, I've told you, I've lived in a lot of campers. I've got nothing against you living in a camper—"

"I don't understand."

He squeezed again and chuckled. "You're not giving me a chance to explain. Some things take more than just a word, you know?"

Huffing, she plopped back down so her cheek was on his chest, eliciting a small grunt from him. "Okay, you're right."

"The irony wasn't lost on me when I met you that you were entrenched in this area and yet lived so simply. And I was the one who usually had one foot out the door and yet had a nice apartment."

She leaned up again to peer down at him. "Do you want to stay at your apartment? I know it's bigger, but what about Frodo?"

"No, not the apartment. Jason can rent it easily to someone else who really wants to live in Baytown. Look, Samantha, I know you own this land and want to build a house on it sometime, but I wondered how much you wanted to live in this camper."

She sucked in her lips. "Honey, I just don't have the money right now to make a down payment for a builder to start working on a house. I figure in a couple more years, if the clinic keeps going the way it is, then I will."

"But what about if you had somewhere else to live until then?"

Her brow furrowed. "You know what I said about your communication? Well, I take it back. I have no idea what you're asking me!"

His chuckle filled her ears, and she smiled.

"Okay, babe, here it is. Betty and Sid want to rent their house. They might come back one day, and until they know for sure, they just want to rent it and not sell. They suggested that I rent it since it would keep me close to the shelter. It's got three bedrooms, an updated kitchen, and two large, updated bathrooms. There's a patio in the back and a front porch."

She pushed against his chest as she rose to stare wide-eyed at him. Waiting to see what else he would say, she finally said, "You want to rent their house? Move into their house? With me and Frodo, too?"

"Yeah, babe. We're all a packaged deal as far as I'm concerned. You, me, Frodo, Pip, and Merry."

A packaged deal. Those simple words stole her breath and caused her heart to stutter. Her fingers flexed into the material of his shirt, needing to hold her legs in place before she melted into him. "Oh, my God, Joseph! I'd love to. I adore my camper but have to admit that sometimes it gets really crowded. And when I'm at your apartment, I love the shower. But then I feel guilty about Frodo."

"We'll go see it tomorrow after we check out the breeder. If you like it, then we'll tell Betty that we'll take it—umph!"

She pitched forward, her lips landing on his, stilling his words... but with other parts of his anatomy responding, she grinned.

Joseph stayed in the background as Samantha toured Bender's Breeding Kennels. Jim Bender had greeted them warmly, his smile wide with pride as he showed them his facility. He brought them inside his house, showing off the awards, medals, and certificates of his dogs and their offspring that had gone on to win at shows and competitions. The ruddy-cheeked, barrel-chested man was dressed comfortably in jeans and a denim shirt with his kennel's logo stitched over the pocket. His hair was still dark, although hints of silver were beginning to show.

Joseph looked up as an attractive woman walked in, her blonde hair pulled back into a sleek ponytail and her makeup subtle. She reminded him of one of the owners of the Georgia peach orchard he'd worked in, a mixture of casual country while their appearance still screamed they were the landed gentry. He had no doubt this woman's clothes and leather boots were expensive while appearing casual.

"And here's my better half, Paula." Jim threw his arm

around the woman, giving her shoulders a squeeze. "I was just starting to show them all our awards."

Paula preened, her hand waving toward the cabinets filled with ribbons and plaques. "As you can see, we only breed the best."

"My dogs have gone on to be champions for years," he said, puffing out his chest.

Samantha glanced at the buttons on his shirt, wondering if they would hold. "I know the recognition goes to the breeder as well as the owner."

"Oh, yes, indeed. I sell the champion pups to owners who will show them, and when they win—and they always win—then as breeder, I get the honors. And the money when more people want my dogs."

Paula slipped from the room, returning after a moment with a tray carrying glasses of lemonade. They sipped their drinks as they continued to listen to Jim expound on his dogs' bloodlines. A beautiful German shepherd wandered the house, his noble bearing giving evidence that he was in charge of his domain.

"I'm a little bit bigger than some breeders," Jim said as they walked out the back door and down the path toward the pristine kennels, each with their own run. "I have several dams and sires. All certified purebred by the American Kennel Association. All with excellent ratings and certification by the OFA. I get top dollar for the puppies and have several litters each year. Once I retire a dam, I'll have another one ready to breed."

"And their vaccinations?"

He chuckled and hooked his thumbs in his belt. "Now, don't get upset that I don't use your clinic—"

She threw her hands up in front of her and shook her head. "Not at all. To be honest, I don't have the time to handle your level of operation. Your location is closer to Maryland, so I was curious considering veterinarians are licensed by state."

"I've got somebody close by in Maryland that I can use if there's an emergency. But a good friend of mine is a veterinarian in Virginia Beach. Granted, it takes him about ninety minutes to drive here, but I make it worth his while. He handles all the examinations and vaccinations."

By now, they'd circled around the expansive kennels. Two men came from a small barn, both pushing wheelbarrows that appeared to be full of dog food.

"Let me introduce you to my employees. This is Lionel Watson and Alejandro Cortez." Joseph and Samantha greeted the men who stopped and offered the barest hint of a nod. Jim continued, "Lionel is from the Eastern Shore and Alejandro comes across the bridge from Norfolk several times a week. Don't know what I would do without them."

While Samantha seemed completely taken with the beautiful German shepherd specimens, Joseph attempted to view the space with a suspicious eye. He didn't know what he thought they might find... *a large animal so obviously a wolf in the kennel right next to the other dogs?* Before coming, he'd asked Samantha if she would recognize a full-blooded wolf or even a wolf-hybrid.

She'd replied that not having much experience it would be harder but that wolves had fixed fur along their neck and back, called the cape, which dogs don't have. But she'd admitted that a hybrid could have that. She had told him that a full-blooded wolf would have smaller, rounded ears.

As they were finishing their tour, Samantha turned toward Jim. "I understand some of your dogs go for training with the military."

"Yes, there's a trainer in Maryland that I've used. In every litter, I evaluate each dog. There are some that I can tell are going to be a champion show dog. Others, loyal pets for the discriminating owner. Others, high intelligence and yet would not be a dog for show. Usually, I'm able to provide two to three dogs a year to be trained. Every dog I've ever sent for training has always been picked by either the military or law enforcement."

"I worked with the dogs when stationed in Afghanistan," she said, immediately drawing Jim's attention.

"You were a veterinarian over there?" Jim asked, not hiding his surprise.

She nodded, her fingers running through the fur of the dog at their side. "Army."

"Well, lucky you. To be able to work with those dogs... who knows? You might have worked with one of mine. Yes, yes, lucky you."

Jim moved on to the next kennel and continued talking about his dogs, but Joseph kept his eye on Samantha. A smile stayed plastered on her face, but he noted a specter of sadness moved through her eyes.

Fuckin' idiot, Jim! Who the fuck would think anybody was lucky to be over there?

Their tour came to an end, and they thanked Jim and Paula for their hospitality. Climbing back into Joseph's SUV, Samantha's attention was focused on the pictures on her phone, pleased that Jim had allowed her to take photographs of his facility and some of the dogs. Looking back, Joseph noticed Lionel and Alejandro standing near the barn, their arms crossed over their chests, scowls on their faces, and eyes staring straight at the vehicle as they pulled out of the drive.

As he started to turn onto the road heading back to the main highway, Samantha's hand snatched over and clamped onto his thigh. "Turn the other way. I want to see if this road brings us around to the back of his property."

He did as she asked but swung his head around to look at her. "What are you looking for?"

"I don't know. Mostly just curious. His kennels looked amazing, and it's obvious he's spent a ton of money on it. Of course, his dogs bring in a lot of money as well. I guess I'm just wondering if we saw it all."

"You think he's got something hidden somewhere else on the property?"

"It's so hard to imagine him risking his reputation as a champion breeder, but his property is not too far from where my client said their dog came from."

Joseph slowed as they continued on the road curling around to the back of the acreage. "Don't you think he would've been looking if he had a dog run off?"

"Not if it was a hybrid and shouldn't have been here to begin with."

They peered through the thick woods that lined the property but could see nothing untoward. She rolled her window down, and he cut the engine so she could hear. The sound of dogs barking in the distance could be heard, but there was no way to discern if they were the dogs from the vendor kennel or somewhere else. Sighing, she leaned back and rolled her window up.

"Disappointed?" he asked.

She scrunched her nose as she shook her head. "Not really. On one hand, it was great to see such a beautiful kennel and meet someone who so obviously loves their animals. On the other hand, I guess I was hoping I could find something definitive to report to Liam." She huffed loudly, her hands waving in the air. "It's just so ridiculous. Wolves are considered an exotic animal, protected state-by-state, and regulated state-by-state. But then, that just makes some people traffic them or own them illegally and make money off of it. Then each state can regulate hybrids. And some states, like Virginia, allow each locality to regulate them. And while a full-blooded wolf can't be owned, a hybrid could be seventy-five percent wolf or more."

She rubbed her forehead and said, "Honestly, I just don't want to see unsuspecting owners end up with an animal that's supposed to be a family pet that could have tendencies of non-domestication. On top of that, the idea of breeding these animals to use them in dogfighting makes me sick."

"I'm sorry, babe. I know you were hoping to find

something more definitive. I gotta tell you, the looks of his employees made me wonder if he was up to something."

"I know! As friendly as Jim was, Lionel and Alejandro gave off a private air." Leaning back in her seat, she said, "Enough of this for now. Are you ready to show me Betty's house? Or rather, I should say your house as of this weekend."

He looked over, thrilled to see the smile back on her face. With one hand on the steering wheel and the other clasping hers in her lap, he nodded. "Babe, as of this weekend, it's *our* house."

Samantha stood in the living room and looked around. *Home*. Well, her new, temporary home as of yesterday. Obviously, it was much bigger than her camper even if it didn't quite feel familiar. She was glad it came furnished considering neither she nor Joseph had any furniture of their own. When Betty and Sid moved out, they left the major pieces of furniture, only taking personal items with them.

The sofa was a bit worn, but that only served to make her cringe less since Frodo had claimed it as his. At the moment, he was attempting to sleep on one side of the large cushions with Pip and Merry curled up next to him. She had brought her colorful pillows and bedspread from the camper, making this house feel a little more like her own space. She'd also brought her Lord of the Rings statuettes and placed them on the mantle.

It had only been a couple of weeks since Joseph told her about his new plans, but she'd witnessed a spark light up inside of him. They'd spent each night together, either in her camper or his apartment, but he'd admitted he preferred her camper. When she'd asked why, his answer was simple. *"Your camper feels more like a home."* She agreed on principle with him, her camper having more personality. But Joseph wasn't a small man, and with him, Frodo, and now the kittens, the camper certainly felt more crowded. Although, thinking about the way he curved his body around hers at night when they slept, she smiled.

Earlier in the week, she'd visited him at work. She had been drawn to the sound of barking in the main area of the shelter. Her heart had warmed when she spied Joseph sitting at the edge of a kennel, a thin dog slowly creeping from a blanket in the corner over to where Joseph held out his hand. Not moving for fear of interrupting their interaction, she'd held her breath as the frightened dog made his way to Joseph, who barely moved as the dog first sniffed, then allowed his head to be rubbed.

A memory struck her, one she hadn't thought of in years. Her grandfather had taken her out on one of his farm rounds. The animal being treated was terrified, shying away from them. Her grandfather had her sit quietly with her arm outstretched and her palm up until the frightened animal came over. She was thrilled, and her grandfather had said, *"Some animals, like some people, warm slowly to others. But once the trust is gained, the loyalty is forever."*

Now, standing in their new home, she let the cares of the day float away. It was not large by any standards and yet felt huge compared to what she'd been living in. Glancing to the other side of the room which held the dining room table, she smiled. A full-size table with four chairs called for her to invite someone over, just knowing she now had room for them.

Two of the bedrooms were small but perfect for the pets, an office, guest room, storage, or whatever they wanted. The master was bigger, and the en suite bathroom was to die for. As soon as her gaze had landed on the soaker tub and separate shower, she'd squealed, eliciting laughter from Betty as well as a wide grin from Joseph.

After moving in, that had been the first luxury she'd engaged in… a long soak followed by Joseph climbing in with her and both discovering bathtub sex for the first time.

Hearing a noise in the kitchen, she looked behind her. She imagined the older house had had a wall that divided the space, but when it was renovated, the area was opened and a granite-topped island now delineated the rooms. Joseph had opened the oven door and was lifting out a pan of lasagna. He laid it on the stovetop before placing another pan of buttery garlic bread inside to toast. The scents wafted past, and her mouth watered.

"I thought I'd miss my camper."

He turned and looked toward her, lifting a brow.

"I thought it would be hard to give up… to give up my own space."

He leaned his ass against the counter, placing his

hands on the edge behind him. "And what do you think now?"

Her smile widened and she inclined her head toward the oven. "Considering the meal that you're cooking right now could never be accomplished in my camper, I think this house can feel very much like a home!"

He chuckled, nodding. "The square footage is not a lot more than what I had in Jason's apartment, but there, I was alone. Well, I was when you weren't with me."

She walked forward and leaned over the pan with bubbling tomato sauce and cheese melted on top, sniffing in appreciation. "It was nice when I stayed over with you, but it was farther from work, and I had to hurry back to Frodo."

He leaned around her and kissed the top of her head as he snagged the plates. They bypassed the counter and sat at the table. A gentle breeze blew through the open windows but made little noise. She heaved a sigh. "I admit that I miss the sound of the Bay nearby."

"You'll still build your house by the water. It's just that now you have something more than a camper to live in."

"My camper was tiny, wasn't it?"

He halted mid-bite and held her gaze, then chewed and swallowed before replying. "Babe, I've lived in a lot of places in my life. My parents' house was huge, although my grandparents maintained a modest home even when they had the money to buy something much larger. Of the two of those, I always preferred my grandparents' house. In the Navy, I was in a bunk room with a lot of others. Once out and on my own, I slept on couches in someone else's house, tiny apartments barely furnished, and more than my share of campers. I've never judged anyone on where they lived, but yeah, it bothered me that you were in a camper because I never felt like it was safe enough or good enough for you."

Warmth surrounded her heart, but just when she was about to speak, it seemed he wasn't finished.

"You deserve whatever you want to have, be it palace or just a little home by the sea. Hell, if you wanted to build a mansion by the water, that'd be good, too. But, I know you… you'd rather have a simple home that's full of pets and kids and a man that'll consider it an honor to wake up to you every morning after holding you all night."

If she thought her heart had warmed earlier, his last statement sent a blast of heat straight through her. Pets? *Absolutely.* Kids? *God, I hope so.* A man? *Dare I hope it's you?*

"What are you thinking, babe?"

"That I want pets and kids with you." As soon as the words rushed from her mouth, she winced. *So much for coy finesse.* Blushing deep red, she blurted, "Sorry. That was—"

"Perfect. Fuckin' perfect." His grin widened and his white teeth showed against his tanned skin and lush lips. "With you, there's never any bullshit."

A hasty gulp of air sucked in before she pulled her lips in, pressing them tightly together. "Really? You didn't think that sounded weird?"

A deep, rumbling chuckle erupted. "No, Samantha. I

never thought I'd hear those words from any woman, especially a woman as perfect as you."

Joseph adjusted his night vision goggles. An easy purchase from one of the local stores, he also checked the camera he'd purchased online that allowed night photographs. He'd kept them tucked out of sight in his truck to keep Samantha from becoming curious. A casual conversation with Dylan had given him more information as to what the concerns were about a possible wolf-hybrid breeding business in the area. He was willing to let them wait to see what happened, but when Samantha mentioned she'd like to check out the back of the Bender Breeders' property when no one was around, he knew he needed to step in.

He had no idea what he was looking for, but the idea of Samantha trying to be sneaky—or trespassing on private property, which could get her arrested—did not sit well with him.

So, here he was, his truck parked a mile away, and he was slipping through the underbrush and woods that filled the rural area. While trespassing wasn't in his vast resume, with the use of the goggles, he could easily maneuver between trees, over fallen logs, and past the brambles that grew nearby.

He remembered Jim had said he owned thirty acres that bordered Maryland on one side and an inlet coming in from the Chesapeake Bay on another. Dylan had mentioned that the Virginia Marine Police were aware of the possibility of the illegal transportation of exotic animals by water. One of the original Baytown Boys that Joseph had met through the American Legion was Callan Ward. Callan had formerly been with the Coast Guard Station in Baytown and now worked with the VMP. With Callan's input, he figured Dylan had the most up-to-date information when he said the VMP had so far not discovered any evidence.

Continuing his trek around the perimeter, he discovered one of the inlets and followed along the border of Jim's property. He was not surprised to discover more than one pier. Most houses that back to water on the Eastern Shore had a pier, but he noted it was not the one he'd seen closest to Jim's house that was probably used for personal boating. Continuing forward, he spied a small barn deep in the woods, completely surrounded by trees.

He halted, wondering if a security system was in place. If the barn was used for anything illegal, Jim certainly wouldn't want it to be found. But, on the other hand, a security system could trigger questions by the authorities if they happened to find it. He listened carefully as he scanned the area. He'd heard dogs barking earlier, but now the woods were quiet as though whatever might lurk in the shadows was listening. He made it to the back of the barn without observing any cameras. At first, he did not think the structure had any windows and was hesitant to go through the front door. Circling around the back, he spied a small window near the roof line.

Quickly climbing the closest tree, he shimmied out

onto a thick limb so that he could peer through the glass. With his night vision goggles, he spied the interior divided with fencing, creating individual crates. From his perch, he could see two large dogs, one in each crate. Three smaller dogs were in another crate.

They certainly appeared similar to the dogs that Jim was breeding, but Joseph was suspicious at the reason these dogs were being kept separate. Balancing precariously, he slid his camera from his pocket and snapped as many pictures as he could, hoping at least one would be able to give evidence as to what kind of dog or hybrid was housed in this barn.

Backing toward the trunk of the tree, he easily climbed down and began to retreat, trying to follow the same path to his SUV that he had taken inland. He was relieved when it came into sight but remained cautious. Even if Jim Bender was not involved in anything illegal, the breeder might shoot first and ask questions later if he thought someone was a danger to his dogs.

It wasn't until Joseph was driving south on the main highway through the Eastern Shore toward home that he allowed himself to breathe a sigh of relief.

Arriving back at the house almost an hour later, he spied the lights on in the living room and Samantha's truck in the drive. She'd had a late call, and while he was glad she was home safe, he'd wanted to get home before her. He'd sent a text earlier, indicating he would be late getting home.

Home. The word slammed into him, squeezing his heart. He'd never referred to any place he'd lived as 'home'. He might have told someone that he was going back to 'his place', referring to wherever he was currently sleeping, but never 'home'. Now, the idea that he had a place with multiple rooms, a big kitchen and bathrooms, nice furniture, was colorfully decorated, and a woman he loved waiting inside... the thought almost took him to his knees.

Walking into the living room, he grinned as Frodo lifted his large head and looked at him through baleful eyes as Pip and Merry snuggled up against his warmth. *Oh yeah, a place filled with animals definitely makes it feel like home.*

Turning toward the kitchen, his gaze landed on the reason Frodo had offered a sympathetic stare. Samantha sat on a kitchen stool, her narrowed-eyed glare pinned on him. Her long hair was piled on top of her head, a few damp tendrils hanging about her shoulders. Dressed in drawstring pajama bottoms, a tank top that left little to the imagination, and a kimono robe flowing about her, he wanted to sweep her into his arms. Before he had that opportunity, she turned the laptop sitting on the counter around to face him.

Swept away with the feeling that he was about to step on a landmine, he said, "Hey, babe. Was your call out okay?"

Without replying, she tapped her finger onto the laptop screen filled with the map of the Benders' property he'd been studying earlier in the evening. Lifting a brow, she asked, "Instead of talking about my call out, why don't we talk about why you were studying a map of Jim Bender's land?"

He sighed, planted his hands on his hips, and

dropped his chin. Staring at his boots for a moment, he hated that she'd discovered what he'd been doing before he had a chance to tell her. He lifted his head as he heard her slip from the stool, her sock-covered feet silently bringing her closer to him. Her hands landed on her hips, mirroring his position. Her dark eyes stared up at him, a furrowed crease between her brows.

"I was going to tell you when I got home, and that's the truth. I just didn't want you to worry ahead of time."

Her mouth dropped open as she shook her head. "Worry?" Her eyes widened as she continued to shake her head slowly. "Okay, I wasn't worried beforehand. I just wondered why you were checking on the Bender property. Now that you've said *worry*, I *am* worried! What's going on?"

He pulled off his jacket, hanging it on the coat rack next to the door. With his phone in his hand, he nodded toward the counter. "Let's sit, and I'll explain everything." He placed his hand on her arm and gently directed her back toward the counter, murmuring, "We've got better light here."

Her brows snapped together again, but before she had a chance to ask more questions, he slid onto the kitchen stool next to her. Twisting so that he faced her, his legs spread slightly so that his knees were on either side of hers, he held her gaze. "Let me start off by saying that I know anything I find out would be inadmissible for law enforcement because yes... I was trespassing."

She gasped, the quick intake of air accompanying her eyes widening even more.

"Out of curiosity, I looked up Jim Bender's property

after thinking about how many acres he said he owned, especially since it partially borders the Maryland line and has water accessibility to the inlets of the bay."

Her brow stayed crinkled, but the glare had left her eyes to be replaced with a gleam of interest. Her tongue darted out to moisten her bottom lip as her shoulders relaxed ever so slightly.

Encouraged, he continued. "I have no idea if there's anything going on besides Jim Bender breeding top-quality, champion dogs. And, I suppose, it makes more sense that if someone *is* illegally breeding wolf-hybrids and selling them across the Bay for use in dogfighting, there'd be a lot of people needing the money in this area, not a well-to-do man like Jim Bender."

"What about Lionel or Alejandro? They acted like they didn't want us there."

Nodding, he said, "Yeah, I thought about that. And the fact that they come over the bridge from Norfolk. But, if he was going to breed, he would hardly do it on the back of Jim's land."

Her nose scrunched, and he leaned forward and kissed her lightly. He caught her grin, and said, "Sorry, but I couldn't resist."

Her lips quirked upward as she leaned forward and placed her hands on his thighs. She nibbled on the corner of her bottom lip before saying, "This is nuts, you know. But… I've been doing a little research myself and reached out to a few of my vet school colleagues that I thought might have some information."

He squeezed her hands in encouragement, curious to see what she had to say.

"While German shepherds have certainly been used for dogfighting, there are other dogs that are much more common. Down through history, mastiffs, St. Bernards, Great Danes, and the Newfoundland were used as fighting dogs because of their size. Nowadays, none of those make the list of popular fighting dogs. The dogs used today are usually medium-sized and sturdy, like the bull terriers and bulldogs, Doberman, rottweiler, Akita, to name some of the most popular. And yes, German shepherds still make the list even though they're not at the top, although the Caucasian shepherd is a more likely dog for fighting."

"Caucasian shepherd?"

"They were bred in the Caucasus region of Armenia and Azerbaijan. They are dominant, powerful, quick, strong, and extremely territorial. They were actually bred to fight off wolves."

"But what if they were hybrids? Would adding in purebred wolf genes to any of these dogs' genetics make them more likely to want to defend their territory?"

She shrugged, her face pinched. "I don't know. There's no information about that... no case studies, no research, no historical data."

They sat quietly for a moment, then he jerked slightly, capturing her gaze again. "Samantha, we're going about this all wrong. It doesn't matter why somebody might be breeding purebred wolves illegally. It doesn't matter if a hybrid makes a better fighting dog. If somebody's breeding them, then it's illegal. On top of that, if they're breeding them *and* selling them, that's illegal. If they're breeding them *and* selling them to be used in dogfights, that's also illegal. In other words, the *why* doesn't matter. It's just whether or not someone has a full-blooded or even a wolf-hybrid here on the Eastern shore."

Nodding quickly, her eyes brightened. "You're right! We don't have to figure out why someone is doing what they're doing. I just want to know *if* they're doing it!"

He pulled out his camera and laid it on the counter. "Then I guess I should show you what I found."

Samantha eagerly leaned forward to see what Joseph wanted to show her. He'd sent a text earlier so she knew he wouldn't be home when she arrived, and she'd used the quiet time to luxuriate in the bathtub. She'd dressed in her pajamas, sliding her arms into the silky, brightly colored kimono robe that had been a Christmas present from her mother the previous year. She wouldn't have purchased it herself but couldn't deny how much she loved the feel of the silk and the colors simply made her happy.

And she'd been happy that evening until she opened up the laptop to check her email, instead finding a detailed map of the Eastern Shore with a close up on the Bender property filling up the screen. She'd had no idea that Joseph was researching a plan to check it out in person at night. Now, with their subsequent conversation, she shoved all those thoughts aside and watched as Joseph explained what he found in the photographs.

"I followed along the back of the property, seeing

they had a number of little piers and wharves all along the inlet. I know that's not unusual, but it certainly wasn't where the larger one behind their house was located. I then found a small barn."

"A barn?" Nibbling her lip, she pondered the implications, shaking her head. "Actually, Joseph, that's not unusual. On a large piece of property, or even a small one, there can be lots of sheds, outbuildings, garages, barns... it might even be a place to store equipment or tools."

"I know, I know," he agreed. "That's why I decided to take a look inside."

She gasped, her eyes wide. "I can't believe you did that! First, you were trespassing. And then you were breaking and entering?"

"Trespassing? Yes. Breaking and entering? Absolutely not. I had no idea if he might have security around, but I did climb a tree and look inside the one window. The barn contained dogs."

Still aghast that he would go to such measures, she was even more aghast at his pronouncement. They leaned their heads together and looked at the photographs on the tiny camera screen. She squinted as though that would clear the picture well enough for her to absolutely discern what animals she was viewing. "Will these come up on your laptop?"

With a quick sync and a few taps on his laptop, he brought up his photographs. There, on the much larger screen, were the ones he'd taken.

"How did you get these in the dark?"

"It's a special camera I bought just to take these pics in the dark."

She jerked her head around again. "I can't believe you didn't tell me you were going to all this trouble. You know, I'd have gone with you."

"Oh, no, babe. There's no way in the world that I'd have let you go with me."

Huffing, she asked, "Sexist?"

"Not at all. I knew when I went on the Bender property I was trespassing. And if they called the Sheriff's department and I was arrested, I'd have to deal with the fallout. But you are the area's only veterinarian, and the last thing you need is to spend the night in jail for trespassing."

That he was looking out for her warmed her heart but didn't surprise her. Leaning forward, she kissed the underside of his jaw, then turned back to the laptop screen. The photographs were grainy, making it difficult to discern any specifics about the canines.

"What can you tell?"

"I'm not sure. If I could see their ears, I'd be able to discern if it was a full-blooded wolf." Cold crept through her, and she twisted around to look at him. "Joseph, this is crazy. There's no way someone has a full-blooded wolf here. That would be nuts!"

His intense gaze held hers, and he gave her hand a little squeeze. "Babe, there's a lot of people who do crazy-ass things. And if big money is involved, that makes the stakes even higher."

Thoughts churned in her head as she tried to make sense of everything. "So... if we go on the assumption that this is a pure-bred wolf or even a wolf-hybrid, both illegal in this area, then they could sell wolf-hybrids that were fifty percent or higher wolf on the black market. It could be to individual buyers who just want a dog like this or for a more nefarious purpose, such as dogfighting or someone else who wants to breed."

"Sounds right," he said, nodding, his gaze moving between the screen and her face. "I guess I don't even know what I hoped to accomplish with this, but seeing this barn with these dogs kept completely separate from his breeding setup, it makes me suspicious. I just don't know if we have enough to go to Liam to see if they can open an investigation."

Her cheeks puffed out as she exhaled loudly. "I still say someone other than Jim is the leader of this... he gets too much money and too much recognition to ever risk it on illegally owning an exotic animal or breeding it."

"Lionel or Alejandro?"

"That'd be my guess. How far away from the house is this barn?"

"It's at the far end, near the Maryland border and near one of the inlets. He's got close to thirty acres, he said, and it's mostly thick woods. This barn is a couple of miles from the house and buried deep in the woods."

She jumped as another thought slammed into her. "What about the wild dog sightings? Could one of these hybrid animals have escaped? They'd have to let it go, not willing to be found looking for something that they should have never had to begin with."

"What about the dog that was brought to you by that

man and his son? The one you were a little suspicious of?"

"I have no proof that it was anything other than just a full-blooded dog. I'd have to have genetic testing done to see if it was part wolf."

"Can you do that?"

She snorted. "Yeah, I can do a blood test to send off. But genetic testing isn't cheap." She caught the roll of his eyes. "Oh, is this going to be one of the times where you tell me that you've got the money?"

"Yep. I've got the money, so if you can get the blood work, send it in, I'll cover the cost."

Not used to someone offering money, for an instant she hesitated. Then she thought of getting the proof to see if someone really did have a wolf or hybrid in the area. A slow grin curved her lips, and she said, "All right. I'll do it."

Two days later, with Bosco muzzled, she drew a blood sample from his leg. Mr. Tolson rubbed his whiskered chin as he watched carefully, an anxious expression on his face.

"I didn't tell Jonny what we were doing today, figuring he was in school and wouldn't know. But you tellin' me that this dog might be part wolf makes me nervous. He's been real good around us, but that don't mean nothing if he's got some wild in him."

"We'll get the results back in about two weeks, Mr. Tolson. As soon as I do, I promise to let you know what

I find out. Until then, I would just continue to treat Bosco the way you have, with a lot of love. But, to be extra cautious, you might make sure that Jonny is never alone with him. I have no way of knowing if Bosco would react negatively to certain stimuli, even if he is a full-blooded dog. Puppies can be very rambunctious, so it's hard to tell."

Mr. Tolson's shoulders slumped, and he nodded as he gently rubbed Bosco's head. "Okay, Dr. Collins."

With Bosco's leash snapped back onto his collar, Mr. Tolson turned to leave. Samantha placed her hand on his arm, drawing his attention back to her. "I know this is difficult, but I want to thank you. If there's any chance at all that Bosco could have been bred as a wolf-hybrid, that's illegal in this area. And we need to know that."

Ducking his chin in response, Mr. Tolson and Bosco left the examining room. Samantha closed the door behind them, staying in the empty room for a moment. She slumped back against the door and dropped her chin, sighing heavily. *This sucks. This just sucks.* Inhaling deeply to re-center her mind, she left the room and walked to the back workroom. Labeling the blood work, she packaged it up just in time for it to go out with the mail.

At the end of the day, she walked into the work-room, seeing Annette, Brentley, Tonya, and Susan. "Wow, we aren't usually all here at the same time."

"We want the scoop, Doc," Tonya ordered, cocking her hip and tapping her foot.

Not knowing what she was referring to, Samantha's

gaze darted from one to the other. "Scoop? What scoop?"

"The scoop on the shelter's new management," Susan said, a wide grin on her face.

Hiding her sigh of relief, she lifted her brow. "Oh? I thought you knew that Joseph Hernandez is the new manager."

"Yes," Tonya quipped, her gaze narrowed, "But you never told us that he is the Joseph that you've been seeing. *Your* Joseph."

Chuckles erupted from the others as she blushed. "Y'all are worse than a bunch of little gossipy women! But yes, *my* Joseph is taking over the shelter."

"I couldn't believe Betty was giving it up," Susan said, leaning back in her seat, shaking her head slightly.

"I don't think she would if it wasn't for needing to be with family somewhere else," Annette added.

"I also have it on good authority that you've changed residence," Tonya pressed, drawing the attention from the others.

"Okay, yes, I have moved out of my camper for now. Joseph and I are renting Betty and Sid's house near the shelter."

Brently laughed. "Got a truck that works... got a place to stay that's close to here and won't blow over in a storm... sounds like you're moving up in the world. Gee, boss... I think you'll be able to pay me after all."

The other three women swung their gazes between Brentley and Samantha. She smiled and said, "Looks like this is as good a time as any to announce that I have offered Brentley full-time employment as a veterinarian, effective as soon as he graduates in a few weeks and passes his boards."

The room was filled with congratulations and laughter. Samantha felt the weariness from earlier ease with the happy atmosphere. She walked to the refrigerator and pulled out a bottle of sparkling water. "Okay, I know this isn't champagne, but since Brentley and I shared his news, we can celebrate."

As they toasted the success of the clinic, she relaxed. Susan turned to Samantha and asked, "Was there something wrong with the Tolsons' puppy? I saw him bring him in."

"No, but I wanted to do some bloodwork, and Mr. Tolson agreed." Seeing the curious expressions, she shrugged. "Believe it or not, there's the possibility of someone in the area breeding wolf-hybrids. There's also been some sightings of what a couple of farmers have called a wild dog. I have no idea if any of the rumors are true or not, but I decided to send off testing to make sure."

The others' eyes widened as they stopped their celebration and stared at her. She looked at her staff and added, "There's even the possibility that it could be tied into illegal dogfighting in the Norfolk area."

"Who would be doing that?" Annette asked, plopping down onto a stool.

"I have no idea. But Joseph is keeping an eye out at the shelter, talking to a few people, and I'm doing the same. If you hear anything, be sure to let me know."

Susan shook her head slowly. "I overheard Mr. Tolson muttering as he left that he was going to warn others that there might be a dangerous dog in the area. I had no idea what he was talking about."

Samantha remained quiet, but it struck her that she wished she had told Mr. Tolson to not tell anyone about the blood test on Bosco. *I'd hate for him to inadvertently tip off someone.*

As they finished their cleaning and prep for the next day, she waved goodbye as they all moved through the lobby toward the door. She spent a little time in her office, finishing her reports and emailing a few veterinarians that she knew worked with exotic animals for information. Closing her computer, she readied to leave then remembered she wanted to double-check the vaccination supply. Joseph had said that three puppies had come in, and if the clinic had enough, she'd take them to give to the dogs. If not, she'd have Annette order more.

Opening the door, she was pleased to see that it appeared the latest order of rabies pharmaceuticals were there. She moved three to the side but hesitated. Deciding to count again, she huffed as she discovered they were two short. *Only two... but still! How hard can it be for the staff to document correctly!* Grabbing what she needed, she locked the vault securely and headed to her truck, anxious to see Joseph in his new environment.

22

Joseph had finished in the cat room and was almost finished with hosing down the kennels. He'd spent time researching animal shelters and was forming an idea of ways to make this shelter better for the animals. Hearing someone walk into the room, he looked over his shoulder expecting Samantha. Instead, he was surprised to see Callan. "Hey, man, what brings you here?"

Callan grinned as he walked closer. Tall, his dark hair trimmed short, he was still wearing his Virginia Marine Police uniform. "I thought I'd stop by. Sophia and I are thinking about getting a dog and want a rescue. I had a dog growing up, but once in the Coast Guard, I couldn't have a pet. Now that we're settled in Baytown, I think we're ready."

"The way everyone else is having babies, I'm surprised the two of you aren't!"

Callan laughed and shook his head. "Hell, we just got

married. I'm sure babies aren't far off, but we'll start with a dog."

"Any particular breed?"

"Honestly, we're fine with a mutt. We'd like something with a sweet disposition and probably not too big."

"Well, take a look around to see if there's one you like. Otherwise, I'll keep a lookout and let you know when something comes in that you might be interested in."

They spent a few minutes walking up and down the aisle, talking about the different dogs as they petted each one.

The front door opened, and Joseph turned to see Samantha hurrying toward him. Her dark hair was pulled into a ponytail although tendrils had come loose and waved about her face. Her eyes were bright as they stayed pinned on him.

"Sweetie, I got the blood work on the Tolsons' dog sent off to the lab for the DNA test to see if there is wolf in him… oh… Callan! I… uh… didn't see you there." She made big eyes at Joseph while mouthing 'sorry'.

Callan laughed and shook his head. "Sounds like I just overheard something I wasn't supposed to." He glanced between the two. "You don't have to say more but… *wolf?*"

Joseph wrapped his arm around her as she sighed.

"I guess you've heard that there may be someone on the Eastern Shore who is breeding wolf-hybrids. I had a client that found a puppy and I… well, I have no proof, but thought I'd check to see if it was pure dog or had some wolf in it."

Callan's chin jerked back slightly. "Wow. I knew that Liam wanted us to keep an eye on some of the inlets, mentioning the possibility of dogs being sold and taken to Norfolk for fighting, but that's hard for us to do. The VMP stationed here don't have enough manpower to watch all the inlets. Plus, it's not illegal to sell or buy or transport dogs. I'm afraid it would be for the local police to actually catch the dogfighters to put them away."

He rubbed his chin for a moment, then looked back at the couple. "But wolf? If we knew for sure someone was transporting a wolf-hybrid, then it would be illegal in this area."

"But there's no way for you to tell," she said. "Not unless it was a full-blooded wolf because they look different than a dog. Even then, you'd probably have to have a DNA test to prove it, and that can take a couple of weeks."

Nodding slowly, he grimaced. "Sorry, guys."

She waved her hand dismissively. "Oh, Callan, the Virginia Marine Police do a lot... don't apologize over something that you can't control." She glanced around. "Were you looking for a dog?"

"Actually, yes. Joseph was showing me what the shelter has now. Sophia and I are hoping to adopt a dog soon."

Joseph gave her a squeeze, saying, "Babe, I'll walk Callan out while you inoculate the puppies."

The two men walked toward the front, then shook hands. "I'll let you know what comes into the shelter."

Callan hesitated, then said, "Joseph, just gotta say that I'm real glad you've decided to make the Eastern Shore your home. You're well-liked and everyone in the American Legion thinks you're perfect for this shelter and..." He turned to look toward the back. "And for Sam."

Grinning, Joseph glanced at Samantha bending into one of the kennels, laughing as the puppies jumped around her. "I appreciate it, Callan. I'm the lucky one."

Waving goodbye, he walked to the back and watched as she inoculated the dogs. "Is this something I can learn to do?"

"Yes, for everything except rabies. For that, a veterinarian has to be the one to give it." She twisted her head around. "That reminds me... someone on my staff is still not marking the rabies vaccinations down correctly! I'm missing two more."

Locking up the shelter, they drove her truck down the lane to the house. As they entered, he turned the problem of her vaccinations over in his head. She let Frodo out into the yard as Joseph fed the kittens. When she walked through the back door into the kitchen with Frodo, Joseph leaned his hip against the counter and crossed his arms over his chest. "Babe? What purpose could someone have for taking a rabies vaccination?"

"Taking it?"

"Well, stealing it."

She poured food into Frodo's bowl, then twisted to look up at him in surprise. "There's no real black market for rabies vaccinations. So, selling it would make no sense."

"Even if it makes no sense, what could they use it for?"

She stood back, allowing Frodo to dive into his food, her gaze drifting to the side. He could see the wheels were turning behind her dark eyes when suddenly, her brow knit, and she shot her gaze back to his face. "To give to someone who either can't afford them or doesn't want a veterinarian to know."

"Like someone who is illegally breeding animals?" As soon as the words left his lips he watched the blood drain from her face. His hand reached out as she rushed to him, her fingers clutching his arms, her eyes wide.

"Joseph, if you're right, then someone on my staff is stealing! Someone on my staff is giving or selling the rabies vaccinations! Oh, my God! What do I do? Who do we call?"

"Take it easy, babe. All we have right now is just an idea… a speculation."

She nodded, her head moving in ungainly jerks, and he pulled her close, wrapping his arms around her. "Shhh, it's going to be fine." After a moment, she nodded against his chest and leaned her head back to peer up at him.

"I just can't think that it's one of my staff. Joseph, that actually hurts my heart."

He had no reply but held her close, enveloping her into his embrace, hoping it offered comfort.

Jerking again, she blurted, "It can't be Brentley. He hasn't been with me for all that long." As soon as the words left her mouth, her brow crinkled again. "But then I can't really say exactly when things started disappearing. And he has a lot of vetmed school debts." Looking up, she sighed. "But Susan? Tonya? Annette? They've been with the clinic longer than I have!"

"Sweetheart, making yourself upset about this now won't help. We don't even know if our supposition is correct."

"You're right. I think I need to pull my list from the clinic and cross-reference dates to make sure I have my information correct."

"Then we can go to Colt with our suspicions. Give him the information, let him know when this started, let him guide us in what we need to do." She nodded again, and he gave another squeeze to maintain her attention. "But babe? Don't do anything to give away your hand. We don't want the person to know what you're thinking."

"You're right. But it's going to be hell working with everyone, wondering who might be a thief!"

Meows from below caused them both to look down, and Joseph smiled as Samantha let go of him and bent to scoop up Pip and Merry. He rubbed their heads with his large hand, then bent to kiss Samantha's forehead. "Take the cats into the living room with Frodo and play with them for a little while. We've got leftovers I can heat up, and I'll have dinner ready quickly."

Glad that she didn't argue, he watched her walk into the living room, a kitten in each hand, cooing and talking to the animals. True to his word, it didn't take long for him to set leftover fried chicken, reheated macaroni and cheese, and salad onto the table. As they ate, he kept the conversation light even though he could see the stress in the slight lines on her face.

After dinner, he read while she channel-surfed. After she'd sighed for the hundredth time, he closed his book and tossed it onto the coffee table. Standing, he pulled her to her feet and said, "Let's go, babe. You need your rest."

By the time he'd checked the security of the house and finished in the bathroom, she was already in bed. Flipping off the lights, he slid underneath the covers and wrapped his body around her, pulling her back tightly to his front. Nuzzling her ear, he whispered, "Let all those thoughts out of your mind. Just relax and sleep."

She twisted her head to the side so that their mouths were close. "I don't think I can sleep, Joseph."

Their hands were clasped in front of her, and he gave a little squeeze. "You got a cure for insomnia?"

"Yeah. You."

Not needing any more encouragement, he shifted slightly so that his mouth landed on hers. She yielded immediately, and his tongue slid between her lips, gliding over the minty-toothpaste freshness, tangling with her tongue. He snaked one hand underneath the hem of her camisole and drew it up over her head, shifting again so that he could kiss along her jaw, down her neck, to her full breasts where he pulled a nipple deeply into his mouth.

His fingers drifted over her belly, feeling her twitch when he moved over her tickle-spot. His hand continued its path, sliding between her legs, dragging through her folds, finding them slick and ready. Inserting his forefinger into her channel, he thrust while his thumb circled her clit. Her back arched as a groan erupted, his assault ongoing. His teeth nipped her breasts, his erection pressed hard and firm against her hip, and his fingers worked furiously inside her sex. She finally cried out, her inner muscles clenching around his finger. Slowly pulling his finger free, he lifted it to his mouth, sucking her juices before taking her lips in a kiss once again, allowing her to taste her essence on his tongue.

She kissed him back with abandon and shifted to her back. He rolled her forward before thrusting his large thigh between her legs. Without words, she lifted her leg as he guided his aching cock into her channel from behind.

This angle presented a different sensation, and if her moans were any indication, she felt it, too. Tight, slick, the heady scent of their arousal filled the air. With one arm under her neck, his hand curved downward to cup a breast, his other hand continuing its ministrations on her clit as his cock pistoned, his pelvis hitting against her ass.

"Come on, babe," he grunted.

"I'm…"

"Come on." His lower back was coiled and tingling, his orgasm not far off. Pinching her clit with one hand while pinching her nipple with the other, he powered through as she cried out, arching her back and pressing her ass toward him. His release blasted from him, and he could swear sparks flew behind his tightly closed eyelids. Continuing to pump until every last drop had been wrung from his cock, he buried his face in her neck.

Finally, opening his eyes, his chest heaved with the exertion, and her panting breaths forced air from her lungs as well. Their sweat-slicked bodies stayed curved together until their heartbeats began to slow, beating in unison. His cock slipped from her warmth. "Think you can sleep now?"

Laughter barked out as she turned to face him. "Yeah, I think you wore me out."

They kissed, soft and gentle, the silky touch of lovers' lips. Separating, he mumbled, "Be right back. Stay put, and I'll get a cloth." They had dispensed with condoms weeks ago since she was on the pill and they were both clean. But he loved taking care of her. After cleaning himself, he wet a cloth with warm water and stalked back into the bedroom, finding her lying on her side, her head propped up with her hand, and her eyes pinned on him. The grin on her face sent electricity straight to his heart.

Gently cleaning her, he tossed the cloth back into the sink and crawled between the sheets once more. Tucking her in close, he was glad that she settled quickly, her breathing soon indicating she had found slumber.

He lay, his chin rested on her head, and thought of their situation. *She is getting the paperwork tomorrow to check the vaccinations, but I'm calling in Colt and Liam. Might as well get them prepped for the investigation.*

23

Samantha was exhausted. Her muscles were tired, and she was sure her bones hurt as well. She'd spent the day darting around, trying to keep her eye on everyone at the clinic. Particularly if any of the staff were going in and out of the pharmaceutical closet. They were busy, and as usual, inoculations were being given. Susan, Tonya, and Brentley were dispensing medications.

While trying to see clients and keep an eye on the staff, she'd plastered a smile on her face in an attempt to keep anyone from being suspicious that she was watching them. But her cheeks hurt from her fake smile, and her frustration mounted as soon as she would come out of an examination room only to realize that she'd been unable to keep an eye on everyone else.

"Are you okay?" Annette asked when Samantha walked past the reception desk to enter her office.

"Yes, I'm fine!" She inwardly winced at her overly bright-sounding words and wasn't surprised when her astute office manager narrowed her gaze at her.

"Samantha, you're as nervous as a cat with his tail under a rocking chair. You've been flitting around all day."

Unable to think of an excuse why her behavior would be off, she shrugged. "You're right. I'm just having one of those days where I feel kind of nervous."

"Nervous?" Tonya walked by and leaned her hip against the reception desk. "About the clinic?"

Glad that there were no clients in the lobby at the moment, she lied, "Yeah, sometimes I get keyed up about the business. Just want to make sure we're running efficiently."

"Well, if we all ran around every day like you are today, we'd be bouncing off each other," Susan laughed as she walked in and glanced at the computer screen near Annette. "Thank goodness, we have a break. If you guys don't mind, I need to go to the back and eat."

Tonya and Brentley headed to the workroom with Susan, and Samantha was torn. She wanted to follow them to keep an eye on what they were doing and saying while knowing she needed to start printing off the spreadsheets of rabies vaccinations ordered and used in the past year. Tossing another wide, fake smile toward Annette, she headed into her office.

It took a while to pull together and compile all the records, but she finally had what she needed printed off. Not wanting the others to see what she had, she bent and shoved them into her bag next to the desk.

Annette popped her head in, eyes wide, and called out, "You're needed out here!"

Jumping up, she rushed out to see a sobbing client carrying a blanket with blood on it.

"He ran right out in front of me! I don't know how bad he's hurt! But I know he's in pain!"

She scooped the blanket-wrapped injured cat and rushed to the back, calling for the others, leaving Annette to adeptly calm the owner. Susan and Brentley left the workroom to continue seeing the afternoon clients while Tonya immediately jumped up to help Samantha.

Upon examination, she was relieved to see that there did not appear to be any internal injuries, but the cat's back leg was broken. Surgery was required to pin it together, and she and Susan worked on the leg for the next two hours. By the time the grateful owner was sent home and the cat was resting comfortably in a recovery crate, the day was almost over.

Brentley offered to stay, but she waved him off, telling him to go home and she'd have him see the morning clients the next day. Susan and Tonya left as well, leaving her with Annette. Walking to the front, she stopped by the pharmaceutical closet and shook her head. She had wanted to try to keep an eye on who might be taking extra drugs during the day, but it was an impossible task. *Going through my list will be the only way I can determine who is more likely to have helped themselves to extra doses of the rabies vaccination and medications.*

Going into her office, she grabbed her bag, then looked over to see that her computer screen was still filled with the spreadsheets from earlier. Shutting them down and turning off her computer, she flipped off the lights and walked back into the reception area just as Annette was ready to leave.

"Samantha, I know you want to check on the cat again. I'll lock the front door as I leave that way, and you can take care of the rear door since I know you're parked in the back."

Waving toward Annette, she called out, "Thanks for everything today, and I'll see you tomorrow."

Walking through the back once again, she checked on the cat, satisfied that he was fine. As she moved down the hall, she checked the pharmaceutical closet once again. Opening the door, she shook her head. *Ugh! I'm so obsessive now, it's almost like I have no control!* But as she looked into the refrigeration storage vault, she noticed they were two vaccines short. *I was just in here! I just looked!*

The reality slammed into her that Annette was the only one who had still been in the building. She slammed the door and secured the storage. She set the alarm and locked the back door before racing to her truck. Tossing up thanks to Jason and Joseph that her truck was in good working order, she quickly left the clinic and drove toward the highway. Her luck was holding as she spied Annette's car at the red light. Slowing, she still made it through the light but was far enough behind her that she hoped she would not be seen.

She started to call Joseph, then decided to wait. *Let's see where Annette is going first!*

"Come on, boy, let's wait up front." Joseph rubbed Frodo's ears, leading him toward the lobby. He occasionally took the large bloodhound to the shelter, giving him a chance to socialize and exercise while Samantha was at work. He had finished for the day but was waiting for Colt and Liam, having asked both men to come over. Since Samantha's clinic was in North Heron but Jim Bender's land was in Acawmacke, he thought it made sense to bring both sheriffs into what he and Samantha were discovering.

He looked up as the front door opened and the two men entered, both tall, well-built, dark-haired, and wearing the tan uniforms of their jobs. Both gave an air of competence in their manner. But Joseph had noticed a change in Colt since Carrie had come into his life. Gone was the taciturn man to be replaced with someone who smiled more often. Inwardly chuckling, he knew the same could be said about himself.

Liam had always struck him as fun-loving, certainly in their dealings with the kids on the AL ball teams. But now, as the two men approached, he saw the intelligent interest in the eyes and had no doubt they were both ready for whatever information he could give them.

"Colt, Liam," he greeted.

"Joseph," they said at the same time.

"What's up?" Colt asked as he settled into the chair that Joseph indicated. Liam followed suit and Joseph joined them after locking the front door and turning off the Open sign. Frodo sniffed the feet of the two sheriffs, then walked back over to Joseph, turned around in a circle, and laid down next to his chair.

He leaned forward, his forearms resting on his knees, and said, "Samantha may have stumbled onto a clue into the wolf-hybrid business on the shore." Colt and Liam's brows lifted, and their posture imitated his as they leaned forward as well.

"She's noticed for a long time that some of her vaccinations have gone missing. Not a lot at a time... maybe only one or two, but it's been consistent. She doesn't handle the ordering and she's not the only one administering them, so it was easy to overlook. When Tom abruptly left the clinic to her, she was unprepared for the business aspect and said it took her a bit to get up to speed. She relied heavily on the others to do the jobs they'd always done. But once she noticed the discrepancies, she talked to her office manager who admitted that they'd had some shipments come in where she hadn't counted all the pharmaceuticals, simply putting them into the storage or refrigerated storage container as needed. Plus, Samantha is out in the field some, and she has a vet intern working with her. She feels badly that things were missing without her noticing, but now she's keeping track and is continuing to have the... well, thefts. Someone at the clinic is stealing rabies vaccinations."

Colt glanced toward Liam and then back to Joseph. "I understand this is a problem in my county since that's where the clinic is, but what does this have to do with wolf-hybrids?"

"According to Samantha, there's no black market for

vaccinations, so no need for someone to steal them to sell. That means that someone is probably using them. Using them for animals that can't or shouldn't be getting them through a vet."

He saw the questions in Colt and Liam's eyes. Sucking in a deep breath, he plunged ahead. "Okay, I'll let you know now that I was trespassing to see if I could find any evidence. Trespassing on Jim Bender's back land."

"Bender's Breeders?" Liam asked, brows lifted.

"Yep."

"What did you find?" Liam continued.

Realizing Liam didn't bother to tell him what he did was illegal, he moved ahead with his story. "There's a small barn on the back of the property, buried in the woods but near one of the little piers. It contains some large crates with a couple of big dogs. There's also a group of about three pups I could see as well." He leaned back and grabbed a folder from the counter behind him, pulling out several printed photographs. Handing them over, he watched as the two men eagerly looked at them. "It's grainy and isn't evidence other than he's got dogs—or something—there. Dogs? No problem. But wolves or wolf-hybrids? I know that's illegal on the shore."

He remained quiet for a moment, allowing them to study the photographs, giving them a chance to sift through the possibilities.

"If he's keeping a wolf-hybrid on his property to breed… " Liam began, his question hanging.

"Samantha can't imagine it's Jim."

That caught their attention as they both lifted their heads from the photographs. "What do you mean?"

"She says that Jim Bender makes a lot of money selling his pure-bred dogs. He knows his dogs can be subject to genetic testing from a potential buyer to make sure of their pure-bred status. He's not about to risk his reputation in the business to introduce a wolf."

"Then who?"

"That's not for me to say, although I didn't get a good vibe from his assistants when Samantha and I visited Jim's kennels. I know Jim said Alejandro comes over from Norfolk a couple times a week."

That raised the eyebrows of the sheriffs, both directing their stares onto Joseph. He threw up his hands. "Like I said… I'm not into the *who*. I just want to make sure Samantha is safe if she has someone at the office stealing and that there are no wolf-hybrids loose in the counties."

"Shit," Colt cursed. "Does Sam think there are?"

Before Joseph had a chance to answer, Liam ground out, "The wild dog reported?"

"I don't know," Joseph admitted, "but Samantha has taken blood samples from a puppy that an owner found, and she had concerns about him. The results won't come back for a bit. She also said that if some of the hybrid dogs that didn't get sold or didn't have the right appearance, they might be let loose."

"We need to talk to Sam again," Liam said.

"She's on her way here." Looking at his watch, Joseph jerked his head back slightly. "I thought she'd be here by now. She was coming after she gathered the records at the clinic to see the discrepancies in vaccines ordered and used."

Right on cue, his phone vibrated. Looking down at the screen, he smiled. "Hey, babe. Putting you on speaker. I've got Colt and—"

"It's Annette, I'm sure of it!" Samantha cried out.

"What?"

"Annette! I'm sure she's the one who has taken the vaccinations."

"Where are you?"

"I'm following her—"

"God dammit, Samantha. What the fuck are you thinking?" He leaped from his chair, Colt and Liam already on their feet.

"Calm down. I just followed her to the turn beyond Bender Kennels. It's around toward the back of the property. I'm not going any further, but I wanted you to know. I stepped out of my truck to see if I could see or hear anything, but I can't."

"Sam, this is Liam. I'm on my way. I'm calling for backup but will tell them to approach quietly."

"I'm getting back into my truck. Should I stay here?"

"No! Get in the truck and drive away. Let Liam do what he needs to do!" Joseph yelled, not caring what Colt or Liam would have advised.

Muffled noises sounded over the phone before her voice cried out. *"What— No—"*

The call disconnected. Joseph stared in stunned silence for a few seconds before hitting the call button again. It went straight to Samantha's voicemail. Jerking his head up, his heart lodged into his throat, but he managed to choke out, "Fucking hell. Something's happened to Samantha!"

Colt and Liam were already on their phones as they rushed out of the shelter. Joseph followed, fear coursing through him, Frodo at his heels.

24

Her truck door was open, and Samantha had one foot inside with her phone plastered to her ear when she was jerked back and to the side. "What?" Her phone was ripped from her hand as a heavy force shoved her body forward, smashing her face into the side of the truck. "No!" Pressure was forced onto the back of her head and someone's full body was pressed against her back, pinning her in place. Instinct had her try to push against the cold metal door with her palms, but the pressure increased, stilling her movements.

Hot breath puffed against her ear as the assailant leaned in. "Don't move."

"Wh... what..."

"You back off. Back the fuck off. Do your job and stay out of everything else."

"I... I—" Her words cut off as the pressure on her back increased.

"Last warning—"

"You can't let her go, man. She's got to come with us," another male voice said from behind.

"Fuck no. Right now, she knows nothing, but—"

"I'm not taking a fuckin' chance!"

Fear tearing at her heart, she kept her eyes shut, swallowing deeply as her breath panted from her lungs. The two men's argument swirled around her, but she remained still. Not that she had much of a choice. The pressure on her back and head kept her immobile. With them behind her, she forced her eyes open, not expecting to see anything, but caught a glimpse of the man holding her when her gaze landed on the sideview mirror of her truck.

Alejandro.

The pressure suddenly fled, causing her body to slump against the side of the truck, her knees buckling. A hand closed tightly on her upper arm, and she was jerked backward. Twisting to the side, she observed that Lionel had stepped forward, pushing Alejandro to the side.

"Stay on your feet, bitch. I'm not carrying your ass," Lionel ordered.

As he dragged her past her truck and down the lane toward a path heading into the woods, her head snapped around and she spied Alejandro walking behind, a scowl carved onto his face. His black eyes held hers for a moment, but she read nothing in them. Blank. Even if he'd tried to get Lionel to let her go, it was clear he was doing nothing now.

Joseph flashed through her mind. *He said he was with*

Colt and Liam. They'll come. Surely, they'll come. But what will they find?

Entering the woods, she had little time to focus on anything other than staying upright. Spindly pine saplings slapped at her legs and arms, tripping her feet. The ground was soft and covered with a layer of dead leaves, hiding the dips in the path. Stumbling, her arm ached where Lionel's grip was unrelenting.

The farther they walked the underbrush grew more thickly, and she could barely make it through. Finally, they came to a small shed, and Lionel whirled her around, shoving her face against the wooden side. "No!" she cried, sucking in a gasp, sure that she was about to be killed. Instead, Lionel whipped a handkerchief around her head and tied it over her mouth, forcing her teeth apart. Her hands were pulled behind her and wrapped together. Seeing the end of the restraint, she recognized a thin, rope dog leash.

"Open it," he growled, and she watched as Alejandro bent to the door and unlocked the padlock holding it shut.

Before she had a chance to think of running, Lionel gripped her arm again and forced her to bend before shoving her into the small space. The dirt floor rose to meet her face, but she managed to jerk her torso upward, landing only on her knees. The door slammed shut behind her, the lock clicking back into place. She heard footsteps walk away but couldn't tell if it was only one or both of them.

She jumped at the sound of a man's voice on the other side of the door. "It'll be okay. I promise."

She leaned forward to listen closer, but all she could hear were the two men arguing as they were both walking away. She had no idea which one had spoken to her nor did she know what he meant.

Looking around, she was grateful the shed was old and cracks of light penetrated the slats of wood. Crawling forward on her knees, she maneuvered to peek through one of the slight openings closest to the sounds of retreating men. Seeing both of their backs disappear through the woods, she breathed a sigh of relief, knowing they'd left her alone and alive for the time being. Breathing deeply, she fought to steady her heartbeat. After a moment, she felt calm descend, and if the gag wasn't pulling against her mouth, she would've smiled. They had not only left her alone, but they'd seriously underestimated her.

Staying on her knees, she relied on her small stature and flexibility, remembering how she'd surprised her fellow soldiers when she was able to escape restraints. Working her wrists to loosen the leash as much as possible, she shimmied her arms over her hips before plopping her butt on the dirt. Now, she was able to maneuver her wrists up the back of her legs and bring her arms to her front.

Lifting her hands over her head, she was able to grasp the ties of the handkerchief. Only able to use one hand, she managed to loosen the knot at the back of her head and wiggle her forefinger into the opening. The material stretched and she pulled at the knot. Bringing her hands back to the front of her face, she removed the binding. Wiggling her jaw, she was grateful for the freedom, hating the way the gag had pressed against her tongue and rubbed the corners of her mouth.

Peeking through the opening in the slats again, she listened carefully but couldn't see or hear Lionel or Alejandro's presence. Working her hands back and forth, she continued to loosen the leash until she was finally able to slide one hand free. Jerking it off the other hand, she rubbed her wrists, wincing at the sting of her abraded flesh.

Pushing against the door, the padlock and latch was old and rusted but held firm. Looking around, she tried to find a weak spot in the structure. Sitting on the floor, she leaned back, placing her feet on the wall. Kicking out with both feet at the same time, she felt the shock of pain reverberate up her legs, but the wood didn't yield. Growling in frustration, she tried several more times but to no avail. *Of all the times to not have my old boots on!*

Resting for a few minutes, she continued to look for a weak plank of wood, thankful that the sun was still able to pierce the darkness inside the shed.

Frodo sat in the passenger side of Joseph's SUV as he sped north on the main highway, following Liam and Colt's vehicles. His heart in his throat, he gripped the steering wheel tightly. Barely heeding the vehicles in front of him, his mind was filled with Samantha and what might be happening to her. His gaze flicked over to the small-town sign on the side of the road, mentally calculating how much longer they had to get to her.

Seeing a traffic light turn red ahead, he cursed loudly, but then, as Colt and Liam had flipped on their flashing lights and sirens, he stomped on the accelerator and followed them through.

Colt's jurisdiction ended at the North Heron and Acawmacke line, but considering the vet clinic where the thefts had occurred were in his county, Joseph had heard Liam call for Colt to come along. He assumed Liam had called for backup when he observed the other Acawmacke Sheriff SUVs following closely.

Frodo let out a loud bay, and he spared a quick glance to the side. "Hang on. We're going to get her, boy." Now, he just wished he could calm the knot in his stomach as easily as he spoke the words to Frodo.

Still gripping the steering wheel, he forced his mind to clear, knowing Samantha needed him to keep his wits. *Where is she?* He thought about the thick woods around, heavy with underbrush, and the soft ground leading to the bogs near the inlets of the bay. *Did someone take her? What if she's not with her truck?* Frodo bayed again, the deep bark from the bloodhound resounding in the vehicle. Joseph swung his head around, the reality of Frodo's abilities hitting him. *Thank fuck he's with me!*

His wheels churned the last few miles, and gratefully, the turnoff leading to Bender's Kennels was just ahead. Liam passed the turn to the Benders' drive, continuing onto the road where Samantha said she'd parked. Looking ahead, her old truck was pulled to the side of the road, no sight of her around.

Skidding to a stop, he leaped out of the SUV, slapping his thigh as he called to Frodo. Snapping a leash onto the dog's collar, he ran forward. He reached for the door handle, but Liam stopped him.

"Don't tamper with evidence."

Leaning forward, he peeked through the driver window and saw her bag laying on the passenger seat. Fear clutched at his throat as vicious scenarios ran through his mind. "She would never willingly leave her purse." Frodo tugged on his leash, and Joseph looked down to see the dog sniffing Samantha's cell phone on the ground. The screen was cracked, and he started to reach for it, halting when one of Liam's deputies reached down with gloves.

Helplessness coursed through him, and he whirled around to pierce Liam with a glare. "I'm taking Frodo. He can track her." Ready to go rogue if he had to, Liam nodded before ordering several arriving deputies to go with him.

With gloves on, Liam opened the truck door and pulled out Samantha's purse, handing it to Joseph. He held it in front of Frodo, and commanded, "Samantha." Frodo's baleful eyes looked up at him as though chastising. He needed no new scent to follow his mistress. With nose to the ground, he headed toward the woods, and as Joseph followed, he noted the disturbances in the dirt path as though someone had been dragged along. Glancing back at the deputies trailing, he knew why Liam had sent them along. *If I get my hands on the bastard who took Samantha before they do, there won't be anything left!*

The only thing allowing him to hold onto his sanity

over the fear of what might've happened to Samantha was Frodo following her scent. The bloodhound never stopped to look around but stayed right on the trail through the woods. They left the main path and maneuvered through the underbrush. The disturbance in the dirt and broken twigs along the way gave evidence that the path they followed had recently been traversed. He focused on each footstep landing firmly and the feel of the leash in his hand. Tethering his mind to something tangible kept him from thinking of Samantha being taken down this path and what he might find at the end of it.

Suddenly, Frodo stopped and lifted his head. Joseph halted behind the dog and threw his hand up so the deputies behind him would quiet, also. Frodo let out a deep, loud bay, and Joseph's heart leapt into his throat at the resounding cry.

"Frodo! I'm here!"

Hearing his mistress call his name, Frodo bounded forward, nearly dragging Joseph off his feet as they crashed through the woods, coming upon a tiny shed not tall enough for an adult to stand in. Frodo ran to the door, and Joseph's knees buckled when the tip of a forefinger poked through a hole. "Samantha!" he roared.

"Joseph? Oh, my God! You're here, you came!"

He was at the door, pushing Frodo to the side so that his finger could touch the tip of hers. It was only fingertips, but the feel of her skin was a balm to his raging heart. One of the deputies behind him radioed that they'd found her. "Babe, are you hurt?"

"Mostly my pride at being taken. I was able to get my

restraints off and the gag out, but I'm not wearing the right shoes to be able to kick out part of the wooden planks."

"Back up to the other side. Protect your face. I am going to kick the door in."

He heard her scramble and then lifted his foot, kicking with all his might. His boots went through two of the planks next to the door. Dropping to his knees, he grabbed the splintered wood and jerked it away. Ready to crawl in to get her, she was already at the opening, her head popping through as she crawled on her hands and knees through the dirt. Trying to assist her to her feet, Joseph was hampered as Frodo pushed his way in, licking his mistress' face.

A barrage of emotions crashed over him as he pulled her into his arms, each so overwhelming as they vied for first place in his mind. Elation and gratitude warred with rage. Love for her warred with absolute hate for whoever had caged her.

Barely aware that one of the deputies was speaking to him, he kept his arms tightly around Samantha. Finally, the man's voice cut through the red haze and he turned with her in his arms.

"Do we need an ambulance?"

"Yes—"

"No—"

Joseph's brows snapped together as Samantha's answer had contradicted his. "Babe, we need to get you—"

"No, I'm fine. What we need to do is get those bastards! It was Lionel and Alejandro. They are the ones who took me, although I swear, I think Alejandro didn't want to. But I don't know who they're working for."

He'd catalogued bruises on her arms, red, abraded flesh on her wrists, and the edges of her mouth and cheeks were bruised from a too-tight gag. Her fingers were dirty from trying to escape, and she had multiple scrapes on her arms and neck. And yet her dark eyes were snapping with anger, and the tightness around his heart lightened, knowing she was ready to kick ass.

"Compromise, babe. We go get the bastards, and then you get checked out."

She winced slightly as she smiled and nodded. "You got it."

He set her feet onto the ground, making sure she was steady, but she immediately squatted to offer love and thanks to her faithful bloodhound. Standing, she nodded toward the deputies before turning her gaze up toward him. "Okay, let's go."

25

After receiving a hug and visual scans of her injuries from Colt and Liam, Samantha stayed tucked into Joseph's embrace. She was itching to confront Jim Bender but could feel the tense rage kept barely under control from Joseph. They walked toward the Benders' house, staying just behind Liam.

Jim stepped out onto the porch, swept his gaze over the gathering deputies, and cocked his head to the side. "Sheriff Sullivan. Doctor Collins. What brings you—" His eyes widened as Colt stepped out of his vehicle. "Sheriff Hudson? What the hell's going on?"

"We're currently searching your property for two of your employees... Lionel Watson and Alejandro Cortez."

"What the hell for?"

"Samantha was out here earlier. Followed Annette Carson from the clinic out here. Annette is suspected of stealing pharmaceuticals from Sam's clinic. We have reason to believe that they may have been brought to your kennel. Plus, your two employees kidnapped Sam. My deputies have just rescued her from a small shed near the back of your property."

Jim's spine straightened as his ruddy cheeks grew redder. "What are you insinuating? I told Doctor Collins that I didn't use nor did I need her services." He dropped his gaze to her. "Is this some way to try to get back at me for not using your two-bit clinic? One call to my attorney and you'll find you won't have a clinic anymore!"

Paula pushed against the screen and walked out onto the porch, stopping next to Jim. Her hair was slightly mussed, and her cheeks were flushed as though she had been running. Clearing her throat, she placed her hand on her husband's arm. "Jim, dear, what on earth is going on?"

"The sheriff says that Lionel and Alejandro kidnapped Doctor Collins and that some woman named Annette from the vet clinic has been bringing vaccines here. Get me our attorney's number, Paula. I'm calling him right now!"

"Now, Jim... we don't want to be rash, honey. Think of your blood pressure."

"I don't give a god damn about my blood pressure—"

A growl erupted from deep inside Joseph's chest as he stalked forward, starting up the steps, only halting when Liam's hand landed on his chest. Ignoring Liam, he stared up at Jim and Paula. "Samantha was here, following Annette. Then suddenly, she was cut off when your two goons took her. Mark my words... if I have to tear this place apart, I will find them. And after I find them, I'm coming after you." His final word was empha-sized with a finger jabbed straight up toward Jim.

Samantha settled her hand on his waist, feeling the tension in his muscles. As angry as she was, the last thing she wanted was for Joseph to get arrested for threatening someone. "Sweetheart," she whispered, catching and holding his gaze when he swung his head around to peer down at her. "Let them do their job. It's the only way to make sure they're stopped."

Before he had a chance to respond, everyone's atten-tion was diverted as Hunter Simms, a narcotics detec-tive for Colt, pulled up in a North Heron Sheriff's SUV. Samantha had first met Hunter through the American Legion but became friends through his wife, Belle. And as Hunter climbed out of his SUV, he opened the back door and hauled out a handcuffed Annette.

"Stopped her car as she was heading back south. Seems she's got a lot to say," Hunter said as he marched her forward.

"Who the hell is she?" Jim bellowed.

At that question, Samantha swung her attention back toward Jim. Either the large man was a very good actor or he truly didn't recognize Annette. A gasp from Paula had everyone turn her way. Her eyes widened as she stepped back, her gaze leveled on Annette, her mouth tightening into a pinched, thin line.

"It's her," Annette said, her arm raised and her finger pointing toward Paula. "She's the one I bring the vaccines to."

"You stupid bitch," Paula said, her voice low but shaking.

Jim turned to look at her, his face slack. "What's she talking about, Paula? What does she give you?"

"Mr. Bender, on suspicion of illegal drugs being brought to your property, suspicion of wolf-hybrids being bred on your property, and the kidnapping of Doctor Collins on your property, my deputies are already searching," Liam said.

From the side, she heard another gasp.

"Oh, God, Sam. You were kidnapped? I... I had no idea." Annette's eyes were wide, her face pale as she stared at her.

"But you obviously had no problem stealing from the clinic and delivering vaccines here, did you?" Samantha's voice was steady even though her insides quivered. Still running on nerves and adrenaline, she tried to ease the pounding of her heart.

Annette began to shake her head slowly back and forth. "I never meant for any of this to happen. It was Tom. I did it for Tom."

Samantha jerked as though punched in the gut. Joseph wrapped his arm over her shoulder and around her chest, pulling her in tight as Frodo pushed his way forward, his body leaning against her and his nose nuzzling her fingers.

"Tom? What are you talking about?"

"Shut up!" Paula shouted toward Annette before looking down at Liam. "I'm saying nothing without an attorney!"

"You're wasting our fuckin' time, Annette," Joseph growled.

Colt turned toward Annette. "I'd advise you that if you've got something to say, now's the time to do it."

Annette swung her head around and looked at the Benders surrounded by law enforcement. "Wolves. She has a full-blooded wolf that she breeds. I don't know who she sells them to, but Tom Robertson used to supply her with vaccines."

"Shit," Samantha said, her voice soft. Even though she'd had suspicions, hearing it from Annette was still shocking. "A full-blooded wolf?"

Liam now focused his attention on her. "Sam? What do we need to know once we find the animals?"

"We need to maintain everyone's safety, but treat the animals humanely. When I thought there might be wolf-hybrids here, I had already looked up rescue operations. Pennsylvania has a wolf and wolf-hybrid sanctuary. There's also several in the country that offer Wounded Warriors an opportunity to work with the animals in their sanctuary as well. First and foremost, we need to contact the Eastern Shore Wildlife Rehabilitation Center. They may not be able to take in the wolf while we find a sanctuary, but they'll be able to humanely contain it. The same goes for the wolf-hybrids."

Liam swung his head around toward one of the other detectives and nodded. "Make the call. Get them here ASAP."

"I can help."

Everyone's attention swung back to the porch where Jim stood apart from Paula, his face now pale and lines having deepened in the last few minutes.

He started down the steps, his hand lifted in front of him. "I have no idea what any of this is about." He glanced behind him at a glaring Paula, her lips still pinched, before turning back toward Samantha. "I have no idea about a wolf... or hybrids. Hell, I have no idea about you being kidnapped by my employees. Or what the hell Tom Robertson used to do. I don't even know what my wife has to do with all of this." He sucked in a ragged breath before pulling himself up to his full height. "But I can damn well help. I've got sturdy pens that can hold whatever animals you find. I don't want my dogs exposed to anything wild, but I've got pens that we use to transport the dogs. They'll be fine until you can get someone here." His brow scrunched. "But I have no idea where to look."

"I saw them in a small shed on the back of your property near the Maryland line," Joseph said.

"When I bought this property fifteen years ago, there were some old outbuildings that used to be used by some weekend fishermen," Jim said, shaking his head. "I haven't looked at them in years. I never even go out to the far reaches of my acreage."

"Well, someone has." Joseph looked down at Samantha. "You stay here. I'll lead them to the shed."

"Oh, no, I'm not staying here. I'm going with you!"

"Show us where it is," Liam called out, and as she followed Joseph and Frodo, she glanced to the side to see Colt leading Annette into the house along with a deputy that was guarding Paula. She wanted to hear what they had to say but was more interested in finding the animals. *I understand the four-legged ones... they just want to live their lives naturally.*

They spent the rest of the afternoon at the barn Joseph had discovered previously. The deputies had entered first, making sure the animals were contained in their pens. As soon as she was given the all-clear, she'd rushed in, anxious to see what was there.

She had stood, her breath stuck in her throat at the sight of two wolves, each in separate areas. The hair on the back of their necks stood up as their eyes glared toward the intruders. And she was dumbstruck with the beauty and majesty of the animals that should never have been restrained. The yips and barks coming from several other pens drew her eye, and she'd smiled at the energy of the pups. Looking toward Liam, she'd shaken her head. "I can't tell you if these are purebred wolf pups or wolf-hybrids."

"That's okay, Wildlife Rehab is on their way, and they'll take them all in. Once we know what we're dealing with, then the animals will be turned over to them."

Joseph had stayed outside with Frodo, and when she left the barn, she walked directly into his arms. His embrace enveloped her, and he'd kissed the top of her head as he held her tightly. Once again, Frodo had leaned his weight against her leg and sniffed her fingers. They'd stayed entwined for several long minutes as law enforcement moved in and out of the barn. Several members of the Wildlife Rehabilitation Center finally arrived and took charge of the scene along with the deputies.

Liam had walked over to the couple, nodding his thanks toward Joseph before looking down at Samantha. "This is going to take a while, and you're not needed for this. I hate to add more on to you, but you're going to need to come to the Sheriff's station. We'll need statements from you as we're continuing our investigation. Colt has first dibs on Annette since the thefts occurred in his county, but he'll be at my office with her for now. Once we know the whole scope, she'll probably be charged in both counties."

Following Liam back out of the woods, she'd jerked slightly as they made their way toward Joseph's SUV. "My truck! I need to get my truck."

"Don't worry about it now," Liam had said. "Just in case Lionel and Alejandro don't confess, we'll have your truck to collect evidence."

Her face fell and Joseph grunted. "Babe, it'll be fine. I promise, nothing will part you from your grandfather's truck for long."

Now, Samantha looked around in curiosity at the room in the Acawmacke Sheriff's Office where she, Joseph, and Frodo waited. One of the detectives had brought Frodo a bowl of water as well as cups of coffee for both she and Joseph. Taking a sip of the brew that was much better than she thought it might be, she hoped the caffeine would help get her through the rest of the day while not keeping her awake once she and Joseph got home.

Liam walked down the hall, caught her eye, and waved for them to follow him. Standing, they stepped into a conference room with a large table in the center. Once seated, Frodo laid down at her feet. She glanced over at Joseph and whispered, "Frodo doesn't want to leave me."

Joseph wrapped his arm around her and pulled her in close. "He's not the only one. I don't want to let you out of my sight." His gaze dropped to the bruises on her arm, and his jaw tightened.

With her hand on his thigh, she rubbed gently. "I'm fine."

Before he had a chance to retort, Liam, Colt, and Hunter walked into the room and sat down. Liam began, "Because this case is in two jurisdictions, Colt and I will be working together. The theft of drugs took place in North Heron, and Hunter will be working with you to determine what had been taken and when. Although, I'll say that Annette is being very forthcoming."

Hunter nodded, opening a file onto the table and glancing at the contents before lifting his gaze. "I know Annette was your office manager and had been working in the clinic before you came along. She was originally hired by the previous veterinarian, Tom Robertson. They became friends and she discovered he'd had a relationship with Paula Bender—"

"Paula Bender?" Samantha blurted, jerking back in surprise.

"According to her, Tom had an affair with Paula years ago, but it didn't last long. She says Tom had money problems, and Paula offered a solution. Paula knew the money that could be made if she could sell wolf-hybrid puppies, especially if they had fifty percent wolf in them. In order to do that, she needed a full-blooded wolf. It took her a while to make contacts, but she finally did. And it looks like she managed to pay off several employees to keep everything off of Jim's radar."

Joseph kept his arm around Samantha but leaned forward, his gaze intense. "How the hell did he not know what was going on?"

Hunter shrugged. "Jim's got a lot of acreage and only uses a small portion for the house and his breeding kennels. The rest of it he just lets grow wild, having no interest in it other than to give him privacy. Especially the back acres that border on the inlet near Maryland. His entire focus was centered on his legitimate breeding business, and he cared little for anything else."

"Tell me more about Tom. That's what I'm interested in," Samantha said. "I worked with him. I knew him." She threw her hands up into the air and huffed. "Of course, I also worked with Annette. This makes me wonder if I know anything!"

"Whenever Paula needed medication or vaccinations for her wolf-hybrid pups, she turned to Tom. It was easy for him to get them and provide them to her. For this, she paid him and he made extra money on the side."

"But Annette?"

"She discovered the discrepancies in what she'd ordered and what was being used. Tom confessed everything to her, but because she liked him, she remained quiet. When he left to return to his family, Paula offered Annette the same deal. Provide medications and she'd earn extra money."

"But the rabies vaccination isn't proven to work for wolf-hybrids, much less on wolves," she continued to protest.

"That was a chance Paula was willing to take. She had a middleman that was making private arrangements to sell the pups, and she just claimed that they had been vaccinated."

"What about Lionel and Alejandro? How do they fit in?" Joseph asked.

At that question, Samantha watched as Hunter shared a look with Colt and Liam before turning his attention back to them.

Clearing his throat, Hunter continued. "One of the places the middleman was selling pups to was a drug dealer in Norfolk that was running high-end dogfighting. Not the kind where people made cheap bets, but the kind where people with real money bet huge sums on the dogs. He'd found out about the wolf-hybrids and figured they'd make the best fighters."

Gasping, Samantha shook her head. "That's not necessarily true. Even if it was, that's horrible!"

"Whether it's true or not didn't really matter. If people thought they had wolf in them, the betting odds were higher. A fuck ton of money could be made on these fights."

She slumped against Joseph. "I swear this makes me feel sick."

"I want to know what's gonna happen to the fuckers because they took Samantha—"

A knock on the door interrupted, and she looked up in surprise as Alejandro walked in. Joseph shot to his feet, his fists raised as he started toward the newcomer.

Alejandro also raised his arms, but his hands were not in fists. Instead, his palms were out, placating. "I came to apologize, Doctor Collins. I never meant for you to be taken and that's why I tried to let you know that I'd come back for you. Once I heard there was a commotion going on up at the house, I knew I needed to keep up with Lionel so that he couldn't escape."

"But... I don't..." she stammered, her hand resting on Joseph's back as her gaze never left Alejandro.

He glanced toward the side of the table where Liam, Colt, and Hunter sat before reaching into his pocket and pulling out a badge, hooking it onto his belt.

She gasped. "You're..."

"I'm undercover for the state police, Doctor Collins. I've been in Norfolk, infiltrating the gang running the dogfights and managed to get hired by Jim Bender. At first, he was on my radar, but I was gathering evidence that Paula was the one in charge. My case was almost complete with Annette and Paula and Lionel. I had planned on turning in evidence against Annette today and then having Paula and Lionel arrested. But then you showed up, and Lionel went rogue."

Alejandro nodded toward the others before leaving the room. Samantha kept her hand on Joseph's back as he looked down at her, and she chuckled. "I don't know about you, Joseph, but I feel like my head is spinning!"

The rest of them stood as well, and she leaned her weight against Joseph as Frodo took to his feet and stayed right next to her legs.

"I'll come by the clinic in a couple of days to get any pharmaceutical discrepancies you uncover," Hunter said.

"Can I ask what will happen to Annette?"

Colt replied, "The thefts of the pharmaceuticals took place in North Heron, and that's where she's being charged. Right now, she's in the Eastern Shore Regional Jail. She'll probably be able to post bail and be out until her trial, but be wary. Don't have any contact with her and don't let her back into your clinic."

Samantha nodded, but it was Joseph who said, "We'll get the locks changed tomorrow."

He escorted her out, Frodo staying close by. When he opened the passenger door to his SUV, Frodo jumped up into the seat and then crawled into the back. She put her foot on the running board but squealed as Joseph scooped her into his arms, setting her carefully into the seat. He leaned forward, cupped her cheeks, and kissed her gently. Keeping his forehead pressed against hers, his warm breath coasted over her face.

"I was fuckin' scared, babe. Fuckin', fuckin' scared."

"I'm okay, sweetheart. We're going to be fine."

"I know that now, but I didn't know that then."

For a moment, she hesitated, both reveling in the feel of his face pressed to hers and worried that the emotions of the day might be so overwhelming he'd want to bolt.

He leaned back so that his gaze was pinned on her and said, "You and me, Samantha. Together, always."

His words shot straight through her, erasing her fears, knowing he was in this to stay. "Are you sure?"

"How can I go wrong? I've got Sam, Frodo, Pip, and Merry. I've got the best at my back, and I'll always have your back as well."

Laughing, she threw her arms around him and pulled him tight. "Take me home, Joseph."

He rounded the front and climbed behind the wheel, taking them home.

2 6

"You know this is crazy, right?" Tonya stomped around the workroom, waving her hands. "I mean, unbelievable, batshit kind of crazy!"

Samantha's grin spread over her face. She had called her employees in on a Sunday to let them know what was happening, glad she had a day to prepare before the next work week began. And just as she supposed, her staff was as astounded as she had been. "Yep, I know. Unbelievable, batshit crazy."

Tonya whirled around in the middle of her rant and pointed her finger at Samantha. "And you! You got kidnapped and hurt!"

"Hey, I've got some bruises, and while it could have been a lot worse, I'm fine."

"All for money," Susan said, shaking her head slowly, her brow crinkled. "It's just so hard to believe what Annette did. It's hard for me to think of Doctor Robertson selling our vaccines, but... it seems worse with Annette."

"Because she was our friend, not just a boss," Tonya declared, finally plopping into a chair, her rant seemingly over for the moment.

"It was all for money," Samantha agreed. "Paula for not being satisfied with just Bender Breeders. Tom for being involved with Paula and then agreeing to inoculate animals that he knew were illegal in this area. Annette for wanting to ingratiate herself with Tom, and then when he left, realizing she could make money. They were all motivated by their own greed."

With those words, the gathering sat quietly for a moment. Finally, Brantley looked over and asked, "What happens now? How does this affect the clinic?"

"Well, thankfully, our clinic was never directly involved other than being a place where the drugs were stolen. I'm sure there'll be questions when the story hits the news, but I can't imagine any fallout for us. We keep doing our job, doing it well, giving as much as we can to the community while running a business."

"What about an office manager?" Susan asked.

"I'll put out an advertisement tomorrow, and I have a feeling that in this area, we'll have a lot of applicants. I don't want to wait long to hire someone, but I really want to hire the right person. They need to be trustworthy, honest, friendly, hard-working, and love animals. Until then, we'll all pitch in to make sure the clinic runs smoothly."

"On a happier note, how are things at the shelter and with Joseph?" Tonya asked, a smile finally curving her lips.

"The shelter is great, and the shelter manager is even better," she laughed.

"And Betty's house? Is it working out for you?" Susan asked. "It sounds romantic." Her eyes cut toward Brentley, and he held her gaze for a few seconds then ducked his head.

It happened so quickly, Samantha wondered if she had imagined it but grinned at the thought of those two getting together. "Yeah, it's great. But we hope to start building a house on my land to replace my camper within a year... maybe a little longer."

She glanced at the clock on the wall, then looked back at her staff, her heart glad she had these people working with her. "Okay, everyone, head home and be ready first thing in the morning."

She locked the doors after the others left, promising she was leaving soon as well. She just wanted to take a moment to be alone in the clinic. She wandered through the rooms, the equipment and spaces clean and disinfected. The supplies in the cabinets and closets were in order. The pharmaceuticals were carefully stored and had been checked so that she could make her report to Hunter.

She wandered through the empty exam rooms, her mind filled with the many animals she'd treated and the clients she'd comforted. She stood at the door to her office and thought of the older veterinarian who'd built the business, Tom, who'd continued it until greed set him on a different path, and now it was Hoofs and Paws... her very own.

Closing the door, she locked the building securely

and turned, startled to see a black motorcycle parked in the front. A large man sat astride, his thick, jean-covered legs extended to either side, and his worn, black boots firmly planted on the pavement. A faded T-shirt covered muscles but allowed his tatted arms to show. A black leather vest with patches sat easily on his wide shoulders. His helmet was off, and his thick, dark, wavy hair hung to his shoulders, a blond streak in the front falling into his face. A scruffy beard covered his jaw, and reflector glasses covered his eyes.

"Looking for a ride?"

His low voice rumbled from deep inside his chest and it jolted straight through her. "With you? Always." She laughed and ran toward him as he shoved his sunglasses up onto his head. The lines on either side of his eyes deepened and a white-toothed smile spread across his face.

She stopped at one of his legs, her hands moving to clutch his cheeks as she kissed him. It only took a second for the kiss to flame hot as it always did. Tongues tangling, they drank each other in.

Finally, pulling back, her chest heaved as she dragged air into her lungs.

"Damn, babe," he groused. "I was going to take you for a long ride, but now, I just want to take you home."

"How about the camper? Far enough for a little ride, and there's a bed with the sound of the Bay at the window."

His lips curved again, and he jerked his head toward the back. "Then climb on, babe, and hold tight."

With more practiced ease, she swung her leg over

the seat and squirmed until she was pressed chest to back, crotch to ass, wrapping her arms around his waist.

With a roar, they launched out of the parking lot heading to their past… and their future.

Click below for the next Baytown Boy, Liam's story…
Sea Glass Hearts

Cael

Jaxon

Jayden

Asher

Zeke

Cas

Lighthouse Security Investigations

Mace

Rank

Walker

Drew

Blake

Tate

Levi

Clay

Cobb

Hope City (romantic suspense series co-developed

with Kris Michaels

Brock book 1

Sean book 2

Carter book 3

Brody book 4

Kyle book 5

Ryker book 6

Rory book 7

Killian book 8

Torin book 9

Saints Protection & Investigations

(an elite group, assigned to the cases no one else wants…or can solve)

Serial Love

Healing Love

Revealing Love

Seeing Love

Honor Love

Sacrifice Love

Protecting Love

Remember Love

Discover Love

Surviving Love

Celebrating Love

Follow the exciting spin-off series:

Alvarez Security (military romantic suspense)

Gabe

Tony

Vinny

Jobe

SEALs

Thin Ice (Sleeper SEAL)

SEAL Together (Silver SEAL)

Undercover Groom (Hot SEAL)

Also for a Hope City Crossover Novel / Hot SEAL...

A Forever Dad by Maryann Jordan

Letters From Home (military romance)

Class of Love

Freedom of Love

Bond of Love

The Love's Series (detectives)

Love's Taming

Love's Tempting

Love's Trusting

The Fairfield Series (small town detectives)

Emma's Home

Laurie's Time

Carol's Image

Fireworks Over Fairfield

Please take the time to leave a review of this book. Feel free to contact me, especially if you enjoyed my book. I love to hear from readers!

Facebook

Email

Website

ABOUT THE AUTHOR

I am an avid reader of romance novels, often joking that I cut my teeth on the historical romances. I have been reading and reviewing for years. In 2013, I finally gave into the characters in my head, screaming for their story to be told. From these musings, my first novel, Emma's Home, The Fairfield Series was born.

I was a high school counselor having worked in education for thirty years. I live in Virginia, having also lived in four states and two foreign countries. I have been married to a wonderfully patient man for thirty-five years. When writing, my dog or one of my four cats can generally be found in the same room if not on my lap.

Please take the time to leave a review of this book. Feel free to contact me, especially if you enjoyed my book. I love to hear from readers!

Facebook
Email
Website

[f]

Made in the USA
Middletown, DE
23 April 2021